He t_____
your turn."

The instant Blair curled her fingers around the cold metal, they began to tremble.

With a terse sigh, Caleb wasted no time in stepping behind her, and before he thought, he placed his arms around her and gently turned her slender frame toward the target, all the while helping to hold the gun steady.

Blair fought to hang on to reality as fervent desire jolted through her with a force that sent her senses reeling. She was completely and hopelessly enraptured by his big brawny body. All Blair's senses were attuned to this man whose arms felt like velvet chains around her.

Caleb coughed. "Remember," he said, "to keep both hands under it, arms straight and wide stance."

"I'll try," Blair responded in a whisper, her mouth dry, as if it were crammed with sawdust. If only he weren't so close . . . if only he weren't *touching* her.

Dear Reader,

When two people fall in love, the world is suddenly new and exciting, and it's that same excitement we bring to you in Silhouette Intimate Moments. These are stories with scope, with grandeur. These characters lead the lives we all dream of, and everything they do reflects the wonder of being in love.

Longer and more sensuous than most romances, Silhouette Intimate Moments novels take you away from everyday life and let you share the magic of love. Adventure, glamour, drama, even suspense— these are the passwords that let you into a world where love has a power beyond the ordinary, where the best authors in the field today create stories of love and commitment that will stay with you always.

In coming months look for novels by your favorite authors: Maura Seger, Parris Afton Bonds, Elizabeth Lowell and Erin St. Claire, to name just a few. And whenever you buy books, look for all the Silhouette Intimate Moments, love stories *for* today's women *by* today's women.

Leslie J. Wainger
Senior Editor
Silhouette Books

IMRL-7/85

Mary Lynn Baxter
When We Touch

Silhouette Intimate Moments

Published by Silhouette Books New York

America's Publisher of Contemporary Romance

SILHOUETTE BOOKS
300 East 42nd St., New York, N.Y. 10017

Copyright © 1986 by Mary Lynn Baxter

ISBN: 0-373-07156-6

First Silhouette Books printing August 1986

America's Publisher of Contemporary Romance

Printed in the U.S.A.

Books by Mary Lynn Baxter

Silhouette Special Edition

All Our Tomorrows #9
Tears of Yesterday #31
Autumn Awakening #96

Silhouette Desire

Shared Moments #24

Silhouette Intimate Moments

Another Kind of Love #19
Memories that Linger #52
Everything but Time #74
A Handful of Heaven #117
Price above Rubies #130
When We Touch #156

MARY LYNN BAXTER

sold hundreds of romances before she ever wrote one. The D&B Bookstore, right on the main drag in Lufkin, Texas is both her home and the store she owns and manages. She and her husband, Leonard, garden in their spare time. Around 5:00 every evening they can be found picking butter beans on their small farm just outside of town.

Chapter 1

Blair Browning winced as she felt the warm trickle of blood on her tongue. Slowly she unclamped her teeth from her lower lip.

Keep your cool, she warned herself. *All you have to do is tell him to go to hell and show him the door.*

"Blair, for chrissakes, don't look at me as if I've just sprouted two heads."

Feeling like someone who has suddenly been deprived of breath, Blair forced herself to glance a second time into the face of the man watching her.

Jack Worrell. Ex-boss. Old friend. Or so she had thought— At the moment his countenance looked anything but friendly. His near-white brows were settled together in a frown and a muscle worked overtime in his jaw, a living testimony to his exasperation.

Today he looked more than the sixty-odd years Blair knew him to be. His close-cropped white hair highlighted the bald spot on top of his head. And if she wasn't mistaken, his tall, lanky frame was just a tad more stooped than she remembered. Though he spoke with his usual slow Southern drawl, there was nothing slow about his mind or his sharp, piercing eyes. Eyes that were now boring a hole through her.

"Blair, can't we at least discuss this with some degree of civility?"

Blair swiped across her lower lip with her tongue, stalling for time, knowing that she had to have all her faculties about her to fight this man, for she knew from experience that when Jack Worrell wanted something, he always got it. And right now he wanted her to return to work, back to the type of work she now abhorred and had sworn never to do again.

Puncturing the heavy silence with her sudden movement to the nearest window, Blair stared out into the sunlight dancing across the busy San Francisco street. She blinked several times, hoping against hope that this intrusion into her life was only a figment of her imagination and would suddenly disappear like a puff of smoke.

Worrell tried again, his voice effectively bringing her back to the matter at hand. "Blair, you haven't even heard what I have to say."

Her back to him, Blair refused to give an inch, knowing if she did, he'd take a mile. "That's just the point, Jack. I don't want to and don't intend to hear what you have to say. You're wasting your time and mine." Suddenly having gained the courage to meet his challenging gaze once again, Blair spun around. "I told you I was through when I walked out three years ago and I meant it, Jack. So do us both a favor and leave me alone."

If possible, Worrell's thin face tightened even more, yet he boldly took a few steps toward Blair, determination dogging each tread of his feet.

When he was almost within touching distance he stopped. His features softened considerably and his tone took on a pleading note. "Blair, you know I wouldn't ask you to do this if it weren't urgent, a matter of life and death."

Thrusting her hand behind the heavy mane of hair that graced her neck, Blair rubbed the tight muscles. "Oh, Jack," she whispered, "how can you ask me to come back after all that's happened, after all I've been through?"

Worrell sighed before delving into his coat pocket for his pipe. That, too, never changed, Blair thought irrationally, watching as he poked a finger into the large bowl before replacing the finger with a match. In a moment a fine cloud of smoke colored the air between them.

Worrell and his ever present pipe had been a standard joke between her and Josh. *Josh.* It was three years since the quiet, kind man who had been her husband for only two short years had been brutally gunned down in the line of duty.

Blair squeezed her eyelids shut. She simply could not handle this, she thought. Not now. Old friend or not, Jack Worrell had to go.

"Sorry," Worrell said, fanning awkwardly and stepping back. "Damned rude of me to blow smoke in your face."

"Jack, please," Blair began. "Just—"

"No, Blair, I can't go," he interrupted, having read her mind correctly. "Not now. Please just hear me out and then if you still want me to go, I will." The pleading had shifted from his voice to his eyes. "Deal?"

Blair averted her gaze and began chewing on her lower lip again. *Don't do this,* an inner voice warned. *You'll regret it, Blair Browning, just as sure as God makes little green apples.*

"Blair?"

Defiance flared briefly in her eyes, then died. "Oh, all right," she snapped, knowing that she had no choice if she was ever going to get rid of him. So why did she feel as if she had just chosen her coffin and was about to add another nail to it?

Brushing past him, she made her way toward the brightly colored couch that occupied one corner of her office, and she gestured for him to take a seat. Worrell complied with apparent relief. Blair followed suit, positive she would be better off hearing what he had to say sitting down. Her legs were capable of giving way at any moment.

Another silence fell between them while Worrell toyed with his pipe, before shoving it back into his coat pocket. Blair held on to her patience by a mere thread. Then, locking his eyes on her, Worrell asked, "Does the name Paul Tanner mean anything to you?"

Blair didn't hesitate. "No, not right off the top of my head. Why, should it?"

Worrell buried his back deeper into the plush cushions. "No, not really, although he's in the public eye quite a bit. In fact, for the past few weeks, his name and picture have been plastered all over the society page in the *Herald*, each time linked with a different woman."

"What does he do besides squire women around?" Blair asked, not because she was interested but because she wanted desperately to bring this scenario to an end and get back to work. She had photographs in the darkroom that needed her attention. And she had a model due for a photo session soon.

"At one time, Tanner made millions in the real estate business," Worrell replied. "But after squandering most of it away on several bad investments, women and high living, he's broke and has been for some time."

"Why would a real estate investor be of any interest to the FBI?"

"Tanner is a former counterintelligence officer," Worrell announced slowly, each word punctuated with a hint of suppressed violence. "He's suspected of already having sold the identity of U.S. double agents to a spy for the Soviet KGB, with plans to sell more. He must be stopped before he can do further damage to national security and place other lives in jeopardy."

"Oh, no," was all Blair was capable of saying as it dawned on her that Josh had also been a counterintelligence officer. But what did all this have to do with her? she wondered. How could she possibly help? She hadn't even held a gun in three years, for god's sake. She fought back the new surge of panic that rushed like hot bile up the back of her throat.

"That's what I think, too, and worse," Worrell finished bleakly. "And I intend to stop that bastard before he can do any more damage."

Blair busied herself removing a patch of lint from her coffee-colored slacks. "Believe me, Jack, I sympathize with you and agree wholeheartedly that a man like Tanner must be stopped, but surely you don't think—" She paused, looking at him now, her eyes wide and troubled.

"That you can help," he said, finishing her sentence, leaning eagerly toward her. "You're the key to stopping Tanner cold, and you know that. Why, Blair, you were the best at garnering information that no one else could get in a million years. Your beauty draws men to you like moths to light." Ignoring her muted cry, he went on, "You can take up exactly where you left off with your code name, The Beauty, and—"

Blair lunged to her feet, oblivious to the fact that the bones in her legs felt like jelly. "No!" she shrieked. "I won't do it! And you have no right to ask me."

"Please, Blair—"

"Don't you dare 'please Blair me,' Jack Worrell. I won't do it. Read my lips. I won't have any part of your plans." Tears darkened her eyes, though she battled fiercely to curtail them, feeling her control slipping with each word she uttered.

Worrell was standing now, too, towering over her, and this time his voice matched the coldness in his eyes. "Dammit, Blair, I'm not asking you to return to the bureau permanently, only to help us out with this one assignment, to put scum like Paul Tanner behind bars where he belongs."

Shaking her head, Blair replied, "The answer is still no, Jack." Tears were streaming down her face. "I've lost it. I've lost my nerve; I'd be more of a hindrance than a help. See—" she held out her hands to him; they were shaking like a leaf "—just thinking about it does this to me. Anyway, that part of my life is behind me. In case you've forgotten, I shoot pictures now instead of guns." Her eyes implored him. "Please . . . I'm just now beginning to live again."

And she was. At age thirty-five, three years after Josh's death and her resignation from the FBI, she was making great strides in recovering from the past, in gluing the pieces of her life back together. With the help of a friend, she had become a free-lance photographer specializing in both men and women's fashions. And she had just begun to tackle this new career with a flourish and enthusiasm that had been missing from her life for so long.

Because she coveted her newfound peace and security, she was adamant in not wanting anything or anyone to interfere with her life. Returning to a career she had come to fear, as well as loathe, was certainly not in her plans.

"Would it make any difference if I told you that we think Tanner was responsible for Josh's death?"

It took a few seconds for Worrell's words to soak into Blair's befuddled brain, but when they did, she grabbed her stomach and reeled as though she'd just received a life-threatening blow.

"Oh, no," Blair whimpered, pain pinching her features.

Suddenly afraid she was going to keel over, Worrell reached for her and led her like a baby back to the couch. Once there, Blair closed her eyes and let her head sag against the cushions.

Worrell cursed silently, striding briskly toward the opposite end of the room where a tiny bar was located. He jerked open the refrigerator door, only to curse again, this time aloud. It was empty except for a bottle of Coke.

Well, it would just have to suffice, he decided, and wasted no time in half filling a glass. Rapidly closing the distance between them, Worrell eased himself down beside Blair and, hiding his concern said gruffly, "Here, drink this."

Blair complied, but with an unsteady hand. Miraculously, the cold liquid seemed to do the trick—her heart no longer raced like an out-of-control locomotive—or maybe it was that she had something concrete to hold on to. Her fingers clutched the glass in a death grip.

"Thanks," she murmured at last, trying her best to regain control of her shattered emotions. It was a long time since she had experienced the acute sinking in the pit of her stomach and the dull ache around her heart—not since Josh's death and the loss of their unborn child. *Don't, Blair. Not now. Don't think about that now.*

Breathing deeply, she struggled to sit up, still clinging to the glass as though it were a lifeline. "You certainly haven't lost the ability to deliver your bombshells, Worrell. No, sirree, you were right on target with this one."

In spite of himself, Jack Worrell smiled, though more from relief than from her caustic remark. He was extremely grateful to see the color blooming once again in her cheeks and a bit of her fighting spirit return. For a moment he'd been afraid he'd gone too far.

"Let's just say I had to get your attention," he admitted, the smile having completely disappeared. He was all business. When Blair remained stoic, he went on. "I'm desperate—we're desperate. We need you and if it takes playing dirty . . ." His sentence trailed off, leaving Blair to reach her own conclusion.

She stood up and slowly walked the short distance to her desk, then leaned against it, her whole body suddenly feeling as limp as a wet dishrag.

"Tell me everything you know about Tanner's involvement with—Josh," she demanded quietly, crossing her arms and hugging them to her breasts as though to shield herself from Worrell's answer. Just mentioning Josh's name still had the power to cut her insides to ribbons. There was so much pain, so much guilt associated with his death.

Worrell sighed, brushing his fingers roughly across his head, but he didn't flinch from the coldness in Blair's eyes. "For starters, did you know that Josh was a double agent?"

"I suspected as much," Blair reflected sadly. "But of course that was something we never discussed. It was taboo."

"Well, Tanner was aware of it."

Blair's eyes widened. "Do you think he knew Josh?"

"More than likely. That's why we're concerned about the safety of a lot of double agents who, like Tanner, worked with the U.S. Army Intelligence and Security Command."

"What else?" she asked in a voice laced with pain.

"From what we've been able to piece together, when Tanner got into deep financial trouble, he needed a quick way to come up with megabucks. That's when we think he first made contact with the Russians and began trading names for money."

Blair avoided his eyes, knowing what was coming next.

"Josh and another agent were operating under the code name, Royal Miter, that night when Josh went to the railroad depot to give bogus information to that KGB agent. The Russian was waiting for him, thanks to that sonofabitch Tanner."

And Josh never knew what hit him. Blair cringed against her thoughts, once again replaying that fateful night in her mind. If only she'd been with him, she agonized, maybe she could have done something. If only they hadn't fought that morning when he'd tried to convince her to quit the bureau because she was pregnant. If only she'd loved him more. If only...

"I want that traitor!" Worrell raged, drawing her out of the painful past. He was pacing back and forth in front of her, his right hand doubled into a fist and slamming into the palm of his left one. The sound shook the room. "I want to see him sweat when I get his ass in a vise."

"No more than I do." Her throat was so clogged with emotion that she could barely speak. Yet her mind was churning the entire time, cold logic giving her the strength she needed to endure this moment.

"Then for heaven's sake, Blair, help us," Worrell rasped. He had stopped his pacing and was staring at her, his mouth clamped together in a grim, straight line. "Do you want me to beg? Is that it?"

Slowly Blair released her pent-up breath. "No, Jack, you don't have to beg."

Worrell blinked, afraid that he had heard her wrong, that he was misinterpreting her softly spoken words. Then Blair spoke again.

"Just tell me what you want me to do," she said.

Caleb Hunt felt as though something had crawled into his mouth and died. His mouth tasted as foul as the last bottle of cheap whiskey he'd consumed the night before. God! When was he going to learn he was too old to hoot with the owls?

He moaned, then blinked several times, wondering what the hell had awakened him suddenly at this ungodly hour of the morning. It was Saturday, wasn't it? His day off? Or was it? Right now, he couldn't even tell anyone his name much less what day it was.

Damn, but he'd done it last night. He wondered how Candace was feeling?

Then, thrusting thoughts of her aside, he concentrated on the more pressing problem—the loud noise banging against his head like a jackhammer. Suddenly realizing what it was, he leaned over and groped for the button on the alarm clock. Finally he bingoed, though he paid for the sudden movement with another excruciating pain to his right temple.

Knowing that he couldn't wait another minute to brush his teeth, pain or no pain, Caleb very gingerly moved to the edge of the bed, where he even more carefully forced his body into an upright position. Again he winced as another sharp pain darted through his skull.

Caleb had just taken his first step toward the bathroom when he was suddenly halted in his tracks. "Damn!" he muttered, glaring at the beige telephone on the bedside table, before lifting the receiver to his ear.

"Hunt here," he barked.

A deep chuckle filtered through the line. "Well, Caleb my man, you sound like your usual charming self."

"Cut the crap, Worrell, and just tell me what you want at this hour of the morning?"

Worrell laughed again, Caleb's surly manner completely lost on him. In fact, he'd have been shocked if Caleb behaved otherwise. It was a known fact that Hunt made the most of his time off duty. Yet on the job, Worrell could find no fault. He was head and shoulders above the other agents.

"Get down to the office pronto," Worrell demanded.

"Hell, Jack, it's Saturday."

"I know it's Saturday," Worrell said with forced patience, almost as though he was talking to a small boy. "It may be Saturday, but there's work to be done. And it can't wait until Monday.'' He paused. "Don't worry, Hunt, you'll be more than compensated for whatever inconvenience this may cause you."

Even though Caleb still hadn't gotten it all together, positive he had a bowling ball on his shoulders instead of a head, he was nevertheless aware of the sarcasm in his boss's voice.

"I don't give a damn about the money and you know it!" Caleb grated. "But I would like a day off occasionally, you know," he added, his voice dripping with his own brand of sarcasm.

"I couldn't agree more. You do have a right to bitch loud and long, but can you wait till later? This matter is urgent."

Caleb was fully alert now. "Why didn't you say that to begin with? I'll be there as soon as I shower and throw on some clothes."

No goodbyes were exchanged as Caleb slammed down the receiver and headed toward the bathroom. Fifteen minutes later he was dressed in a pair of jeans and a chambray sport shirt. Ignoring the dull thud in his head, he flexed his muscles, trying to get the circulation flowing. The hot shower had helped, and he no longer had that foul taste in his mouth. But his head ached unmercifully. Just as he hurriedly tucked his shirttail inside his jeans, another sharp pain zinged through his head.

"He winced.'' What had gotten into him last night? he asked himself again. It was a long time since he'd tied one on like that. If his thoughts served him correctly, it was when his divorce had become final. That had definitely called for a celebration.

Caleb grimaced against the memory, refusing to dwell on that painful part of his life, though it had taught him a hard lesson. He had learned that marriage did not mix with his type of work. No sirree, marriage was not for him. An occasional one-night stand with a woman was all he needed to keep him sane.

The past night, however, was the second time he'd taken out Candy Miller, a fellow agent, and for a reason he couldn't explain, he'd enjoyed himself. Was it because she knew the score, that friendship was all there would ever be between them? Or was it because she understood his work and he could relax with her? Probably a little of both, he thought with a sardonic twist of his lip.

Yes, give him a woman who knew the score every time. Places, and women lost their allure when they became too familiar. Thankfully, his life-style provided him with a great deal of variety in both areas.

Suddenly he shook his head, his eyes dipping down to the gold watch on his arm. "Dammit, Hunt," he spit out loud, "get the lead out of your ass and get to movin'."

He knew Worrell would be chomping at the bit waiting for him. Wasting no more time, he strode out of the bedroom and into the kitchen. Although he didn't have time to make coffee, he knew he had to put something into his stomach. It had been rumbling since he opened his eyes.

Caleb jerked open the refrigerator, and his eyes scanned the contents. Empty. Empty except for a jug of orange juice. He grimaced. It would have to do. So much for bachelor life, he thought with bitter amusement, suddenly comparing the empty contents of the refrigerator to the loneliness of his life.

Then, with a disgusted groan at himself for wallowing in self-pity, he grabbed the container and swallowed its contents in several large gulps. What was the matter with him? He had it made, didn't he? After all, he answered to no one, did as he damn well pleased. He had a great job, welcomed the danger and challenge it represented. What more could he want? He liked his life just the way it was.

If booze was going to affect him like this, he'd sure as hell go on the wagon.

With that thought uppermost in his mind, Caleb tromped out the door, and without a backward glance at the place he called home, slammed the door behind him.

Jack Worrell was about to chew the stem of his pipe in two when Caleb sauntered through the door of his office exactly one hour after their phone conversation.

Worrell stood up, a sour expression on his face. "Well, Hunt, it's about time you got here. I was beginning to think I was going to have to roust you out of that damn bed myself." He moved his pipe to the other side of his mouth.

"Well, I'm here now, so you can relax," Caleb said easily, completely undaunted by Worrell's tirade. He knew just how far he could push his longtime friend and boss, but right then he was in the driver's seat. Worrell needed him.

"And you look like hell, too," Worrell added sharply. "Were you afraid they were going to quit making the booze before you got your fair share?"

A smile toyed on Caleb's lips. "Something like that, but don't worry, I'm up to hearing what you have to say." He paused. "But only if you don't talk too loud." This time his lips broke into a full-fledged grin.

Worrell answered his smile, showing a bottom row of stained teeth, then said roughly, "How 'bout a cup of coffee?"

"Thought you'd never ask," Caleb quipped, crossing to the bar next to the floor-to-ceiling windows that were adjacent to Worrell's desk.

After he poured himself a generous amount of the hot liquid, Caleb's gaze wandered to the windows where he looked down into the streets alive with tourists on that early May morning.

The quarters of the Federal Bureau of Investigation were in an unpretentious high-rise building sandwiched in the heart of downtown San Francisco. Both his and Worrell's offices were on the twenty-first floor, giving them a view of the city's skyline, enhanced by the brightly colored cable cars, restaurants of all sizes and kinds, condominiums inhabited by the rich and famous and, last but not least, the Golden Gate Bridge, shining like a beacon from its home on the bay.

Even though Caleb had only been there for three years, having been transferred from the Los Angeles office at Worrell's request, he loved the city. It had become home to him.

"If you're through daydreaming," Worrell snapped, "we'll get down to business."

Caleb took a swig of his coffee and, turning, propped himself against the countertop on the bar and said, "I'm all ears. Shoot."

"Do you ever look at fashion magazines?"

Caleb's dark eyebrows shot up. "What the hell kind of question is that?" he asked.

"One that I expect an answer to."

"Well, in that case, the answer is no."

Worrell removed his pipe from his mouth. "That's what I was afraid you'd say. So the name Blair Browning doesn't mean anything to you?"

Caleb thought for a moment, bouncing the name around in his head. "As a matter of fact it does." He ignored the way Worrell's eyes lit up and went on. "Fashion photographer, right? Saw an article about her in the paper awhile back. I'm not in the habit of reading fluff like that, but for some reason that caught my attention." He paused and took another sip of coffee. "She was a Stephens if I remember correctly. Born with the proverbial silver spoon in her mouth."

"One and the same," Worrell said, excitement edging his voice. "And believe it or not, she used to be an agent— worked for me for five years before she quit. It was exactly one year before you came aboard that she resigned."

Caleb's mouth gaped open, then clamped shut. "Ah, come on, Jack, surely you're puttin' me on."

"Sorry to disappoint you," Worrell said coldly, "but it's the truth. She was a damned good agent and I'd give my eyeteeth to have her back."

"Why did she leave?" Caleb asked, intrigued in spite of himself.

Worrell sighed. "Her husband, who also worked for us, got killed and then she lost their baby. Something snapped; she couldn't handle it anymore."

Silence greeted his words.

After a moment, Worrell continued. "We haven't been able to prove it, but we're positive that Tanner was responsible for her husband's death." He paused. "When I told Blair this, she agreed to come back and help us stop Tanner once and for all."

"And?" Caleb had the gut feeling he wasn't going to like what was coming next.

"And you're to work with her, and be her contact. I'm—"

Caleb jumped up, his eyes suddenly as cold as ice. "Now wait just one minute, Jack! My vacation starts next week and you promised me nothing would interfere with it!"

"I'm turning her over to you," Worrell continued as though Caleb hadn't even spoken, the tone of his voice still smooth and unerring. "I want you to give this woman everything you've got. Think of her as a new recruit. You can do it and I'm not accepting any excuses. Okay, I know I'm reneging on your vacation, but I promise I'll make it up to you."

Caleb's expression was thunderous. "Get someone else, Jack. I haven't got the time or the inclination to—"

"Caleb," Worrell interrupted, this time with steel underlining each word. "I'm not giving you a choice. You *will* do as you're told."

"Dammit, Jack, why? There are others just as capable of playing pussyfoot with the Browning woman. She's nothing but a spoiled rich bitch and you know how I feel about that type of woman."

"I'll pretend I didn't hear that, Caleb," Worrell said coldly. "She's got the means of getting to Tanner, if anyone has. And I'm counting on you as a professional not to let your prejudices get in the way. And though I don't owe you an explanation, I'll tell you this much. I need the best man for the job and you're it."

And he was. Caleb Hunt was a fighter. He grew up on the streets of Los Angeles, responsible for himself since the age of fourteen. He traded four tough years in the army, serving in the special forces, for a college education. From there he went to law school.

Nothing had ever been given to him. Everything he had acquired was earned the hard way, through the school of hard knocks, he was fond of saying. He was one of the bureau's most sought-after agents; his mind and instincts were razor sharp and he had the cunning and the stamina to carry out a job no matter how difficult. He did not know the meaning of the word fear.

He also had the power to shrink the enemy with the cold, calculating sharpness of his black eyes, and he could break a man's neck with his bare hand. If there was trouble, Caleb Hunt was definitely the man to have on one's side.

"And if I refuse?" Caleb's softly spoken words split the silence like a bullet hitting a tin can.

Worrell didn't hesitate. "You won't. I know you too well. You've never turned your back on a challenge. And anyway, your job means more to you than your pride."

Caleb knew he'd lost the battle, but not the war. "All right, Jack, you win," he said.

Worrell hid a triumphant smile as he reached for a folder stamped TOP SECRET and handed it to Caleb. "For you, it'll be a piece of cake. You just wait and see."

"Only if I can train her at my cabin," Caleb added lightly, watching the smile suddenly disappear from Worrell's lips.

Silence.

"Well, what's it going to be, Jack? Do we bargain or not? I'm not going to let you cheat me out of my time at the cabin. Not again."

Worrell scowled. "What you're asking is against the rules and you know it," he said.

Caleb shrugged. "So? Rules are made to be broken?"

"If I let you do this, I could get my tail in a crack."

"You'll think of a way out. I have every confidence in you," Caleb replied, his lips twitching.

"Oh, hell," Worrell growled, "go ahead. But get out of here before I change my mind."

Caleb brought his eyes down from the light fixture and grinned into Worrell's glare.

Later, as Caleb made his way out into the sunshine, the grin faded. He realized his victory was a hollow one.

He didn't want the assignment, cabin or no cabin. And he couldn't help but feel as if he was about to be shoved out of an airplane without a parachute.

Blair's well-ordered life was suddenly blown to smithereens. Since Jack Worrell had walked out of her condo two days before, nothing had been the same.

After getting her commitment to help, Worrell had told her very little. He'd said that she would be expected to find the list of agents' names that Tanner had, and the exact time and place for the next exchange between him and the Russian. Then he'd filled her in on Tanner's background. At the door, he'd added that the agent who'd be working with her would be in touch. In the meantime, she was to sit tight.

That was a lot easier said than done. She had taken long walks, she had exercised until she had to crawl into bed at night, but nothing seemed to cure what ailed her. She was afraid. Fear flowed through her veins like ice water.

The last thing she wanted was to rejoin the ranks of the FBI, even if it was only temporary. But what choice did she have? None. She had to do it, wanted to do it, especially in the light of what Worrell had told her.

If indeed Paul Tanner was responsible for Josh's death either directly or indirectly, then she would do more than her part to make him pay. The circumstances surrounding Josh's death had haunted her for three long years. Maybe after this assignment, she could lay the ghosts to rest.

According to Jack, she had the perfect cover. Paul Tanner liked beautiful things, including women and houses. Collecting both seemed to be his forte. And she had just been commissioned to do a layout for *Home Beautiful* magazine. Paul Tanner's estate in San Andreas would more than qualify. There was no doubt in her mind that she could charm him into letting her do the article and take the pictures, hence putting her into direct contact with him.

Still, it wouldn't be easy. She had been away from the bureau for so long that she was out of step, out of practice with using her beauty as a tool. But where there was a will there was a way. She would make it work.

Now, as she waited for further instructions from the Agency, she tried to keep her mind on track, figuring out a way to juggle her commitments so that her assistant could carry on in her absence.

Later that afternoon, she had interviews set up with models competing for spots in a fashion show she was to photograph.

She peered at the list of names, keeping her fingers crossed that she would be through with her work for Worrell before the show came about. She had exactly two months. The show could make or break her as a professional; she just had to be able to do it.

So intent was she on her work that Blair failed to hear the impatient sounds coming from the reception area. The jiggling of her office doorknob brought her to full attention.

Her frown deepened, as she remembered that Lisa, her assistant, was out to lunch.

"Just a moment," she snapped, dropping her pen and getting to her feet, irritated with the untimely interruption.

Then, suddenly and without warning, the door flew open and a man barreled across the threshold, uninvited.

For a second Blair was speechless, completely taken aback by the large rawboned bulk of the man. But her lack of words was no deterrent to the intruder. Without hesitation, he began closing the distance between them.

Blair squinted and held out her hand, halting the man in his tracks. "Sorry," she said bluntly, "but I don't have any openings for male models."

This time it was Caleb Hunt who was taken aback. She's mistaken me for one of her models! he realized. Dammit, he'd tried to tell Worrell this would never work.

Before he could utter a word, however, Blair sashayed from behind the desk. Her cool amber eyes missed nothing as they traveled from the mop of unruly jet-black hair that grazed a broad forehead, down the harsh uneven features to the dimple in his chin.

"I'm sorry," she said again. "Even if I were looking for models, you wouldn't qualify. I suggest you look elsewhere for employment," she concluded in her most professional tone, though she felt suddenly uncomfortable with the giant of a man towering over her.

Slowly, with disdain oozing from his black eyes and contempt snarling from his lips, Caleb reached inside his coat pocket and pulled out his badge, flashing it before her face.

"Caleb Hunt, ma'am," he drawled sarcastically. "At your service."

Chapter 2

To say Blair was shocked was an understatement. For a moment, the room spun crazily as his deep-black eyes held her captive. Her heart slammed against her ribs while her eyes fluttered shut, and she prayed that when she opened them again he would no longer be standing there.

No such luck.

Caleb Hunt's large frame filled the small room, shrinking it, making it appear that any second it would burst at the seams. A cigarette now dangled between his fingers and there was an aura of intense concentration about him as he continued his sharp perusal of her.

"He's the best in the bureau," Worrell had told her at the door. "So don't worry your head. After all, my dear, I asked you to do this, and I'm responsible for you."

A dull flush invaded her cheeks as the silence climbed to a screaming pitch. Where was Worrell now when she needed him?

God! she was beautiful, Caleb thought, feeling a knot of dread form in his stomach. Damn Worrell to hell! He couldn't take his gaze off her. He simply stood there and soaked up her beauty.

Long hair cushioned her head, forming a charcoal-brown halo around a face of delicate symmetry, a breathtakingly lovely face. Fine dark eyebrows were arched against a peaches-and-cream skin, enhancing the amber-colored eyes, the straight slender nose, the high cheekbones. Her lips, parted now, were edged as though they had been molded by a sculptor with delicate precision. It was a face both soft and aristocratic, a face that stirred one's imagination—his imagination.

Whoa, Hunt! Put the brake on right this minute. This woman's not for you. She's way out of your league. And even if she wasn't, she wouldn't give you the time of day. So back off before you develop a permanent ache in your groin!

Realizing he was staring, Caleb abruptly turned away and crossed the room to a table that bore a decorative ashtray. There he brutally stubbed out the cigarette.

Blair, too, was at a loss for words. In fact, she couldn't have spoken if her life had depended on it. All she could do was stand there wrapped in the silence. She had become hopelessly thick-tongued, inarticulate, unable to give the apology she knew was due him.

Model! How could she have done such a thing? Would an apology suffice, start them off on the right foot? Probably not, she told herself. She had made a faux pas that could not be undone no matter how sincere her apology. Nevertheless she had to try.

Wetting her lips she began, "Mr. Hunt...I'm...sorry."

At the husky sound of her voice, Caleb swung around and made his way back toward her desk. He exuded an animal strength and vitality, she thought. The simple act of crushing his cigarette in the ashtray was tight with violence. And the match he'd used to light it had been tossed away like an explosive.

But the icy glare in his eyes had not thawed one degree when he clipped tersely, "Forget it, Mrs. Browning, we all make mistakes." He paused deliberately. "I'm sure that's only one of many."

The silence lengthened. Nobody moved.

Blair's face turned a brighter crimson, as she once again began feeling defensive under his steady unsmiling gaze. Damn him and his condescending attitude! she fumed. Not a smile anywhere. Just that icy arrogance. Well, she'd show him. She could be as cool and collected as he was.

"What do you say we dispense with the barbs and get down to business," she suggested in the haughtiest of tones.

"You're right, of course," he said, his face once again completely devoid of expression. "Work it shall be."

Blair ran her tongue around her dry lips, trying her best to avoid his eyes. "Would...would you care for a cup of coffee?" she asked, trying to relieve the thickening tension.

"Sounds good," he said politely. Then, usurping Blair, he crossed to the coffee maker, and after latching on to a cup, swung around and asked, "How 'bout yourself?"

"No...no thanks." She forced a smile to her lips. "I've already had enough this morning to sink a battleship."

He almost smiled in return and Blair found herself waiting in anticipation, but the smile never quite materialized. He twisted his head and began helping himself to the coffee.

She was used to men of this type: hard, ambitious, lacking in scruples, capable of anything. She neither admired nor disliked them. They had a job to do. Theirs was not a profession for weaklings.

Sure he wouldn't notice, Blair continued to watch him. He was precise; he never made an unnecessary movement.

His age was difficult to guess, somewhere in the range of forty to forty-five. On closer scrutiny, she noticed that his dark hair was threaded with silver and that his skin had a leathery look, as if he spent a lot of time outdoors.

His face seemed somehow wrongly put together with the shaggy eyebrows, high defined cheekbones and a dark, prominent jaw. Yet he oozed a raw energy that drew attention to the muscles in his arms and thighs, muscles honed to perfection, and not in a gym, either.

And those incredible dark, dangerous eyes, half-concealed by thick lashes, were now resting on her.

She could not turn away. For several long seconds their gazes continued to hold. Suddenly she felt dizzy and light-headed. What had come over her? This man was nothing to her. Why, only a few minutes ago, she would have liked nothing better than to slap that smirk off his face. And now...

Blair was the first to turn away. With as much dignity as she could muster, she walked to her desk and sat down, her legs threatening to cave in beneath her.

With the desk as a shield, she said, "Jack told me you'd go over the game plan with me, tell me exactly what's expected of me."

"That's right, but all in due time, Mrs. Browning. All in due time."

His tone irked her so that she had the urge to scream. But there was something about the man that turned her tongue to stone. Even the palms of her hands were wet and her throat pulsed hurtfully at the thought of carrying on a conversation with him, much less working with him.

"You need to pack your bags." His voice was light, with a metallic base. "We'll be leaving for Colorado in two days."

At first Blair was not sure she understood him correctly, as her mind had wandered again. The vagueness must have shown on her face, because he repeated his statement without being asked.

"Mrs. Browning, did you understand what I said? We'll be leaving for Colorado in two days."

This time Blair heard every word. "What!" Her voice cracked in disbelief.

His exasperation was evident. "You heard me. I have a cabin there and for about two weeks—I figure it'll take that long—we'll be holed up while you go through a crash retraining course." He paused, as though to let his words penetrate, then added, "With me as the instructor, of course."

Blair felt her heart plunge to her toes. *No!* she rebelled inwardly. She simply would not do it. Could not do it. To be alone, at this man's mercy for two weeks in the godforsaken wilds of Colorado, was asking too much. It was as though a red flag was being waved in front of her face. *Worrell.* Just wait until she saw him again, she silently threatened, she'd kill him, that's what she'd do. And in the meantime, she'd take great pleasure in planning how she'd carry it out.

"I take it you don't cotton to the idea?" Caleb drawled. He had lowered his huge frame into the chair in front of her desk and was comfortably seated with a leg crossed over the other knee. As usual, he was eyeing her closely.

He was having a field day putting her on the defensive, watching her squirm, she thought. And to think she was going to be cooped up with him for two long weeks. Heaven forbid!

Refusing, however, to let him know that he had indeed gotten under her skin, Blair drew herself up straight and glared at him.

"You're right, Mr. Hunt, I don't," she said. "And what's more, I don't understand why we're going to *your* cabin and not to the official training camp?"

Caleb didn't mince words. "That's easy enough. I wouldn't take on this assignment unless it was on my terms." He paused. "And the cabin just happened to be my terms."

"I see," Blair commented in a toneless voice. But she didn't see. She didn't see at all. It was ludicrous! It was mad!

Her thoughts were not lost on Caleb. Even though she made an obvious effort to hide her feelings, he could read her like the pages of an open book.

And in that moment, he couldn't help wondering what it would be like to take this particular product of American society to a motel room and stretch her out across a bed. Over the years he'd run across his share of spoiled and frigid women, not excluding his own wife, who were cut from this same bolt of cloth, but he had never accepted them.

He wondered whether this woman—with her designer clothes, her perfectly coiffed hair—would be any different. His mouth twisted sardonically. He thought not.

Again he wondered what it would be like to fill his hands with those voluptuous breasts, whose nipples were visible through the thin silk of her blouse. He was suddenly positive it would be an experience—even an achievement. But thinking about it was one thing; acting upon it was another. After all, he had always abided by the unwritten code, to never mix business with pleasure, which in plain English meant to never get involved with the people he worked with or worked for. It was dangerous just thinking about it.

Anyway, he wasn't good enough for the likes of Blair Stephens Browning, he reminded himself bitterly. She only saw him as a means to an end, and his private fantasies did not figure into it.

Furious with his meanderings, Caleb suddenly delved into his shirt pocket and pulled out another cigarette. He damned well knew his role; he had been playing it long enough, so long that it was natural. No, it would be sheer lunacy to become involved with Blair Browning; it must be avoided at all costs.

"I'm sorry," Blair said at last, "but there's no way I can be gone for that length of time. Jack'll just have to make other arrangements."

Caleb's nostrils flared. "Listen, lady, you might as well come down off your high horse right now. There will be no other arrangements made. And just so we understand each other, I don't like this any better than you do. If I had my way, I'd be a helluva long way from here."

Following his words, a blanket of silence fell over the room leaving the air riddled with suppressed animosity.

"Well, Mrs. Browning?"

"All right, Mr. Hunt, I get your point," she countered with equal hostility, knowing that he was right, that she must go along with the plans that had been made. There was nothing she could do about it short of welching on the deal, and that was out—she had given her word. But more than that, she owed it to Josh and to herself. And the sooner she got the job behind her, the sooner she could go on with her life. Yet, it still didn't make it any easier.

"Good," Caleb said, "because it won't be easy obtaining the information from a man like Tanner; he's a smooth operator, who has the charisma and gift of gab that can charm the horns off a billygoat."

"In spite of the time away from the bureau, I'm not a novice. I know what I'm doing." Blair felt stung by his attitude toward her and her ability to function as an agent. There was no way she would give him the satisfaction of knowing that she was afraid, that fear had been her constant companion since Worrell had walked out of her condo.

His mouth quirked. "For your own good I hope to hell you're right, because if you're not completely committed to this endeavor, you'd best get the hell out now. It's going to be tough, Mrs. Browning."

Blair raised her head and looked into his eyes. They were as cold as a glacial pool and about as inviting. "Just tell me when we leave."

Finally alone, Blair wilted back down into her chair, mortified at the sudden and shocking turn of events. In just two days' time, her life had taken a 180-degree turn.

Surely this was some kind of horrible nightmare, she tried convincing herself, and in a moment she would wake up and her life would be back on its right axis? But she knew that it was no dream, that it was a cold fact of life, especially when Caleb Hunt's face leaped to the forefront of her mind.

"Arrogant bastard," she mumbled aloud, picturing the contempt in his eyes when he had looked at her, which was often. In fact, it seemed to have been his favorite pastime.

Oh, she was aware that she had made him fiercely angry when she had mistaken him for a model—she couldn't help but smile, knowing that for a brief moment she'd had the upper hand, catching him off balance for once—yet she sensed that for whatever reason his resentment went much deeper.

Well, the feeling was mutual, she told herself with a savage twist of her shoulders. But the ridiculous thing was that when he'd walked into her office, she'd been intrigued. Was it that brooding air about him? Or the male magnetism he wore like a shield? Or was it simply the way he looked at her with both disdain and scorn?

No man she could recall had ever looked at her with anything less than admiration and, more often than not, desire. Her sensuous beauty attracted men like bees to honey and turned heads wherever she went.

However, none of that admiration had been present in Caleb's eyes. Oh, there had been laugh lines around his eyes, showing that he could relent, but it was obvious they hadn't been reinforced lately.

So what? she asked herself belligerently. She didn't think any more of that angry man than he did of her. The feeling was mutual, one of antagonistic dislike. And there was only a matter of days before she had to meet him at the airport. How was she going to cope? She honestly did not know.

It was the telephone that brought an end to her frantic thoughts.

With a heartfelt sigh of thanksgiving, Blair grabbed the receiver, and slinging her hair back from her ear, murmured, "Hello?"

"Blair, how's it goin'?"

The cheerful sound filtering through the line made Blair go weak with relief. She sank back into her chair while her fingers relaxed their tight grip on the receiver. She didn't know whom she'd been expecting to call, but she was glad it was Kyle Palmer, the man who had taught her everything she knew about photography. In doing so he had saved her sanity. She owed him much more than she could ever repay.

"Blair?" he said again in answer to her silence.

Shaking her head to clear it, Blair finally said, "Fine . . . just fine." The moment the little white lie left her lips, she raised her head upward with a silent prayer of forgiveness.

Kyle wasn't convinced. "Are you sure? I don't know, but you sound harassed."

Blair took a deep breath. "Well, my morning has been rather distracted," she admitted lamely, warning herself that she must be careful. She could not afford to let her deep-seated unrest show. Her work for the FBI was not something she could share with anyone, not even her family. And Kyle was quick to pick up her moods, as they had shared long hours of late.

"Have you been to lunch?" he inquired, tactfully changing the subject.

Blair glanced down at her watch. Two o'clock. She'd had no idea it was that late. "As a matter of fact, I haven't."

"Then let me treat you to a quick bite?"

"That would be great, only I promised Mother I'd be out there this afternoon." Regret gave her voice a gravelly, husky tone.

"You couldn't make it later—the visit, I mean?"

Blair hesitated, sorely tempted, only to decide suddenly against it, not because she particularly wanted to drive out to the Stephens mansion; she actually dreaded it. Being around her mother was trying at best. But on the other hand, she wasn't in the mood to exchange light conversation when her insides were in such a turmoil.

"Why don't we make it tonight, instead?" Kyle asked, making no attempt to hide his eagerness.

Blair smiled, picturing him standing up, bending over his desk, never able to control the huge supply of nervous energy that drove him like a master. She was sure his hands were shuffling through a stack of photographs while he was talking to her, his sharp green eyes not missing a flaw in any of them.

Most women, she'd venture to say, would consider Kyle handsome, with his ever present mischievous grin and the mop of curly sandy hair that was forever falling across his forehead. But to her he was just Kyle, her dear friend and mentor.

Suddenly realizing that she was wool-gathering, Blair laughed and said, "Sounds like a winner to me."

"Great. I'll pick you up about eight." He paused, then added, "Are you sure there's not anything wrong?"

"Thanks for caring, but nothing's wrong." *Only if you don't count the fact that the bottom has just dropped out of my world, that is.*

"I'll see you tonight, then."

The drive to her childhood home was always relaxing. Blair never tired of gazing at the green rolling hills as her car ate up the miles. The Stephens estate was tucked away in the lush Sonoma hills in the heart of the wine country, only forty-five minutes from the city.

Her mother had ranted and raved when Blair hadn't agreed to move back home after Josh's death. That, however, had been the last thing she'd wanted to do. It was enough at times to weather Sarah Stephens's strong personality from afar, much less at closer range.

Now, as she turned into the long steep driveway leading to the house, Blair rolled down the windows, anxious to soak up the sweet smell of the flowers that so proudly lined the drive on both sides. They were a sight to behold and one that she had tried to capture on film many times, only to come to the conclusion that she could never do so. Those exquisite products of nature were meant to be enjoyed firsthand, not through the lens of a camera.

Shortly the house came into view. It, too, had the power to thrill her. Resting atop a ten-acre, oak-studded knoll, it presented a breathtaking view.

It was a large house, offering total privacy, with four unique bedrooms and baths, a gourmet kitchen, a dining room and a den. But none of these could rival the beautiful redwood deck overlooking the professionally landscaped grounds.

The moment she brought the car to a halt, she unbuckled her seat belt and then, with heavy footsteps, began making her way up the steps.

Just as she closed the front door behind her, she looked up into the face of Ellen Riley, the housekeeper, who was as much a part of the house as the foundation it was built upon.

Ellen was grinning from ear to ear, while her eyes were shining with happiness. "It's about time you came home,

Blair Browning," she chastised, though the grin never left her round face. "Your mother's been about to have a fit, says you've been neglecting us."

"You know better than that," Blair exclaimed, reaching out and putting her arms around the woman she considered to be a substitute mother. More times than she cared to admit, she had gone crying to Ellen with her problems rather than to her own mother. And never had she come away with anything less than her tears dried up and her heart lighter.

"You must be getting senile, Ellen my girl," Blair teased, pulling away from the ample bosom. "It's only been two weeks since I was here." Her eyes twinkled. "Don't you remember, I almost foundered on the strawberry cheesecake you fixed."

"Huh," Ellen said with a snort, looking Blair up and down. "Don't seem to me like you've been eating much of anything. If you don't put some meat on those bones, you're gonna dry up and blow away."

Blair laughed again. "Ah, come on, Ellen, give me a break. You sound just like Sarah."

"Did I hear my name mentioned?"

Blair whipped around and watched as her mother walked toward her. Sarah Stephens was a tall, straight-backed, gray-haired woman with finely formed features and round, intelligent brown eyes. Eyes that could suddenly turn frigid, especially if she didn't get her own way. An attractive woman, some would say, who moved with a purpose.

And her purpose at the moment was to confront her daughter. "It's good to see you, my dear," Sarah announced formally, offering her scented cheek to Blair.

"Same here, Mother," Blair responded, brushing the still-unlined skin with her lips, hating the tension that always hovered between the two of them.

"I'm glad you got here before Thomas left." There was a mild reproof in her voice, letting Blair know that she didn't approve of her being late."

Blair's eyes lit up. "You mean Uncle Thomas is here? Great!" Wasting no more time, Blair turned and made her way toward the back of the house where the den was located, completely oblivious to the opulence surrounding her. Even when she stepped into the large room, where sunshine poured through a dramatic skylight in the beamed-ceiling, the rich surroundings failed to claim her attention. She had eyes only for the man who was curled up on the couch.

The moment he saw his beloved niece breeze through the door, he stood up.

"Oh, Uncle Thomas," Blair wailed, flying into his arms. "It seems like aeons since I've seen you."

"You're a sight for sore eyes, girl," Thomas said, giving her a hearty hug and then pushing her to arm's length. "Your mother and I were talking about you. I had just told her that I was thinking of driving in unannounced and pulling you out of that darkroom and whisking you off to dinner." He tweaked the tip of her nose before he dropped his arms.

"Sounds like a good idea to me," Sarah interrupted, strolling into the room, followed by Ellen with a tray of goodies and coffee. "That will be all, Ellen," she added. "Thank you."

"Mmm, that coffee smells heavenly," Blair said, throwing Ellen a smile before the housekeeper turned and left the room.

"Instead of drinking coffee, you should be thinking of eating a well-balanced meal." Sarah's eyes were closely monitoring Blair, and her disapproval was evident in her tone as she watched her daughter help herself to a cup of the steaming brew.

"Oh, I don't know so much about that," Thomas chimed in. "I was thinking that I've never seen her look lovelier." He paused and cocked his head to one side. "Oh, maybe the circles under her eyes are a bit more pronounced, but that merely adds an air of mystery about her." He grinned, enjoying taking issue with Sarah, though it was done in a teasing, gentle manner.

Blair flashed him a grateful smile. "Thanks, Uncle, for coming to my rescue," she said, loving the sound of his voice: deep and resonant, and humorous like his eyes. "I don't know what I'd do without you."

Truer words were never spoken. In his middle sixties, Thomas Stephens was a fine figure of a man. His mop of silver hair capped off sharp but twinkling gray eyes. He was of medium height with only the slightest hint of a thickening waistline. Blair couldn't understand why he had never married, he had everything going for him: looks, money, power.

He had begun selling insurance as a young man and by the time he was thirty he had formed his own company. From then on there had been no stopping him. When he retired more than a year before, his company had been worth millions.

Sometimes Blair wondered if maybe he wasn't smitten with her mother. When Thomas didn't know he was being observed, there was a certain look in his eyes when Sarah came into the room. If only that were true...

"It's obvious, Blair, that your adoring uncle won't tell you the truth, but I most certainly will."

"Now, Sarah," Thomas began calmly, though his bushy brows were drawn together in a frown.

Blair jerked her head up and around at the sound of her mother's sharp, cold voice. "Please... Mother, I didn't come here to get raked over the coals." Although she made an effort to keep her tone even, she knew she had failed, her ears picking up the slight tremor. Why did she let Sarah get to her?

Sarah stiffened visibly and, ignoring Thomas's loud sigh, continued harping. "You looked completely washed out, as though you haven't slept in a month. It's that job, I just know it. All that traveling and worrying with those temperamental models. And you don't even have to work. Why, you have more money than you could ever spend."

"Mother!"

"All right, all right, I'll hush," Sarah said petulantly, "but only if you'll answer one question."

Although Blair was furious at that point, she knew she'd agree to anything just to shut her mother up. She had reconciled herself long ago to her mother's shortcomings. She knew Sarah was a frustrated, domineering woman who had nothing better to do with her time than meddle in others' affairs, mainly hers.

"What is it?" Blair demanded tersely.

"When are you going to marry Kyle Palmer? It's there for the world to see that he adores you, and I think you're a fool for not accepting his offer."

Her mother had never made any effort to hide the fact that she thought Kyle Palmer hung the moon, that he would make Blair the perfect husband, that he had it all. To Sarah, keeping up appearances was important. Having been reared in poverty, she never forgave or forgot her past. It was only after she married Warner Stephens that she felt her life had begun. Together they made millions in the oil industry in Texas, before moving to California where Warner later died of heart failure. Blair was ten years old at the time.

As a result of her upbringing, Sarah was extremely conscious of social status, of "keeping up with the Joneses." She wanted more than anything for Blair to settle down and marry into the right family. She considered Kyle Palmer the perfect match.

Sarah had been none too pleased when Blair had married Josh Browning, who had lured her daughter into what she termed "the seedy business of spying." She never forgave Josh for that, nor did she ever believe he was good enough for her daughter. The second time around, Sarah aimed to see that Blair did not make that same mistake.

"Sarah, don't," Thomas said, breaking into the silence. "Don't you know when to give up? Blair's a grown woman who—"

"Thanks for the vote of confidence, Uncle Thomas," Blair cut in with a weary sigh. "But don't you know by now that once Mother gets something on her mind, there's no stopping her?"

Even Thomas was unable to do anything with his sister-in-law, Blair knew. He had tried for years to keep her out of Blair's life as much as he could, but Sarah would not listen to reason where Blair was concerned. Since the death of her husband, it was clear that she had made her daughter the focal point of her life.

Slowly, Blair turned around and confronted her mother, her face a waxen mask, her body unnaturally stiff. "I'm going to tell you once and for all that Kyle Palmer is a friend and that's all. I'm not ready to remarry and when I'm ready, if ever, you'll be the first to know."

Putting her exasperation into words, Sarah snapped, "Don't you think you've mourned for Josh long enough?"

"Dammit, Sarah, you've gone too far!" Thomas bellowed, closing the distance between himself and Blair in one stride. "Leave the girl alone."

Although Blair winced in reaction to her mother's harsh words and was holding herself together by a mere thread, her comeback was fierce. "That subject is not open for discussion and if you don't want me to walk out of here and never come back, then I suggest you remember that."

"Sarah, what's gotten into you?" Thomas muttered harshly, putting an arm around Blair and hugging her close against his side.

For a fleeting moment, Sarah's face seemed to sag, or was it just her imagination? Blair wondered as she, herself, sagged against Thomas. "Well, you can't blame me for being concerned," Sarah admonished haughtily, although her bottom lip was quivering.

Blair knew that was as close to an apology as she would ever get from her mother. Suddenly she longed to reach out and touch her mother, close the distance between them, only to realize that she didn't know how.

So instead she said, "I appreciate your concern. Let's just leave it at that, shall we?" Then she smiled, in an effort to take the chill out of the air.

"I'll vote for that," Thomas exclaimed before sitting down in front of the serving tray. "Food anyone?"

Things settled down after that, and the cookies and tiny cakes Ellen had baked were nibbled on and pleasantries were exchanged.

It was only after Blair had walked out to her car a short time later that it dawned on her she had forgotten to give her mother the concocted story concerning her whereabouts the next few weeks. She'd had every intention of telling Sarah that a photography assignment was taking her out of the country.

Blair hated lying, but then deceiving her mother was the least of her worries. Wasn't it?

Chapter 3

Thomas Stephens unfurled his frame from behind the wheel of the Lincoln Continental and made his way up the long walk to the front door of his sister-in-law's house.

After Blair had walked out of the house three days before, he and Sarah had quarreled, something they had never done before. He hoped to make amends, or try to, he corrected himself unhappily. But, dammit, he'd wanted her to see what she was doing to her daughter.

And, in the process, he'd also wanted Sarah to see the type of woman she had become. Selfish. Snobbish. Possessive. All those adjectives fit, and they were just the tip of the iceberg.

Yet, with all those faults, he loved her. He could not remember a time when he hadn't loved her. An older replica of her daughter, Sarah was still beautiful and her figure well preserved. Just thinking about her high, firm breasts caused his breath to quicken.

"You're a fool, Thomas Stephens," he said aloud, slowing his stride to the door.

May God forgive him, but even when his brother was alive, he'd loved her. To his credit, however, it had been his secret and his alone; he'd kept it locked tight in his heart all these years and took great effort to make sure that no one else was aware of it—least of all Sarah.

He always made it a point never to touch her. Even when long periods of time elapsed between meetings, he never so much as leaned over and pecked her on the cheek—a handshake was all the intimacy he'd allow. He couldn't bear the thought of bringing further unhappiness to Sarah. He suspected that her marriage to his brother had not been a happy one, for when Blair was born, Sarah had devoted every minute of time to her.

Thomas had likened it to a rebirth. Sarah, through Blair, felt she had been given another chance to live her life as she'd wanted to, but never could.

Thank heavens Blair was finally pulling away. The scene the other day had proved it; he had never heard her talk to Sarah so strongly. He was glad, yet he couldn't help but worry about Sarah. Hell, she needed him and didn't even know it.

He was tired of being the devoted brother-in-law, Johnny-on-the-spot when things didn't go exactly as Sarah planned. He'd have made his move years before except that Blair towered like a mountain between them. Then, when Blair married, Sarah had buried herself in countless bridge parties, catering to her insufferable snobbish friends—if one could call them friends; Thomas had always thought of them as a backbiting bunch of vipers—and endless rounds of charity functions.

Still, at no time had he ever resented Blair—the others yes, but never Blair. He'd loved her like a daughter, and still did. And when she'd married Josh Browning and gone to

work for the FBI against her mother's wishes, he'd sup-
ported her. Sarah had nearly gone crazy when Blair told her
what she intended to do.

But that was all history and Blair was well on her way to
making a name for herself in the world of photography. He
couldn't have been happier for her. If only Sarah could feel
the same. His patience, after all these years, was finally
playing out. He had made up his mind to make his move
soon or forget it altogether.

Ellen greeted him at the door and informed him that
Sarah was in the den. He lost no time in getting there and
walked through the door just as she was hanging up the
phone. There was a troubled look on her face, making her
look her age.

Thomas felt another premonition of doom twist through
his gut. Another crisis? Would there ever be time for just the
two of them? Suddenly he thought not, and it filled him
with a bitter sadness.

"Oh, Thomas, am I glad to see you," Sarah whispered,
reaching for his hand and then squeezing it before letting it
go.

"Same here, Sarah," he responded lightly, relieved that
she was willing to forgive and forget the angry words that
had passed between them. Then, seeing that she was shaking, he sat down immediately and lost no time in pouring
two cups of coffee from a tray on the table.

"Here, drink this," Thomas ordered. "It'll help calm you
down." Sarah picked up the cup. He didn't take his eyes off
her as she sat down opposite him on the couch. "Now, tell
me first who that was on the phone and then tell me why
you're so upset?"

"It . . . it was Blair."

Thomas raised his eyebrows, afraid that it had been Blair,
yet puzzled that she would be in touch with her mother so

soon after what had transpired between them. "Well, tell me."

Sarah shook her head as though dazed and stood up. "She's leaving on an...assignment. She's...going to be gone for two weeks or longer."

"So?" Thomas couldn't for the life of him understand what all the fretting was about. Blair was certainly no amateur when it came to traveling.

"She refused to give me a hotel, a phone number or any way I might reach her. She...she said that she would be flitting from one location to the next."

Thomas expelled an impatient sigh. "And why does that upset you so much?"

"I don't know," she cried, the coffee cup beginning to rattle in her hands. Quickly Thomas reached for it and set it down before she could drop it. "But I know Blair and there's something wrong, something she's not telling me. I sensed it the other day when she was here, looking so ghastly."

His expression growing hard, Thomas stood up. "Come on, Sarah," he chided, skirting around the coffee table and coming to stand just inches from her. "You're making a mountain out of a molehill." *As usual,* he was tempted to add, but refrained from doing so, not wanting to make matters worse.

Sarah's lips tightened. "I knew you wouldn't understand. You...you never do when it comes to Blair."

A terse expletive zipped through his lips. "Sarah, Sarah, you'd try the patience of a saint." Then he saw that she was really upset. Tears were pooling in her eyes and it dawned on him that she had convinced herself that Blair was in some kind of trouble.

He raked an impatient hand through his hair instead of reaching for her as he longed to do. But his eyes spoke volumes as he stared directly into hers, seeking to reassure her.

"Blair will be just fine," he said softly. When she would have interrupted, he hurried on. "And though you might very well be right and something is wrong, you'll just have to let her work it out for herself."

Sarah, with tears streaming down her face, again reached for Thomas's hand, twining her long shapely fingers around it and clinging as though for dear life.

The gesture was almost his undoing. The blood raced through his body as their eyes continued to hold.

Then Sarah whispered, "Please...would you...hold me? I feel so alone...so frightened."

Feeling as though he'd just received manna from heaven, Thomas carefully folded her into his arms.

And for the longest of time, their tears mingled.

Blair was packed. The taxi was due any minute. And thank goodness, she thought, the dreaded phone call to her mother was behind her. Although she'd hated to break the news over the phone, she'd hated even more the idea of going back to the house and telling her in person. She just hadn't been up to putting herself through another verbal skirmish with Sarah; she had enough on her mind as it was.

Kyle for one. When she'd had dinner with him, she'd had to tell him that she'd be away for a while. He'd taken it in stride fairly well, but she could tell that he wanted to question her in detail.

"Why so secretive all of a sudden?" he'd asked as they were having an after-dinner drink.

"You're imagining things," she returned lightly. "It's just another overseas assignment, no big deal," she added, lying profusely and hating every minute of it.

Then abruptly, he challenged her. "When we're married, I hope you won't run amok without telling me exactly where you're going." He grinned, lightening his tone, though his eyes remained serious.

"I haven't said I'd marry you, Kyle," she said softly, not wanting to hurt him. "You know I don't love—"

"That's all right," he cut in, smiling. "I know the score, but I don't care. I still want to marry you, and I can always hope, can't I?"

Blair sighed. "Just as long as you don't push. I'm . . . not ready yet. I'm already pulled apart, with you on one side and Mother on the other. And both of you know how much I want to get my business off and running." She heard the nervousness in her own voice. "And for some reason I feel like I'm running out of time. Sounds crazy, I know, but..." She had let the sentence play out with a shrug.

Kyle's smile had been sad. "Just don't forget about me...."

Suddenly the sound of the taxi's horn jogged her out of her musings and into action. Minutes later, she found herself in the back seat of the cab with a lump the size of a golf ball lodged in her throat. *There's no turning back now.*

She'd desperately tried to keep her fear under control. But when she was least expecting it, it would rear its ugly head, leaving her feeling weak and disoriented. In defiance, she'd worked that much harder. And the one thing—perhaps the only thing—that had been in her favor was that she had been successful in keeping thoughts of Caleb Hunt at bay.

But now, as the taxi clicked off the miles to the airport, her mind suddenly switched tracks to him. With impending dread, she concentrated on the dark, angry man. Was his deep-seated anger directly associated with her or was it from a past pain or loss? Or was he simply angry? This man with gray weaving through his hair and a mouth that, in repose, looked so soft. Perhaps misleadingly soft. Thinking of kisses, *his* kisses. Suddenly she slipped into a kind of hungry lassitude with a vision of his tongue sparring with hers....

God! Had she completely lost her senses? She had to clear her head, control her mind. Taking deep breaths, she frantically searched for something else to think about, anything that would take her mind off Caleb Hunt and her unbelievable thoughts of him.

What on earth had come over her? Was it just sex, the lack of it taunting her? Of course it was. There had been no one since Josh. Sexual promiscuity was not for her. And though she found it hard to admit even now, sex with Josh had not been all that great. Maybe she was frigid, as Josh had so often accused her, only to apologize later for his cruelty. But she knew she wasn't frigid; it was just that for some unknown reason she was never able to give of herself completely and Josh could never forgive her for that.

Then she'd gotten pregnant in the hope that a child would breach the growing gap between them. Only it was not meant to be....

"Ma'am, what airline?"

With a start, Blair jerked her head up and around, taking in her surroundings for the first time since she'd climbed into the automobile. Making an effort to hold her voice steady, she responded. "Uh, Delta . . . please."

Before Caleb had stalked out of her office—what seemed like a lifetime ago now—he'd told her he'd have her tickets sent to her home. He'd been as good as his word and had included a terse note reminding her to pay close attention to the exact date and time of departure.

Nodding, the driver made the appropriate turn, and within minutes Blair had checked her luggage and was making her way through the terminal, her purse and a carryall in her hands.

And then she saw him.

He was leaning negligently against a wall smoking a cigarette. Again, she wondered how she would cope as despair washed through her with a renewed vengeance.

She doubted she'd survive a second.

As yet he was unaware of her presence, and Blair observed him, noticing again the depth of his eyes, the breadth of his shoulders, the swell of him against his jeans. She looked at his hands, his ears, his neck, the way his hair fell over his forehead and his casual habit of pushing it away.

For a second, her eyes fluttered shut while she fought to control the storm in her stomach.

"Blair?"

Her eyes opened wide, the sound of her name on his lips buzzing inside her head like tiny drills working away at her pressure points.

Caleb had narrowed the distance between them, only a hair's breadth away, or so it seemed to Blair, and was reaching for her bag. Careful not to touch him, she relinquished it, then took a step back.

"Hello...Caleb." She almost choked on the familiar use of his name, though realizing, as he evidently had, that under the circumstances it would be silly to continue to use their surnames, no matter how thick the hostility.

The fact that she had stepped back out of harm's way was obvious to Caleb. Suddenly the softness in his lips vanished; they slipped into a pencil-thin line, and Blair could see his knuckles whiten as he increased the grip on her bag.

"Shall we go?" he said shortly, stepping aside, letting her precede him.

After surviving the hassle of having their bags checked thoroughly, they were finally on the plane, comfortably seated in the first-class cabin. For a moment Blair had been tempted to try and find a seat away from him, but he had been close behind her and she found herself being edged into a row where there were two vacant seats.

He buckled his seat belt and then reached for the pack of cigarettes in his pocket and pointed it in her direction.

"No, thank you," she said. "Anyway, the lights are on; you can't smoke."

With a terse expletive, he jammed the pack back into his pocket.

She wished they weren't sitting together. She was entirely too aware of him. The smell of his cologne mixed with the smell of his cigarettes was potent. He filled the seat; his arm next to hers was veined and powerful. She was careful not to touch him.

Inhaling sharply, Blair forced herself to look at the plane's plush interior. Things had certainly changed since she was with the bureau, she mused silently. Either that or Mr. Caleb Hunt wielded more power than she'd first thought.

The silence stretched between them as they continued to avoid looking at each other.

By the time the smiling flight attendant reached them, Blair's nerves were jumping. She clenched both her hands in her lap.

"Surely you're not nervous?" Caleb said offhandedly, and then turned his attention to the attendant. The lilting soprano voice was coming on to him like a flower to the sun.

Blair kept her head averted, staring out the tiny window, forcing her mind to block out their conversation. And then she heard him laugh.

Slowly, and without conscious thought, Blair turned her head. His eyes were still on the woman, but she was held captivated by the uninhibited movement of his dark head, thrown back in laughter, his white teeth sparkling against his tanned face. His hands were huge, but unlike most big men, his gestures seemed controlled and gentle.

Suddenly Blair was finding it difficult to breathe; it was the sound of that laughter that caught and held her. In response, something deep within her body quivered in a purely sensual reaction. She began to breathe deeply, determined to recover her equilibrium.

God! Blair, you're behaving like a complete idiot. As far as you're concerned, the man might as well be from an alien planet. Just remember that this is just an interlude in your life and when it's over you'll both go your separate ways.

"Would you care for something to drink?"

"Ah, yes—a glass of white wine—please," Blair stammered as she avoided looking at Caleb, although she felt his eyes on her.

"And you, Mr. Hunt?" the redhead purred, widening her smile just for him.

"Make mine a double Scotch."

With a nod and another smile, she moved on. Blair still felt Caleb's eyes on her. Suddenly deciding not to let him intimidate her a second longer, she faced him, returning his bold stare.

When their eyes collided, she felt her resolution weaken. For an absurd moment she saw herself as a fish on the end of a hook, dangling, completely at his mercy. The blackness of his eyes was like the unending reaches of a cold, calm sea. They seemed to look right through her. She shivered.

"Cold?"

Blair forced herself to smile, the resolution once again stiffening her spine. "No... I'm fine."

He wasn't convinced and said as much. "Well, you don't look fine," he said bluntly.

"It just so happens you're right," she said flatly. "I'm not. I don't particularly like to fly." No way was she going to admit that he was three-fourths responsible for her weird behavior.

Caleb raised his eyebrows. "I find that hard to believe," he drawled in a mocking tone, "especially with the type of work you do. I can just picture it now: the glamorous Mrs.

Browning flying to cities around the world snapping her camera among the rich and famous."

When the mockery turned to derision, she wasn't sure, but she was sure she wasn't about to let him get away with his snide remarks. She didn't owe the man a thing.

Smiling innocently, Blair asked, "Exactly what have I done to make you dislike me so much, Mr. Hunt? We might as well clear the air once and for all. Surely it couldn't be because I'm a woman." Her words were drenched in sweet sarcasm.

For a moment, Caleb seemed stunned by her comeback. But then he rallied and Blair thought she saw a glimmer of admiration in his eyes, even before the shadow of a smile lent his harsh features a reprieve.

He had his mouth open to speak when the attendant arrived with the drinks. "We'll be taking off shortly," she said with a smile. "Sorry for the delay, but ground traffic's stacked up."

Caleb merely nodded and when the redhead received no further response, she moved on, though a promise danced in her eyes.

Blair sipped her wine, grateful for the refreshing liquid as it slid down her throat to her stomach. Was he going to answer her question? she wondered. More than likely not. He probably thought she was just being childish and that her question deserved no answer.

Then, out of the clear blue he said, "It's not you personally I don't like; it's what you stand for that rubs me the wrong way."

"Oh, and how is that?" Blair was furious and it showed.

"Money." He finished his drink. "So long as you have money, it buys most things and most people."

"But not you? You don't dirty your hands with it?" She hadn't meant to say that, but his contemptuous attitude grated against her nerves.

His tone was frigid. "If money was important to me, I wouldn't be in this line of work, that's for damned sure."

"Then it has to be the danger that keeps you coming back for more."

"You got it. But then you ought to know that."

"How could I? After all, I don't know anything about you," Blair said. "I only know that according to your superior you're the best and that we'll be working together for the next two weeks."

"And that's all you need to know."

A silence followed his words, and Caleb sensed that his bluntness had made her angry. He lifted his head to look at her with weary resignation, his eyes intent upon her delicately boned profile. He began thinking of the amber-colored eyes that were rimmed with thick black lashes, and her soft, lusciously full mouth, then, with an effort, dragged his thoughts away. His hand closed tightly around the glass in his hand and he had to fight the urge to shatter it into a million pieces.

"Mr. Hunt," Blair said after a minute, saccharine sweetness back in her voice, "has anyone ever told you that you have the personality of a corkscrew?"

The corners of his lips turned up as though he was actually going to smile. He didn't.

Instead, he looked at her curiously and said, "Chalk one up for you, Blair Browning."

Blair turned away in silence, wishing she felt better about having scored at least one small victory over the difficult man who had swept into her life like a raging spring storm. But she did not; she felt depressed.

The silence deepened as Blair leaned back and closed her eyes. Were they ever going to take off? she asked herself impatiently. It seemed like hours ago that they had boarded the plane, though in reality it had been only thirty minutes.

"You haven't fastened your seat belt," Caleb said in his low, gruff voice, jarring her eyes open. He was staring at her, his eyes resting curiously on the taut fabric stretched across her breasts. Blair felt the color surge into her cheeks, objecting to the way he was looking at her, yet curiously excited at the same time.

"Oh," she mumbled, making a feeble attempt at connecting the buckles.

"Let me," Caleb said tautly, reaching across her, his arm lightly brushing the fullness of her breast. Something akin to an electric shock coursed through Blair. Then, with eyes as wide as she could make them, she sank deeper into her seat just as the seat belt popped into place. Had he felt the same jolt of electricity?

She watched as he drew back slowly and gazed down into her face. It was as if he were reaching into her body and squeezing her heart.

Then the moment was no more.

Caleb twisted back around in his seat and immediately reached for the refill the attendant had placed on his tray. In one gulp, it was gone.

"Would you mind not...drinking so much?" Blair asked in a small, dazed voice, still not recovered from that mind-blowing experience of a moment before.

She had spunk; he'd say that much for her, Caleb admitted. But she also had a mouth that had been fed only with a silver spoon. Suddenly he had the urge to take this beautiful woman by the shoulders and shake her.

"I never get drunk," he sneered. "And I don't need a keeper."

The plane was finally climbing toward the heavens. Already the puffy clouds above San Francisco were below them.

Blair accepted a copy of *People* magazine from the attendant and thumbed through it. Out of the corner of her eye she noticed Caleb's eyes were closed; he seemed asleep. She went back to her magazine, but she couldn't concentrate. The pages were a blur. There were too many questions she wanted to ask, and no one to answer them. It was all well and good for Jack Worrell to put her under this man's care, but she couldn't be with him and not know what made him tick. Especially not this man.

Was he married? No. Maybe, she mused, that was his problem. A failed marriage. He had all the symptoms. No doubt about it, he held women in contempt. No, she corrected herself immediately, remembering the way he had laughed at something the attendant had said. It was *her* he held in contempt.

Blair closed her eyes and tried to force herself to relax, not to think about him. It was impossible, as every muscle in her body was stretched like a taut string.

She had never considered herself to be a snob like her mother, although she was guilty, she'd admit, of taking for granted money and the things it could buy. Was that a crime? Did her good fortune make her lord it over the lesser beings of the world? Of course not. Yet, by the same token, she wasn't in the habit of apologizing for her station in life. And she wasn't about to start now.

But this big brute of a man sitting next to her had her on the defensive and she resented the feeling, and him as well, for making her feel that way.

Again she wondered what made him tick. He was like no other man she had ever met. He was so totally rough around the edges, yet so totally sure of himself—a man's man. And when his arm had accidentally touched her...

His eyes were open and fixed on her. The look made her uncomfortable, her thoughts still fresh in her mind. She wasn't used to men looking at her like that, as if they were dissecting her under a microscope.

"Do you think we really stand a chance against Tanner?" Blair asked, hell-bent on making him talk, feeling desperate to know something about him. Anything.

"Don't you?"

"I . . . hope so," she murmured, her expression troubled.

"Don't worry. That sonofabitch's days are numbered."

Just looking at the cast iron strength of his jaw, Blair could understand why Worrell placed so much confidence in him. "I . . . I want him to pay for what he did to my . . . husband."

Caleb's eyes suddenly sharpened like ice picks. "He'll pay."

"If I do my job, that is. Right?"

"That's right," he drawled. "It all depends on you."

"Well, I'm certainly out of practice, I'll be the first to admit that, but as the old saying goes, if you ever once learned to ride a bicycle, you'll never forget how."

For the first time, he smiled at her. Wonders never cease.

"Don't you agree?" she asked, her voice soft and breathy.

"We'll see."

She was frustrated to see his eyes become guarded, and could have kicked herself. He'd behaved like a human for almost a full minute. Blair pushed on, "You don't have much faith in my ability, do you?"

"It doesn't really matter what I think," he said with a shrug. "You were Worrell's choice and that's that."

I guess that's supposed to put me in my place. She answered with a frigid silence.

"Look," he said flatly, "all I want is to get this over with, as much or more than you do, Mrs. Browning."

"I doubt that," she countered sharply, still miffed by his lack of tact.

"What's the matter, you got a fiancé waiting in the wings?"

"No, I don't have a fiancé," she said quietly, stunned that he cared enough to ask.

"That's surprising."

"Why?" Blair asked, taking a sip of her wine and watching him swallow another double Scotch.

"Don't worry, I can handle it," he said, having seen her eyes dip to the empty glass. "Now, to answer your question. You're beautiful and you have money."

Money again. "You're not married?" she asked suddenly, turning the tables on him.

"Not anymore." The tone of his voice didn't invite further questions, but she wasn't so easily put off.

"You didn't marry again?"

"This is a job for single men, Mrs. Browning. You of all people should know that."

Blair's eyes narrowed at his sarcastic tone. "Ah, the job again. You're really into what you do, aren't you? Your job, I mean."

"It's all I have," he said simply.

She peered at him strangely. "What about your family?"

"I don't have a family. I've been alone since I was fourteen."

"I'm sorry," she whispered inadequately, hearing the pain in his voice. Yet he had risen above the circumstances. He was educated and had advanced in the ranks of the FBI, which in itself was no easy feat. Still, it was a pity...

"I don't want your sympathy," he spat violently, showing his uncanny ability to read her mind. "Save it for some poor slob who needs it."

It was clear to her why few people ever got to know the man inside Caleb Hunt. His confession had proved that there was a carefully bricked-up vulnerability inside him. So why didn't she just back off and leave him alone? Why did she care?

Again she was sorry she had taken the seat beside him. But he was there, they were together—albeit poles apart—and whatever happened afterward, she could not ignore him.

An hour later, sleep still proved an elusive prey. Without thinking, Caleb opened his eyes and looked at her. So beautiful. It was just incredible how beautiful she was. He longed for a cigarette but for some reason the no-smoking light was on. Looking at her was like being kicked simultaneously in both kneecaps so that he buckled to the ground.

He bitterly resented that feeling. Besides that, the woman had the uncanny ability to rub him the wrong way. She seemed to delight in setting him off, bringing out the worst in him. That worried him. He knew anger would impair his efficiency and she'd kept him angry ninety-five percent of the time.

So he hated this assignment. So he was forced to take it. So he felt nothing but contempt for her kind.

So what?

He could handle it.

He could handle her.

Or could he?

Chapter 4

Paul Tanner loosened his tie as he strode briskly into his town house, slamming the door behind him. Damn, but it had been a bitch of a day. He was tired of sitting on pins and needles waiting for his financial advisor to get back to him. What the hell was taking him so long, anyway? he asked himself, slinging his tie onto the nearest chair. Then, in a jerky movement, he closed the distance between himself and the bar.

Things couldn't be as bad as they had been presented to him. Or could they? No. He had to believe that Hal Havard was merely trying to put the screws to him, to scare him. Even though he did not like Havard, he was confident he could juggle the books and keep him afloat—at least until he could play his last big ace in the hole. There was money; Havard would just have to find it. After all, wasn't that what he paid that flunky to do, to rob Peter to pay Paul?

"Cool it, Tanner," he said aloud. "Don't let this get to you."

The moment he reached the bar his hand plucked the bottle of whiskey off the glass shelf, and when he did he saw his reflection in the beveled-glass mirror above the bar. He grimaced.

His brown eyes were sporting bags under them that could hold a bowling ball, he thought. But the rest of his face didn't look too bad. He was endowed with crisp, regular features chiseled from excellent bones and tight, clear skin, and a head of thick brown hair with a sprinkling of gray, reminding him of his forty-plus years.

Although considered short for a man—five foot eight—he did not look on that as a handicap. His muscular build and trim waistline had a tendency to compensate for his stature. He walked with confidence in his world of movers and shakers.

With a muffled curse directed toward himself for dallying, he returned to the task of mixing his drink. That accomplished, he took two swigs and then walked to his favorite chair and sat down. To wait. He looked at his watch and noted that it was seven-thirty. Where was Dee? She should have already been there.

Paul Tanner was devoted to two things in life: money and beautiful women. He considered himself to be a connoisseur of both. Unfortunately, money had become a problem the past few years, or rather the lack of it had. But women—never. When he chose to turn on the charm, which was often, they flocked to him.

And right now he needed a woman. Dee Baker, his secretary, was the chosen one. It hadn't been a particularly successful day and, though the drink helped to smooth his ruffled feathers, a woman would finish taking the kinks out of his body. Where the hell was she? A good lay was definitely the order of the evening, he thought. He couldn't say much for Dee's expertise as a secretary, but in the bed she was pure dynamite.

But now he still had time to think. He couldn't believe another real estate deal had gone sour. Was he losing his touch? He'd been counting on putting some money in the coffer until he could get the other deal set up exactly the way he wanted it. His eyes took on a fanatical glint and his mouth followed suit with a ruthless twist. If everything worked out as planned, he could say to hell with his real estate, for he would be a very rich man again.

Suddenly the rattling of the doorknob pierced his thoughts. Without bothering to stand up, he snapped, "It's open."

A young woman in her middle twenties breezed across the threshold. She was pretty with an overabundance of curly blond hair, straight out of a bottle, and large blue eyes. Her sensuous mouth was curved upward in a wide grin.

"Where have you been?" Tanner asked, his voice laced with a deadly calm.

The grin disappeared instantly from the blonde's face as she stopped in the center of the room. Dee Baker was frightened. She knew this man's moods, knew that he was angry and would more than likely take it out on her as he'd done so often in the past.

Although her bottom lip quivered, she managed to push the words through it. "Don't be mad at me, Paulie," she pleaded. "I . . . I went shopping for a new dress for Saturday night just like you told me to. You said you wanted me to look real nice." She paused as though to regroup and then rattled on. "Time just got away from me. You know how it is with women. . . ." She gave a childish shrug and watched as he tipped the glass and drained it of every last drop of whiskey.

Then Tanner stood up, his face no longer pinched with menace. "Come here," he demanded softly.

Recognizing the passion in his voice, Dee raced to do his bidding, an eager smile on her face.

Roughly, Tanner's bullish arms wrapped around her and his lips covered hers in brutal force. Dee squirmed closer. When there was no more air between them, Tanner rasped, "I can't wait another second."

His companion was as eager. While reaching under her skirt, Tanner edged backward, Dee tight against him. When he hit the couch, he fell against it. Theirs was a fusion of lust as Dee fell on top of him. Just as their lips locked together, tantalizingly hot, the phone rang.

Tanner froze.

The phone had no conscience; the sound was like a scream through the air as it continued to ring.

Moaning, Tanner pushed Dee off him, searching blindly for the phone that was within arm's reach.

"Tanner," he bit out.

"It's me, Hal."

"Jesus, Hal! You couldn't have picked a worse time to call."

"Let's face it, Tanner, no time's ever good for you. Just zip up your pants," he said crudely, "and get the hell down to my office."

"That bad, huh?" Tanner asked, his stomach suddenly feeling like a chunk of lead.

"That bad."

"Well, I'm not leaving here for any bad news. Just spit it out, over the phone."

"All right, Paul, have it your own way." Hal paused. "The bottom line is that you're broke. Dead broke."

Tanner felt sick. "There's bound to be something you've overlooked," he said desperately.

Hal's sigh was sharp. "None. Zilch. I'd say you have about a month at the most to come up with megabucks before your lenders foreclose, and in the process squash you like a bug."

"Thanks for nothing, Havard," Tanner yelled, slamming the phone down in its cradle.

Dee was sitting beside him. She flinched. "Paulie?"

His eyes narrowed into slits as he turned toward her. "Get the hell out of my sight. Now!"

Exactly one minute later he was alone. Push had finally come to shove. He'd give those Russian bastards what they wanted, he thought wildly, not just one or two names, but everyone he'd ever known. The whole list, for what it was worth—even the ones already out of commission. But this time they'd pay through the nose, no more paltry sums for him.

Lifting the receiver off the hook, he punched out a series of numbers.

After all, *he* was the one calling the shots.

When the tires squealed against the runway, Blair was stiff with a fatigue that was more mental than physical. She had dozed off and on, only to wake up with a sense of anxiety she couldn't equate with the flight.

They disembarked in silence. Although Hunt did remove her bag from the overhead storage compartment he otherwise ignored her as they walked down the concourse, finally ending up at a rent-a-car booth.

Blair stood quietly to the side while he took care of business, feeling the tension mount inside her like a smoldering volcano. *What am I doing here?* she screamed silently, only to instantly answer her own question. *For Josh. You're doing this for Josh. Don't ever lose sight of that and you'll do just fine.*

Caleb turned around and said impatiently, "Let's go."

"I'm waiting on you," she responded with equal impatience.

His jaw was thrust forward. "We're stuck with a small car, but that's all they had to offer."

"It doesn't matter," Blair said. Her voice sounded odd. Her throat had constricted with the tension of the past few hours, and she could not seem to clear it.

The nondescript compact was waiting for them when they walked out into the Denver sunshine a few minutes later.

Silently Caleb held the door open for her and she got in, passing so close to him he could smell her hair. He found himself wanting to reach out and bury his hand in her silken strands—just to close his eyes and breathe in the smell of it.

Then, realizing how his thoughts had betrayed him, he stifled the curse that rose to his lips and slammed the door closed. *You're just horny, Hunt. Face it. Any warm body would suffice at the moment.* But somehow he knew that wasn't true, and that made him all the madder.

He also knew that something had to give and to give soon. He felt responsible for the time bomb that ticked between them. He knew he'd been acting like an ass and that it was up to him to call a truce. But he didn't know how. This woman beside him, looking so regal, so untouchable, scared the hell out of him.

Caleb had never been afraid of anything in his life and didn't understand or sympathize with anyone who was—least of all himself. *Loosen up, Hunt, for crying out loud! Learn to go with the flow.*

Blair was miserable. Caleb's unapproachable, hostile attitude and anger kept her riding on a fine tension wire. His jaw was clenched as if he had something between his teeth, causing the lines to run deep from the corners of his nostrils to the edges of his mouth. Dark glasses hooded his eyes, and his hands were wrapped tight on the steering wheel.

What was there about this man that affected her as no man ever had, even her husband?

Entrapped with him in the small car, she could feel Caleb's thighs move against hers when he shifted his foot from the brake to the accelerator. And she was acutely aware of the contact, of the molten sensation it created low inside her.

Suddenly she felt overheated and very aware of her breasts, her thighs, her stomach. Keeping her face perfectly blank, she stared straight ahead.

"Hungry?"

His abrupt question startled her. She twisted around to face him. Although the tilt of his lips fell short of a real smile, Blair sensed his mood had changed. He no longer seemed so uptight, on guard. Even his voice sounded free of hostility. A feeling of relief swept through her.

Was this a peace offering?

When she hesitated, Caleb spoke again, answering her question. "Look, I know I haven't been the easiest person to get along with, but…" He paused as if weighing his next words carefully. "Hell, I guess what I'm trying to say is that we're going…"

Again he broke off, obviously unable to say what was on his mind. Blair sat quietly and waited, locking her fingers.

"Dammit, Blair, you know what I'm trying to say," he ground out, swinging his eyes back to the road.

Blair swallowed and found her mouth dry. As this was the closest she was going to get to an apology, she decided to meet him halfway. The fact that he was back on a first-name basis had not escaped her.

"Yes, I know," she said, "and I couldn't agree more." Her voice was unsteady. "I'm…I'm willing to do my part."

There was perhaps a split second when they locked eyes, his dropping to the dusky hollow just visible above the unbuttoned neckline of her blouse, the creamy flesh a hidden allure.

Blair's fingers clutched involuntarily at the seat, feeling her nipples expand and pout against the fabric.

He raised his eyes, but they were as impersonal as a doctor's.

They both smiled.

"Truce?" he asked softly.

She nodded her head and looked away. "Truce. Until this is over, anyway."

"Now back to the subject of food. Surely you must be hungry. You didn't eat a thing on the plane."

Blair pulled a face. "I've never acquired a taste for that food."

His lips curved crookedly. "I know what you mean. You have to be real hungry to eat it."

"I know and I never get *that* hungry."

"It shows," he said in a low voice.

She saw his piercing gaze move quickly over her.

"You sound like my mother." There was a waver in her voice.

"Oh."

"She thinks I'm much too thin."

"Well, I agree. You could use some flesh on those bones."

Suddenly everything became strangely disjointed in the sterile confines of the car as their gazes met again. But this time there was no way for Blair to tell what went on behind his black eyes.

Clearing his throat, Caleb said, "I suggest we wheel into the next fast-food joint and get you something to eat."

"Oh, don't go to any trouble for me," Blair said quickly. "I'm sure I can wait until we get to the cabin."

Caleb shook his head, causing a few strands of hair to tumble across his forehead. "I doubt that. We have a long way to go and it'll be late when we get there."

Blair was silent, mesmerized by those errant wisps of hair. She had to quell the urge to reach out and brush them back in place. *God, I'm really losing it!* she thought, curving her fingers into a ball.

"How 'bout a sandwich of some kind?"

"That's fine," she mumbled, turning toward the window, forcing herself to look at her surroundings.

Denver was no stranger to her, and she loved it. Loved the smell and the feel of the thin dry air as it caressed her skin. And the Rocky Mountains. Nothing could equal or surpass them in her estimation. Their majestic beauty towered over them as Caleb maneuvered the car through the waning sunlight. When she had traveled these same winding roads in the past, she used to think that the road to heaven could not be any more beautiful.

Several times she and Josh had rented a cabin in those same mountains so Josh could ski. Not a skier herself, she had been content to lie around the cabin and read and take long walks. A shadow ran across her face. Those times had been in the first year of their marriage, when they'd been happy.

"Tired?" Caleb's eyes were shrewdly assessing.

"No . . . no," she said, shocked at his sudden show of concern. One minute he was the epitome of rudeness and the next he was inquiring about her health. Would she ever understand what drove the man? No. But then, understanding Caleb Hunt was not part of the deal.

"Why the sigh?" he pressed, carefully steering through a bend in the road.

"Oh, I was just thinking," she said softly. "This part of the country holds memories for me." They were out of the city now and soon they would begin their trek up the mountains.

To Caleb's surprise, he found himself digging deeper, "With your husband?"

For a moment, Blair was disconcerted. "Yes." Her voice came out in a breathy gust.

Drop it, Hunt! he ordered silently, brutally. *Don't, for god's sake, add stupidity to your list of blunders. Leave her*

*be! You don't care about her married life. You don't care
about her, period.*

But for some unexplainable reason, he could not dam up
his thoughts or his flow of words. "How long were you
married?"

"Two...two years." Blair glued her eyes to the window,
although at the moment, she couldn't say what she was
seeing. She was about to cry, though for exactly what reason, she wasn't sure.

Caleb was cursing silently as he took in the rigid set of her
shoulders. He knew she was close to tears and he blamed
himself for it. Damn! The woman certainly knew how to
twist his guts inside out. ·

Battling against the strained silence, Caleb wheeled the
car into a fast-food restaurant as he'd promised and got in
line for the drive-through window.

By the time Blair heard Caleb give the order to the girl
practically hanging out the window, she had recovered
somewhat, making a supreme effort to blot out the pressure that was building inside her.

She faced him with a smile on her lips. "I'd like a cup of
coffee, too, please."

"I was just about to ask if you wanted anything to
drink," Caleb responded unnecessarily, thinking he'd never
heard a voice quite like hers: low, raspy and sensual. Why
hadn't he noticed it before?

Once the ordering was taken care of, Caleb twisted
around to face her, a grim set to his jaw. "Look," he began
uncomfortably, "I didn't mean...to pry." It seemed as
though he were always having to make excuses to her.

Blair held up her hand, stopping his flow of words.
"Forget it," she said. "It's just that I'm still unable to talk
about that part of my life," she added by way of explanation.

Caleb did not reply, as the waitress chose that moment to shove the cardboard tray through the window. Minutes later, they were back on the highway.

Although there was nothing wrong with the sandwich, Blair literally had to force it down. It tasted more like cotton in her mouth than chicken. She chewed methodically.

"No good?" Caleb asked, unconsciously noticing how her hair framed her face in a riot of soft curls.

"It's okay, but I'm not hungry. I guess I'm just tired, after all," she added lamely.

"Why don't you rest?" Caleb suggested. "We have a good two hours' drive ahead of us."

Silently, Blair laid her head back against the headrest with every intention of sleeping. The day had taken its toll on her, stretched her nerves until she could almost feel them on the surface of her skin—exposed and raw. If she could sleep, she knew she would be able to cope much better with what lay ahead of her.

But good intentions turned out to be only that and nothing more. Her eyes fluttered open after only five minutes of being closed. There were just too many thoughts darting across the chasm of her brain.

"Caleb?" His given name still sounded strange rolling off her lips. But she'd promised to meet him halfway in their quest for a truce and she intended to uphold her end of the bargain.

"I thought you were going to sleep," he said, his eyes never leaving the road.

"I tried, but I couldn't." She paused. "I want to talk."

"About what?" His tone was wary.

"Exactly what will be expected of me during these two weeks?"

Caleb's glance swept over her. "Work from sunup till sundown."

Surely he wasn't serious? She pursed her lips. "I may be rusty, but I'm not that rusty."

His face revealed a hint of the old impatience for a moment. "Well, I beg to differ with you on that score," he drawled. "You'll be shocked at how much things have changed and improved over the past few years. Computers have just about completely overhauled our equipment."

"But still..." She felt the color rise to her cheeks.

He ignored her. "Also there's the physical aspect of the training. Before we leave, I'll expect you to be able to run at least three if not four miles a day."

Blair stared at him in horror. "That's ridiculous," she snapped. "Though don't get me wrong," she hurried on to say. "I'm a firm believer in physical fitness but..." Four miles a day! She couldn't think of anything worse. For her that would be pure torture.

"Only when it applies to someone else, right?" His voice was quiet, but she was aware of the unyielding steel in it.

"How can my running four miles a day possibly aid in bringing Paul Tanner to justice?"

His eyes narrowed. "Sharp bodies make sharp minds. Worrell wants you to be just as fit physically as you are mentally. You've already been told that Tanner is no slouch. You have to be prepared to best him on all fronts. And if you're not..." He shrugged.

"I'd better quit before I get started, is that it?" A new spasm of bitterness quivered through her.

"You hit the nail on the head." His tone was acid.

"Don't worry, you've made your point," she said stiffly. "Again. And you can rest assured I won't rock the boat and prolong this venture a moment longer than I have to."

He turned slowly toward her and she felt the impact of his black eyes meeting her with a distinct jolt.

"Good. Then we both understand each other."

Blair swallowed a sigh of frustration and slumped against the seat, nursing the feeling that the props holding up their truce had just cracked.

Chapter 5

Blair."

"Mmm."

"We're here."

The sound of the gravelly voice finally penetrated Blair's fuzzy senses. She opened her eyes and for a moment they locked on the scene around her. She had no idea how much expectancy showed on her face as she stared at the rustic dwelling, sandwiched between two overpowering mountains. Although it was late, just before the sun called it a day, Blair's trained eye soaked up the beauty of the wild country.

"What do you think?"

"It's...beautiful," Blair replied, afraid the sound of her voice would somehow disturb the peace and tranquillity. Then, without waiting for Caleb, she jerked up the door handle and got out. For a second she leaned heavily against the car, her legs feeling wobbly from the long ride. They had stopped only once after Denver and that was to go to the rest room.

Blair sucked the clean air into her lungs, barely conscious of Caleb standing close to her, watching her. There was a fresh scent of leaves and wildflowers, a quiver in the air that she had always associated with spring and nature's rebirth.

They had driven up a rough narrow road, the tall grass highlighted by rippling waves of yellow flowers. Blair was reminded of home, where the spring flowers were also a carpet of color. Home. San Francisco. Suddenly her heart lurched. She was homesick already. Even all the beauty could not disguise the reason why she was there.

"I'm crazy about this place," Caleb said simply. "I come here every chance I get, but with my schedule, it's not nearly as often as I'd like."

"I'm sure it isn't," Blair agreed, her gaze now resting on the small cabin. And that was exactly what it was—a cabin. Made of cedar, it looked lost up against the massive trees and underbrush that surrounded it. Blair hoped it wasn't as crude inside as it appeared on the outside.

"Did you build it?" Blair asked, curiosity getting the better of her.

"Nope," Caleb declared while digging into his pocket for a cigarette. She watched in silence as he cupped his hand around the match, his fingers strong, looking sinewy and brown.

Would his skin be that dark color all over? The intimacy of her thoughts brought a sudden flush to her pale cheeks and sent her heart diving to her toes.

"Actually, a buddy of mine left it to me," Caleb said, between puffs.

"Some friend, huh?"

"Yeah. Too bad he had to die in the line of duty." Pain laced his voice, and he dropped the cigarette and mashed it under his boot.

Blair didn't reply since there was nothing to say. Death was one of the hazards of his job. That was why she hadn't been able to handle it anymore.

Silence reigned for a moment longer, then Caleb said rather roughly, "Let's go inside. I know you're exhausted."

Blair didn't argue, feeling as though she had the weight of the world sitting on her shoulders. Caleb unlocked the door and pushed it open, switching on a light just inside the room. Careful not to brush against him, Blair stepped across the threshold.

Walking into what was obviously the main room of the cabin, Blair could have sworn she had just entered a dollhouse. And when Caleb's large frame followed her, with bags in tow, it seemed to shrink that much more, to take on a dwarflike appearance.

Her eyes scanned the room, noting the tiny kitchen to her immediate right, the breakfast nook adjacent to it, the skylights that opened the downstairs to the evening shadows. To her left, a winding wooden staircase disappeared to the upper level, to what she assumed were the sleeping quarters. Surely she was correct in adding the "s" to the word quarter.

Suddenly her heart jumped to her throat. What if... No. She shelved that thought before it had a chance to blossom. Yet the cabin was so tiny and they were so isolated and after all, he was a complete stranger.... Fear and uncertainty began boiling within her, taunting her with their faces of many colors.

"Well?"

Blair's gaze stopped on Caleb, who was now leaning against the fireplace as though he hadn't a care in the world.

She knew better. Even as rattled as she was, she did not fail to pick up the antagonism in Caleb's voice. *He knows how I feel.*

"It seems comfortable enough . . . all right." She paused, moistening her lips. "But it's so small . . . so . . ."

"Sorry to disappoint you," he hurled back. "What were you expecting, something to equal the size of your house? Or better yet, closer to that of the White House?"

He was glaring at her. Although his lashes were long and thick, they failed to veil the coldness in his eyes. He was remote, detached.

"That's absurd!" she countered. "It's just that . . . What I'm trying to say is . . ." She paused again, wetting her lips nervously. "Are there two . . . bedrooms?" Her voice was so low she could barely hear it herself.

The silence was so thick, so tense, it could go only one way and that was to erupt into violence.

"Put your mind at rest, Mrs. Browning," he sneered. "There are indeed two bedrooms." Caleb's face was savage. "You don't have to worry about the likes of this roughneck crawling in between your sheets and jumping your bones. Anyway, I like my women warm and eager."

His anger cut across Blair's consciousness like an icicle falling, shattering. Her face turned beet-red at this last insult. "And *you* don't have to be crude!" she hurled back.

He snorted and then laughed scornfully.

"I'm sorry if I offended you."

"Whatever gave you the idea I was offended?" His voice was dangerously quiet, taunting.

"Well, I . . ."

Suddenly he shoved his body away from the mantel and raked a hand through his hair. "Forget it. This game is beginning to bore me."

"Please ... if only you'd let me explain." Blair knew she had backed him into a corner, but he had a chip on his shoulder the size of his ego and was a smartass to boot.

"There's nothing to explain. You've made your point." He spoke rudely, irritation lending his voice a cutting edge. "But just so you'll rest easier, I don't want to share your bed any more than you want me to."

Liar! You're a damned liar, Hunt. Just who do you think you're kidding? His eyes were on her now as she stood like a frightened deer in the middle of the room, and it hit him all over again just how beautiful she was: hair soft and shining, skin the color of peaches and cream. She stirred his blood as no other ever had.

You want to get so deep inside her you can't stand it.

He drew a rugged breath through his lungs and with an expletive turned away.

Blair edged backward. "Please, I think I'd better go to my room."

"Lady, I couldn't agree with you more."

When Blair awakened the next morning, the day was just beginning. It was bright, like a newly made gold piece, and she felt the aggravation of the night before drift away like the roll of haze already dissolving over the mountains. Even Caleb's taunting words, "I like my women warm and eager," failed to make her blood pressure rise.

But her heart did skip a beat. Just thinking about Caleb had the power to cause that sensation. He was without a doubt the most irritating, yet the most fascinating man she had ever met.

Following their tiff the previous evening, he'd shown her to her room. After dumping her bags unceremoniously in the middle of the floor and pointing to the bath down the hall, he'd stalked out the door, pulling it shut behind him.

For a moment she'd felt weak with relief at being alone. Then she'd hightailed it to the bathroom, taken a shower and gone straight to bed, but not to sleep. She had lain awake, wild-eyed, on the rock-hard mattress, listening to every sound that came from the next room. Only after she'd heard the springs creak in there did she close her eyes. Surprisingly, she'd slept.

Now, as she stood by the window and watched a bird perched on the limb of a nearby tree sending liquid, sweet notes into the sunny room, she was positive she could cope with the day. She stretched, lifting the tangled mass of curls from her shoulders, and stared out the window a moment longer, soaking up the soothing sunshine.

But then she knew that postponing the inevitable was not the way to get her an early ticket back home.

Quickly she reached down for the largest piece of luggage on the floor and hoisted it on top of the bed and began rummaging through it. Unpacking should take top priority, she knew, but at that moment she couldn't quite bring herself to do it. There was just something so final about filling someone else's drawers with one's personal belongings.

Shrugging these shadows aside, Blair dressed in a yellow cotton shirt and a pair of pleated jeans. Then, grabbing her makeup kit off the desk, she made her way out the door and to the bathroom, relieved to see no sign of her tormentor.

It was the tantalizing aroma of bacon frying that sent her scurrying down the stairs twenty minutes later with her makeup on and her hair swept up on top of her head, secured with two yellow clips.

Caleb was standing at the stove, his back to her. Blair came to a sudden standstill, spellbound by what she saw. His shoulder muscles were bunched together as he wielded a long, sharp-pronged fork in his efforts to cook the bacon. A bear of a man—nonetheless a fine specimen by anyone's standards—his muscles filled out his knit shirt and jogging shorts to mouth-watering perfection. Why she had thought he wouldn't qualify as a model was beyond her.

On legs not quite steady, Blair made her way slowly into the room. Caleb laid the fork aside and turned around.

"Good morning," she said, not meeting his eyes.

"Did you sleep well?" Caleb asked with polite formality, moving away from the stove and reaching for the coffee pot. Without bothering to ask, he filled a cup and held it out to her.

Blair latched onto it and with a brief smile of thanks eased herself down into a wrought-iron chair that matched the table. "I slept much better than I thought I would, actually. The bed reminded me of my own—hard as a brick."

He allowed himself a half smile, no more. "I've just cooked a pan of bacon and eggs. How's that sound?"

"Wonderful." She found herself talking quite naturally. All the hostility that had quivered between them the night before was gone. The ground rules had been laid, the dividing lines drawn. They knew where they stood with each other, and now they could get down to work.

Caleb heaped their plates full of food, and though Blair's eyes widened considerably at the large portion, she didn't say anything, just picked up her fork and began eating. She hadn't realized how hungry she was until the creamy eggs touched her tongue. She shouldn't have been surprised, though, as the chicken salad sandwich the previous day was the last morsel of food she'd put in her mouth.

They munched in silence, the only sound penetrating the room the sounds of nature. The patio door leading to the deck was open, treating them to the singing birds and the rustle of the trees.

When she couldn't eat another bite, Blair pushed her plate aside and watched as Caleb did the same, only his was empty. He lifted his cup and again she was startled by the size of his hands. The cup disappeared as he held it between them. But thank heavens those black, angry eyes no longer made her think of snow and bitter winds, she thought gratefully. This morning they had thawed considerably.

"What's first on the agenda?" Blair asked, before getting up and carting their plates to the sink where she went about the task of cleaning up.

Caleb kept his silence for a moment, lighting a cigarette and studying her, thinking she looked like a teenager, with her slender figure. He could see her collarbones through her thin cotton top; they seemed incredibly fragile, like parts from a frail bird. Her hair looked like burnished silk in the sunlight. He could smell the flowery fragrance of her shampoo. Everything about her was feminine and delicate.

Yes. It was definitely going to be a hell of a long two weeks, he told himself, more shaken than he cared to admit.

Suddenly and roughly, Caleb got up and drained the last of his coffee. "First, I thought I'd show you around, let you get your bearings."

"I'd like that," Blair responded. "Just let me run up to my room and get my sunglasses and then I'll be ready to go."

Thirty minutes later they were on their way back to the cabin. The tour had been short and sweet, with Caleb only pointing out where he planned to build his house when he retired and where he intended to clear the land for a vegetable garden. He'd also told her that he owned 5.2 acres and that he eventually wanted every grain of earth to count for something.

Although he hadn't come right out and said he worshiped the very ground he was walking on, Blair knew he did. She saw it in his eyes, heard it in his voice and recognized it in the proud carriage of his body. He seemed completely at home, as one with this rugged terrain. It suited him. Man and nature alone, against the world.

Now, as they sat down at the table once again with coffee in hand and a cigarette dangling from the corner of Caleb's mouth, they began to work in earnest.

"First of all," Caleb said, eyeing her through a thin haze of purple smoke before grinding the cigarette out in the nearest ashtray, "I want to show you the latest in the electronic bugging devices and show you how to identify each." He stretched a long arm and reached for the briefcase on the floor next to him. After setting it on the table, he popped it open.

When Blair saw all the gadgets lining the bottom of it, she looked up at Caleb, a bewildered expression on her face. "You're right," she said with a sigh, "three years is a long time. Those look like foreign objects go me." *And I don't want to touch them,* she screamed silently. *I thought I was through with all this, for Pete's sake!*

She blinked several times and fought for control.

Caleb was quick to pick up on the bad vibrations. "What's the matter? You look like you've just seen a ghost."

"I...I have," Blair said quietly. "A ghost from my past."

Caleb whipped a hand through his thick hair. "Hell, Blair..."

She stood up and walked stiffly across the room. Her whole body felt as if a magnet were trying to drag it through the floor. "I know," she said in a toneless voice. "You don't have to say any more. I gave my word to Jack and I intend to keep it. Let's just get on with it, shall we?"

Caleb's face spoke louder than words. His tightly drawn lips and his dark expression told her exactly what he thought of her sudden display of emotion.

But dammit, she thought defensively, she wasn't a robot like this man, where everything was either black or white.

There were gray areas in her life for which she didn't intend to apologize.

"Each of these little gizmos is different," Caleb began explaining patiently as she went back and sat down. "And each has a separate function. For instance, these two—" he lifted the microphones out of the case and laid them in the middle of the table "—are to be attached to the phones. The voice quality is excellent, practically no static at all."

Blair looked at the gadgets for a moment and then reached for them. So did Caleb.

Their fingers tangled. Blair froze, her hand feeling paralyzed where he'd touched it. Then she jerked it away, making a small startled sound that she attempted to stifle. It was as if he'd burned himself on her skin.

"Pardon me," Caleb muttered harshly, managing to curl the words around the edges.

Blair would have liked nothing better than for the floor to open up and swallow her. Why did she react so violently to his touch? What must he be thinking?

Again Caleb's expression said it all. His jaw was set in unyielding granite and the cords in his neck were pulsating. But when he spoke his voice was cool and even. "As I was about to say..."

And so it went for two hours without a break, except to refill their coffee cups. By the time Caleb called a halt to the session, Blair could easily identify every piece of equipment and knew exactly where and how it was to be used.

"You're a quick learner," Caleb commented, his eyes now filled with a gleam of reluctant admiration.

Blair was pleased. "You sound surprised," she said huskily, still upset by what had transpired between them, although Caleb seemed to have forgotten the incident as if it had never happened. Yet one could never tell what he was thinking....

"Not really. I knew you had it in you, though for a minute after I opened the case I wasn't sure that you wouldn't freak out on me."

Blair could smile about it now. "Well, for a moment, I almost did."

"You know we've just started." His tone was brisk. "We have a long way to go."

"I know," she answered lightly, stealing a second in which to close her eyes and flex her muscles.

Caleb watched, enchanted by the way her lashes feathered against her cheeks and the way her breasts... *For chrissakes, Hunt! Get hold of yourself. Why, she can't even stand for you to touch her. Where's your pride? Just forget about how it would feel to...*

"Caleb."

He smothered a crude oath and forced himself to speak normally, though his voice held a coarseness that hadn't been there before now. "What?"

"Don't you think that Tanner will check his place for bugs, especially with him being involved in espionage?"

"Not if he doesn't have reason to think he's suspect."

"And you're sure he doesn't?"

"No. I'm not sure of anything. I never take anything for granted. But Worrell says Tanner's a confident bastard and has no inkling that we're on to him."

Blair ran a hand through her hair, flicking it back from her face. "Then I'll just have to make sure that it stays that way, won't I?"

"You got it. The bugs have to be planted in places that he wouldn't suspect, even if he was looking. That's why it's so important for you to gain access to his house and offices."

She chewed at her underlip. "It's too bad we won't be able to use that information in a court of law."

"You have the bloody liberals to thank for that. Depriving them of their human rights, my ass!"

Blair smiled. "I couldn't have said it better myself."

An answering smile crossed his lips, and then disappeared. "But we'll nail him. If you can just find the list of agents' names and then pinpoint the exact time and place of the exchange between Tanner and his contact, we'll be home free."

"As I said before, I'll do my best."

"Let's just hope that's good enough."

"Me too," Blair whispered with a sinking sensation in the pit of her stomach.

Then she stood up and walked to the patio door and looked out, feeling like a bird in a cage. But she couldn't relax, not when she felt his eyes tracking her every move, boring into her back.

"Want something to eat?" he asked casually.

Blair slowly turned around. "Not unless you do. A salad maybe?"

"Well..."

Blair's brows puckered. "Well, what?"

"It's your turn to cook. And I, for one, want more than rabbit food."

The look she gave him would have given lesser men frostbite. "Well, in that case you'll just have to fix it. I don't...have never done much cooking."

"You mean you can't cook!" His voice cracked like a bullwhip.

She stiffened. "That's exactly what I mean."

"Damn! I would have to get stuck with a useless woman!"

Blair's face burned. White rage locked her tongue. Then she rebounded, stepping forward, itching to slap his face. "Why, you...you!" Her voice was taking off in the upper reaches and she couldn't stop it. "You can go to hell as far as I'm concerned!"

Then, for what seemed like an endless span of time, she looked straight at him and he looked straight back.

Tension crackled in the room.

Suddenly and with a muffled cry, Blair whirled and tore out the door, the warm air slapping her in the face. But not even the sun's warmth could dry her tears.

So much for the truce.

Caleb stood rooted to the spot, spitting out crude obscenities, watching as she ran toward the woods. This time he'd really done it. Why hadn't he kept his mouth shut? Why had he gotten so bent out of shape when she admitted she couldn't cook? He answered his own question. It was the old prejudice against money and the things it could buy.

Another obscenity flew from his lips. He couldn't have picked a worse time to further antagonize her, for god's sake. They had just begun to dig their heels in and make real progress with the work. And he had to go and blow it.

Even now, he could still see the tears as they had gathered in her eyes. She'd never looked more beautiful.

"Damnation!" The word exploded through the entire house like a rifle shot, the exact second the telephone rang.

Caleb shook his head savagely, trying to get it back on straight. The two long strides took him to the ivory instrument hanging on the wall.

"Yes!"

"How's it goin', my boy?"

It was Jack Worrell.

"Like hell, if you must know," came Caleb's terse reply.

"What happened?"

Caleb read the sharp concern in Worrell's tone, could see him in his mind's eye, jerking himself upright with his eyes almost popping out of their sockets.

"Forget it. It's nothing I can't handle," Caleb said, lying through his teeth. But the way he saw it, he didn't have much of a choice. He'd be lucky if she didn't demand to return to San Francisco or, worse yet, demand that he be replaced. Well, he had news for her; he'd never failed to complete an assignment yet, and he wasn't about to start now.

"Caleb, don't you dare take that attitude with me. I want to know what the hell's going on."

"Calm down, Jack," Caleb said with more patience than he felt. "It's just a little disagreement, nothing we can't work out."

"Are you sure?" Worrell didn't sound at all convinced. "I won't have you intimidating Blair."

Caleb gave a weary sigh. "Don't worry," he drawled sarcastically. "From now on, I'll handle your prima donna with kid gloves."

"Then why don't I feel reassured?"

Ignoring Worrell's statement as though he hadn't spoken, Caleb asked, "What'd you need?" Worrell wasn't in the habit of making idle phone conversation. Caleb knew something was up or he wouldn't have called.

Worrell came straight to the point. "We have reason to believe that Tanner's going to make his move sooner than we expected."

"That means we have to step things up on our end, right?"

"Right," Worrell confirmed. "Time's of major importance."

"Consider it done."

"I knew I could count on you. I want that guy, Caleb." Worrell's voice was rough. "But I want it done by the book, so that it won't get thrown out of court due to some stupid technicality. Understand?"

"I'll handle my end. Blair Browning'll be ready. This is one I'm going to enjoy handing Uncle Sam on a silver platter."

Some men were born hunters. He and Worrell filled that
slot. It was part of their makeup. It was in their blood.
Caleb was also patriotic, and he made no apologies for it.
To his cohorts in the agency, criminals were the enemy. To
him, they were the subversive, the terrorist, the traitor.
There was no compromise, no middle ground. Seek and
destroy. That was the code he worked by and expected the
men under him to follow. He admired Jack Worrell. They
were akin.

"Ditto," Jack said. "Keep me posted."

"Will do."

Simultaneous with his hanging up the phone, he heard the
scream.

The untamed woods were beautiful. The soft misty green
of spring would soon be turning into the deep emerald of
summer. Blair heard the sweet, clear call of a thrush from
somewhere close beside her as she strolled over the rough
earth.

Tall trees leaned green heads over her protectingly and shy
wildflowers dotted the earth as she continued her march
through the virgin territory, feeling the tension slowly drain
from her.

She had no idea where she was or where she was headed.
She didn't care. Uppermost in her mind was putting as much
distance as she could between her and Caleb. The tears had
long since dried up and most of her composure had returned; surprisingly she felt ready to conquer her problem—Caleb Hunt.

Yes. The walk had certainly accomplished its purpose. It
had cleared away the mental cobwebs, eased the pain of
Caleb's harsh words and strengthened her resolve.

She'd beat him at his own game. She'd show him who was
useless. Suddenly and in spite of the warmth of the sun
peeping through the trees, she shivered.

It wouldn't be easy, because there was something so different about that man. He appealed to her; she hated to admit that, but he did. Yet at the same time he frightened her. That was the crux of the matter. Why? The question nagged at her. She knew the answer; she had sensed it for some time. She had felt it again as their fingers touched for a moment and then drew away.

He was *too* male. In her imagination his sexuality held a tinge of violence. She didn't want to think about what he would be like as a lover. And she didn't want to think of him as a man, naked, making love. But most of all, she didn't want to become involved with him.

A deep sigh shook her slender frame as she paused to rest. That was when she realized that she had walked much farther than she'd intended. But she wasn't lost, she quickly assured herself. If she just turned around and headed back the way she had come, she was bound to come out at the cabin.

Turning around, she began to walk in the direction she had come from. The farther she trudged, the heavier her legs became, and perspiration started to trickle down her forehead and across her back. Anxiously she watched for familiar markings, but the trees grew more dense, and soon she seemed shut off in a green-walled universe from which there was no escape.

"Don't panic, Blair," she said aloud. "You'll make it just fine." Frantically she kept on.

Weariness dragged at her now and her lungs ached with each breath she took. A branch cut across one cheek and a flying varmint followed, its insistent buzzing adding to her increasing nervousness.

She was upon the bear before she was aware of it. The shaggy black shape had reared high to reach a ripened berry on a small tree. Both huge paws were raking the fruit and leaves into its mouth. She stood still, the thought entering her mind that she must run. But she could not.

The great head with its red dripping jaws turned toward her at once, the tiny eyes fastening on her. Then, with a grunt, the big fellow came down on all fours.

Its movement released her from her inertia. She dashed blindly from the spot, not caring in which direction, and she knew she screamed, not once but several times.

And she ran until her heart threatened to burst through her chest.

Then, miraculously the forest opened and the cabin was in sight. With all the strength that was left in her, she ran toward it. She saw Caleb come running out the door. He caught her as she stumbled and fell.

"Are you hurt?" he cried. "Dammit! What is it!?"

Chapter 6

Her words came out like puffs from a small, spent engine. "Got lost ... went in circles ... a bear..."

Caleb continued to hold her at arm's length, trying desperately to make sense out of what she was saying. "You saw a bear?"

"A big one..."

His eyes scrutinized the mean-looking scratch that ran up into her scalp. "He didn't bother you, did he? They're usually as afraid of humans as humans are of them, unless they have cubs."

Slowly Blair's heart stopped its hammering and her breath came easier. She even managed a shaky smile. "I guess you think I'm an idiot, but you can't imagine how scared I was. I honestly believed the bear would have taken after me if I'd stayed rooted to the spot."

She looked so mad, so idiotic, that he began to smile. And once started, it was hard to stop. "You think so, huh?" he finally managed to say.

Now that Blair had calmed down, she could see that Caleb's lips were twitching and his eyes had a mischievous twinkle in them.

"Are you laughing at me, Caleb Hunt?"

He tried to transform his facial features back into their usual severe mask, but the thought of her tearing through the woods, thinking the bear was after her, was too much.

He tossed back his head and laughed out loud. "Why, whatever made you think that?"

For her, he'd only smiled once. Now she was delighted with the result brought on by her utter foolishness. Whether it was because of that or the beauty of the morning, she didn't know. All she knew was that underneath the mask— inside the frigid forcefulness of his expertise—there was a warm man.

Then, without warning, Blair's lips split into a wide grin. "The way you're laughing at me, that's what," she said, her breathing labored.

Suddenly laughter overwhelmed them both and tears came to Blair's eyes before she stopped.

Just hearing Blair's uninhibited laughter made Caleb feel light-headed and slightly unbalanced. The effect was as warm as sunlight and just as potent. Without realizing what he was doing, his hands tightened on her arms and he drew her closer—until they were hip to hip.

For no longer than the blink of an eye, their bodies touched. A stunned heavy silence fell around them as Blair stared at him in disbelief. Suddenly everything was shut down: breathing, talk, laughter. His eyes held hers with a message that needed no words, and her world went into a slow spin.

"Blair..." The words came out sounding guttural, choked.

She tried to speak, but she couldn't say a word. The rawness that was in her throat suddenly moved down into her chest, creating a heaviness in her lungs. Yet she was poised for flight—frightened and vulnerable, her breasts rising and falling with her panic-short breaths.

Time hung suspended.

Caleb inched closer. *Don't do it, Hunt!* He felt sick and stricken on the inside, his brain refusing to respond to the nerve impulses all screaming at him at the same second. *Let her go.*

He smelled like the wind and the sun. She wanted to bury her lips into his warm neck and breathe deeply of him. His breath, minty and fresh, stroked across her face. How she kept from flinging her arms around him, she'd never know.

Abruptly he drew a deep, ragged breath and thrust her away from him. "We'd best see about that scratch on your face."

The other Caleb surfaced. The stranger.

The days settled into a pattern. They worked from sunup till sundown, just as Caleb had promised. Every morning Blair donned a pair of shorts, a shirt and jogging shoes and hit the trail, but only after doing light, stretching exercises in her room. At first she began by walking briskly, then gradually worked into a steady jog.

Following that morning ritual, they sat down at the kitchen table where she was indoctrinated in the newest and best ways to memorize facts and faces, along with refresher courses using certain types of small cameras.

Caleb was a hard taskmaster, though Blair had to admit that he knew exactly what he was doing when it came to his job. He was exact and to the point and showed the patience of Job when she asked him to repeat something.

And though the truce between them was riddled with cracks, it had somehow held, allowing them the long working hours. Yet Blair was aware that it would take only one wrong word or one more accidental touch and the truce would indeed come crashing down on them like shards of glass.

When they were not working, their relationship was a cautious one at best. After dinner, which Caleb prepared with Blair assuming the cleanup duties, they drifted to their separate rooms. But once there, Blair found no peace. Thoughts of Caleb filled her mind and heart.

She had wanted, no *yearned* for him to kiss her that day he'd held her following the incident with the bear. And she was at odds with herself for harboring such feelings, but she couldn't seem to control them. When he'd pulled her to him and she'd felt the hard planes of his body against the softness of hers, she'd melted.... Thank God, he'd had enough sense to pull away, though at the time she'd followed him inside with a muddle of conflicting emotions—loneliness, relief and a haunting ache.

Just thinking about it, thinking about the hunger, the desire pouring from his eyes, gave her the weak trembles.

They were from two different worlds, she kept telling herself, with different goals in life, with nothing in common. Except physically, she corrected herself brutally. But physical attraction would not make for a lasting relationship.

There was no future for them. Even if she allowed herself to become involved with him—of course, she had no intention of doing so—it could go nowhere. They would be headed down a dead-end street with no place to turn around.

No. It was better this way. Once they got back to civilization the temptation would be gone. Albeit she'd still have to report to him, it would be different. It wouldn't be the same as staying with him twenty-four hours a day.

Besides, she'd have her photography work and her family. Caleb Hunt would no longer be a threat to her peace of mind.

Tomorrow—that was the day. She was going home. But where was the sense of relief she should be feeling? Where was the excitement? After all, the dreaded two weeks were at an end.

Now, as she looked out the window of her room and watched Caleb, bare to the waist, swinging an ax, splitting a log into small pieces of firewood, she felt her heart quicken. She couldn't take her eyes off him. It was a beautiful, clear morning and he looked like a giant god with the sunlight dancing around him. His muscles rippled in perfect harmony with the stroke of the ax while a strand of unruly hair bounced across his forehead.

How long she stood there she did not know. When she finally turned away, her cheeks were wet with tears.

"You're a glutton for punishment, Blair Browning," she whispered aloud.

Caleb was enjoying taking his frustrations out on the long, stout log in front of him. He'd already endured as many ice-cold showers as he could; he had no choice but to try something else.

It was a toss-up as to which made him angrier: himself or Blair. He couldn't remember the last time, if ever, he'd walked away from a woman with an aching arousal. To have that happen with her was a double blow to his pride and his emotional insecurity.

Sweat began trickling down his forehead and, pausing, he let the ax blade drop to the ground. With his free hand, he dug in his back pocket, yanked out a rag and mopped his face. It was unusual for him to perspire so profusely, but that morning, beautiful as it was, there was not a breeze stirring. But then, he'd strained every muscle in his body almost to the breaking point.

For what? Blair Browning, that's what. She was fast becoming an obsession with him. He wanted her so badly he could taste it. He wanted to touch those little buns that she paraded around in tight designer shorts, and he longed to fondle those breasts that shifted so enticingly at her slightest movement.

"Damn!" he muttered under his breath and moved restlessly, seeing nothing but her in his mind's eye: the lovely, amber-eyed face, the charcoal-colored hair and the skimpy T-shirt covering perfect breasts.

"Can it, Hunt!" he muttered to himself. From the moment he'd laid eyes on that woman, he'd been behaving as if he didn't have good sense. With a disgusted curse, he jammed the rag back into his hip pocket, picked up the ax and once more began hacking at the wood. He'd known it was going to be tough, that it wasn't going to be a piece of cake being stuck at the cabin with the woman.

Only you didn't figure on it being quite this tough, did ya? He could blame no one but himself. He had wanted to come here. And now he was trapped in a misery of his own making, wishing for the first time that he could match her penny for penny, dollar for dollar.

God, Hunt! What kind of crazy reasoning is that? If a relationship was meant to be between them, they'd accept each other for what they were and to hell with everything else.

You're the one with the problem, ol' fellow. Didn't his idiotic musings prove that? Anyway, Blair Browning was almost a complete stranger.

"That's a lie," he spat aloud, raising his head to the sun. He knew that not only was she the loveliest creature he'd ever laid eyes on, she was also intelligent, thorough and determined to do better than he expected, making him admit that her ability was exceptional. She was a natural: almost perfect recall and an eye for detail. And she had made excellent progress; he could find no fault with that.

Yet, he still hadn't changed his opinion. He was holding strong to his belief that a woman, particularly that woman, should not be matching wits with the likes of Paul Tanner. He thought it stank. And that was what he'd tried to get across to Worrell.

That was why he'd be glad when it was all over and Tanner was out of commission and Blair Browning was no longer his concern, his responsibility. He'd be back in his own little niche and she'd be back in hers.

And never the twain shall meet.

"Hell!" he growled in conjunction with a weary sigh. Then he began stacking the cut wood in a neat pile next to the metal building that housed his tools and various other junk that he used from time to time.

Just one more day, Blair, he promised her silently. *I'll take you home, and next time I see you, we'll smile and talk and I won't feel a thing. Not a thing. I'll make sure of that.*

Feeling confident in his ability to deal with himself and his job, he moved toward the house. There was one more thing that had to be done; he dreaded it like the plague.

His footsteps were heavy.

Blair was thumbing through a magazine when he came down the stairs, smelling clean and fresh from a shower. At first she didn't notice what was in his hand, so caught up was she in the sight and smell of him, finding it impossible to disregard the way his jeans molded his thighs, the way they cupped his manhood, causing a strain on the fabric. . . .

Suddenly the color zoomed up her cheeks, only to recede then just as quickly, leaving her as pale as tissue paper.

"What's...that?" she croaked before she thought, knowing very well what it was.

"What's this? This is protection."

Blair's eyes were wide as saucers. "A gun," she murmured indistinctly.

"That's right." Caleb's tone was low as he held out his hand, the cold metal lying across his palm, gleaming in the sunlight.

Instantly, Blair recoiled as though it was a poisonous snake that could strike at her at any second. Her heart began banging against her rib cage with a vengeance.

"No." She shook her head. "Put it away...please. Get it out of my sight! I refuse to even touch it."

"You have no choice, Blair." Caleb's voice still held that unruffled calm.

Again she shook her head, causing her hair to shimmer like silk, the sunlight hitting it just right. "I'd...never use it." She paused, licking her suddenly dry lips.

The tip of her tongue peeking through her moist lips was almost Caleb's undoing. He felt as if he'd received a crippling blow to the midsection. He winced visibly against the imaginary pain and longed to haul her into his arms and assure her that everything was going to be all right, that nothing or no one was ever going to hurt her again.

Hogwash, man! he rebuked silently. *Here you go again. Just who do you think you are? You don't walk on water.*

Blair's voice droned on, "No matter what happened, I couldn't shoot anybody. Not now...not after...Josh..." Her voice gave way; her throat simply closed up, crippling her speech. She averted her gaze, refusing to let Caleb see how close she was to tears.

And she'd figured she was home free, that the worst was behind her, she thought despairingly.

Caleb hunched down in front of her, one knee resting on the carpet to hold his balance. "Hey," he pleaded softly, "don't make me the booger bear in this. I don't like it any better than you, but it's necessary and you know it. You're just not thinking." His tone was the epitome of gentleness. "No way can I let you go against Tanner unprepared. It would be like sending Daniel into the lion's den all over again. I couldn't live with myself if I did that."

While giving Blair a moment to come to grips with what she had to do, Caleb heaved his huge muscled frame to an upright stance and waited in silence, knowing what must be circulating through her mind. But as he'd already told her, there was not a damned thing he could do about it. The die had been cast. He hoped, though, she would never have to use the gun—God forbid! Just the thought of her encountering that kind of danger made his hair stand on end—but it was his duty to see that she was prepared, no matter what.

A minute later, Blair stood up and turned to him, her face ashen. "I can't. You'll just have to…understand." A pulse in her neck was jumping like an elusive hummingbird.

Caleb stepped closer. "You're fighting a losing battle and I don't know why. The gun's not your enemy. You shouldn't have to be reminded of that."

Still Blair recoiled, backing up.

Ignoring her cringing stance, he hammered on. "Let's go down to the basement. It's set up for target practice."

"Caleb…"

"That's an order, Blair," he said quietly, but Blair heard the steel in the voice. "I'm through playing games. You know what you have to do, so let's not waste any more time."

Blair's eyes once again strayed to the metal object nestled within his large hand. *Okay, Blair, suck it up. You can do it.* And as he had so bluntly reminded her, she had no choice. But all she could think of was this aching, this slow loss from a wound that had never healed. Thirty minutes and it would all be over. She wouldn't think about Josh, how the bullet had ripped through his body. *Oh, God! Just thirty minutes... that's all.*

Wordlessly Blair whirled and began making her way toward the stairs that led to the basement. From behind, she could hear Caleb's heavy tread as he followed.

Just as she reached the entrance she paused, feeling as though she were on her way to her execution. Caleb reached around her and pushed the door open. Once downstairs she paused again and looked around. This was the first time she'd seen this part of the cabin. To her surprise, it was quite cozy. Narrow rollout windows lined the upper wall, flooding the room with light. A table occupied one corner of the carpeted room, while opposite it a cot was set, carefully made up. Directly in front of her was the target area.

"We'll make this as painless as possible," Caleb said, coming to stand beside her. "I promise," he added, an odd timbre to his voice.

Blair swallowed against the lump in her throat and nodded weakly. "I'm ... ready."

"Good girl."

The low, husky tone of his voice feathered down her spine and left her weak. She avoided his eyes, fearful he could read her emotional reaction. Suddenly, she was not sure whether she was more afraid of him or of what she was about to do.

They maintained a safe distance as they moved nearer to the target, stopping only when they reached the correct distance from it.

Caleb faced Blair and held the gun out to her.

"Please, show me. It's been so long, and I was lucky; I never had to fire it."

Caleb's eyes hardened. "You were lucky indeed. I can assure you it's no picnic aiming a gun at another human, even if the majority of those we deal with are the scum of the earth.'' He was silent for a moment, then said, ''All right, since it's been so long and you've never used a .45-caliber automatic, I'll start from scratch, go through the whole spiel.''

''Thanks,'' Blair said, buying more time.

''Watch me now as I cock it, using my left hand.'' He demonstrated and she looked on, still loath to touch it herself, yet knowing she must.

''Here.'' He thrust the pistol at her. ''It's your turn.''

The instant Blair curled her fingers around the cold metal, they began to tremble.

With a terse sigh, Caleb wasted no time in stepping behind her. Without thinking, he placed his arms around her and gently turned her slender frame toward the target board, all the while helping to hold the gun steady.

Blair fought to hang on to reality as a fervent desire jolted through her with a force that sent her senses reeling. She was completely and hopelessly entombed within his big, brawny body. All of Blair's five senses were attuned to the man whose arms felt like velvet chains around her.

Caleb coughed. ''R-remember,'' he said, ''to keep both hands under it, arms straight and wide stance.''

''I'll try,'' Blair responded in a whisper, her mouth dry. *If only he weren't so close... if only he weren't touching her.*

Then, with his help, Blair squeezed the trigger. The loud, abusive sound bounced off the walls and ricocheted around the room, causing her to flinch.

Caleb's arms tightened.

''This one really jerks back, doesn't it?'' she asked, husky vibrations in her voice. She was aware of nothing but the enveloping warmth of his arms.

Without commenting, Caleb pulled away. ''Okay, this is all yours. Make it count.''

Blair stood transfixed, feeling heat at the base of her throat. *You're doing just fine; hang in there. It'll soon be over.* She glued her eyes on the dot in the middle of the maze and, lifting her arms straight and out like an arrow, she fired.

"Good," Caleb praised. "Once more." His voice was as seductive as a gentle caress.

Taking the clip from him, she slammed it up into the handle and raised her arms. This time her hand was anything but steady. She stood there in agony, unable to master her trembling limbs.

"Allow me," Caleb whispered thickly. But instead of locking his hands around hers, he shifted them down to circle her waist.

A tiny gasp of shock parted Blair's lips.

The gun, clutched ever so tightly in her hand, bobbed up and down and around. It took every ounce of strength she possessed just to hold on to it.

"Caleb!" she choked out.

He paid no heed to her strangled cry. From her waist his hands moved up to her bare arm, where they slid upward. Goose bumps broke out like a rash everywhere he touched.

"Blair, Blair," he whispered, his voice faltering. "Feel so good . . . so soft."

Before Blair could utter another plea for mercy, she felt the wetness of his lips nuzzle her neck. Her skin tingled, giving over to an ache deep within her.

Whimpering, her head lobbed sideways like a flower on a weak stalk, as she gave in to the heady sensation his mouth had created.

"Sweet . . . oh, so . . . sweet," Caleb muttered hoarsely.

The feel of his moist lips against her skin was like nothing she'd ever experienced before; it was as though she was being given a glimpse into paradise.

Then, unexpectedly, that delight mushroomed into panic.

Slowly, carefully the buttons on her blouse were opened, one by one.

The gun hit the floor with a thud.

Blair thought for a second she was going into cardiac arrest. "No, Caleb...don't," she groaned.

"Oh, please don't...stop me now," he begged roughly, his warm breath tickling her ear. "We've both been needing, wanting this...."

It was at that moment his hand penetrated the lacy confines of her bra. The bra was the same plum color as her blouse.

The abrasive touch of his fingertips on her bare skin seemed to dissolve her bones. Blair slumped against him, panting.

Simultaneously, a strangled sound tore from Caleb's throat and like those of a blind man, his fingers pursued their target, stroking, kneading, fondling the creamy softness filling his palm.

At the sound of his hoarse moan, Blair turned her head. Their lips met. And clung.

Time became their friend. The kiss was intimate, deep and hot and seemed to last forever.

"Sweet...unbelievably sweet..." Caleb murmured against her lips.

Blair knew she should call a halt to their madness, but she could not. His lips were doing strange exciting things to her insides, making her a slave to his every want and need.

When Caleb finally took his mouth away, Blair made a feeble attempt to move away from him.

"No!" he cried, his mouth once again sipping at her neck, while the palm of his hand circled the exposed flesh of her stomach, slowly, erotically, hypnotically.

When he reached the snap on her jeans what little resistance she had left dissolved into thin air.

From that moment on, Blair was like putty in his hands, to be molded as he saw fit. Caleb, sensing she was not going to fight him, shifted her slightly. Then, as though it was predestined, he placed his hands on her arms and turned her to face him.

Together they sank slowly to the floor, stopping when their knees caressed the rug.

Caleb's brain seemed to be shorting out and the only thing that made any sense to him was the way she looked, the way she smelled, the way she tasted. He knew then that he'd shrivel up and die on the inside if he couldn't have her. To hell with professionalism and responsibilities. He was hovering on the brink. For once he was going with his heart and to hell with the consequences!

With quivering lips, Blair whispered, "Caleb, I..." The tremor in her voice displayed her confusion, the fear bubbling inside her.

"Shh," he murmured, "don't talk, just feel." He saw the tears gathered on her eyelashes and very gently he removed them with his lips, while her heart raced full speed ahead. She clutched at him, and he knew in that instant there was no turning back for either of them.

He pulled her closer. She came without resistance, her mouth parted, hunger and sweetness on her lips. When at last he withdrew his mouth, he lifted his hand to her hair, winding his fingers through it, watching it slide like silk through, around and over his hand.

Blair watched, her heart drumming on the inside. Silently, he placed his hands on her face and drew her forward to his mouth. His tongue caressed her while she answered with her own, a warm, thrust deep. He drank in the taste of her, the heat of his mouth thrilling her.

Her hands slipped inside the back of his shirt, feeling the smoothness of his skin, the tightness of the flesh over his ribs and chest.

At last he broke away, and with ease he quickly disposed of her shirt and bra. Blair couldn't think with his eyes on her, studying her. But then that became irrelevant as his hands held her to his chest, then, sliding back down, brought her to her feet. His fingers took down the panties. She stood naked against him, shivering.

Her clothes were trapped at her feet, and Caleb knelt down and brushed them aside, then drew his hands up the length of her thighs, over her hips, leading her forward, his mouth closing on the wonderfully soft roundness of her breasts. He tugged gently on the small, flattened tips until they formed tiny crests, while her silent cry of desire vibrated against his lips.

They both went a little crazy then.

Blair's hands pulled at his clothes, helping him undress. He heard her soft gasp of pleasure as his skin touched her, body against body.

Giving in to the sensation that she was falling, Blair went limp as Caleb lowered her back down on the rug.

"You're exquisite," he whispered, on top of her. "Your skin—everything. Here. And here. Your breasts."

Blair was on fire for him. She blotted out all conscious thought, all conscious action—for to think would bring the madness to an end. And that was something she could not let happen and survive.

His mouth was scorching her skin wherever it roamed, and with a shuddering cry she opened herself, bending to the convulsive pleasure that only he could bestow.

"Oh, Blair," came his answering rasp. "I can't wait...."

"Yes...please...now," she whispered, thinking he kissed like a god. His fingers were light as moths as they skimmed over her hips, cupping her buttocks, to the inside of her legs.

As he reached her honeyed sweetness, her voice rose in ecstasy followed by a long, trembling gasp and then a cry for more.

"Ah . . . yes . . . oh, yes!"

When he finally thrust into her wet warmth, she moaned, moving with him, making small marks on his shoulder with her teeth as she cried out in silence, a wonderfully fervent cry that spoke in the throbbing cavities of her body.

Her thighs tightened around him, her stomach quivering as she spiraled to that certain high she had never known before—that unduplicated instant of total giving and total surrender.

When it came to her, she screamed against his chest, a muffled sound that nonetheless tore through him, matching his own moment of supreme ecstasy. . . .

Later, as he lay beside her still figure, Caleb felt the first pang of regret and real sorrow. What was she feeling? he wondered. He didn't know, but he could guess. Her back was turned away from him and she was curled up in a tight ball like a newborn baby. Asleep? He thought not. No more than he was.

Stifling a harsh sigh, he reached over and latched onto his shirt. He spread it over her naked limbs and then, not bothering to cover his own nakedness, he curled his arms behind his head and stared up at the ceiling, silently calling himself vile names in rapid succession.

Red-hot fury raced through him. *Damn, damn, damn!* How was he supposed to fix what he'd just done? More to the point, how had he lost sight of the fact that Blair Browning was an assignment and only that? And after all that severe talking he'd given himself! She was not for him and never would be. And for his own well-being and sanity, he had to keep his hands off her, never touch her again.

No! he revolted silently. Then cold reality set in again. He had to give her up; he knew that. It was the only way. Yet in the wake of this self-punishment, his gut instinct told him that it was going to be the hardest thing he'd ever done, especially after he'd sampled the delights of her body, heard her mewing sound when he'd lost all control. Suddenly his body went rigid as another stab of desire went through him.

Love? Could this be love? Again the word *no* flashed in his brain. Absolutely not. That was out. He couldn't let her get inside him. He wasn't about to get hit by that same tank again; it hurt too much. When his first taste of love and marriage had turned sour, he'd locked the door on that emotion. Blair deserved better.

"Blair..." He had to begin the healing process, make her understand his side. "We have to talk."

She was not asleep, but how she wished she were. Then maybe she could have escaped from the despair that was tearing her to pieces inside. Clutching the shirt to her breasts, Blair rolled over and looked at him, her face splotched with dried tears. "Please, there's nothing to say."

A jolt of pain went through him. He reached for her.

She recoiled. "No... don't touch me."

"I'm sorry." He spoke in a cramping, unbending voice and there was a bleakness in his black eyes that knew no depth.

"No apologies necessary," Blair said dully. "I just want to go home. Today."

Caleb stared at her and they spoke a silent farewell. Then slowly, feeling his insides unraveling thread by thread, he got up and slipped into his pants, a sadness sucking him under,

like someone pushed into a deep, dark well out of the warm
sunlight.

And he was very much afraid he would never feel that
warmth again.

Chapter 7

Home. At last.

It was a good feeling, or it should have been, Blair corrected herself, adjusting her eyes to the heavy glare of sunlight pouring through her office. But her life was in such turmoil that nothing made sense to her anymore. She blinked and slumped against the windowsill and stared outside.

The sky was a high, deep blue, unblemished, showing spring at its finest. As usual, the street below was crawling with the businessmen who were eager to shed their dull meetings for a chance to taste the crisp, vibrant air.

Not Blair. Not today, though she usually never tired of roaming the city. The jammed-up houses that were stacked like colored blocks carefully down the hills continued to hold a fascination for her as did the hilly streets that never failed to lure one toward the dazzling blue water. And right then she would have liked nothing better than to chuck it all and head for that water.

But that was out. She was punishing herself.

She changed her position, continuing to squint against the light that bounced off the building across the street. For a brief second she closed her eyes, seeking relief. None was forthcoming.

What had possessed her to make love with Caleb Hunt? For that was exactly what it was. It wasn't just sex. She guessed that was what bothered her more than anything. At that very moment, she could still feel the impact of what they had done.

When she had issued her ultimatum to be taken home, Caleb had taken her at her word, seemingly as eager to go as she was. After packing and closing up the cabin, they had driven to Denver in silence, and during the subsequent plane trip only a few words had passed between them.

When they arrived in San Francisco, ready to go their separate ways, he'd reminded her coldly, "You know what you have to do. I'll be in touch." So far she'd been spared that torture.

From the time she had slammed her bags down on her bed, she hadn't stopped. It was as though she'd purposefully jumped on a treadmill so as to have no time to call her own.

The first thing she'd done was to let her mother and Kyle know that she was back. However, her motivation had been questionable. She hadn't been able to decide if it was because she'd been anxious to see them or if she hadn't wanted to be alone with her thoughts.

Sarah had insisted she come to dinner and bring Kyle. She had. And to her surprise the evening had gone well. She'd glossed over her absence, and because her mother was so delighted to have her back in the fold, she hadn't asked too many questions.

After that, Blair had plunged head first into her photography work. Lisa had done a good job of keeping their heads above water in her absence, but there was so much that her assistant could not do. The responsibility of the fashion show rested with her.

Now, two days later, she couldn't run from her conscience any longer. Payday was here.

Again she asked herself what had possessed her to become involved with Caleb? To go to bed with him, of all things? Not only had she been mortified then, but she was equally as mortified now, though the blame could not be laid at anyone's feet other than her own. Still it smarted. Smarted that she'd given in to him so easily, actually encouraged him to make love to her.

After the way he'd treated her, what woman in her right mind would have allowed that to happen?

"Me," she whispered aloud. "A gullible idiot, who for a moment simply lost her head."

At first, she had wanted to see if she could get under Caleb's closed exterior and shatter his cool control, determined to awaken some type of emotion in him. Well, she had certainly gotten more than she'd bargained for. She knew now she had played dangerously and that what she had thought would be fun and games turned out to be deadly serious.

But when he'd touched her with his large hands, his firm lips, something inside her had dissolved, opening a reservoir of feelings she'd had no idea even existed. Yet that was still not reason enough to have behaved so brazenly, so foolishly, so totally out of character.

It wasn't love. Of that she was sure. Suddenly her face drained of every bit of color and her blood turned to ice water. Oh, God, surely not! It just couldn't be. How could she love a man she'd known only two weeks and didn't even like, to boot? She couldn't. Just thinking about it was insane. That was what it was, insanity in its advanced stages.

Furthermore, how could she even be attracted to a man whose work had drained all the human elements from him until there was nothing left beyond a great body and a su-perefficient mind?

But she knew with the assurance of death and taxes that now that she'd been a part of him, she would have a hard time getting him out of her system.

If ever.

Blair did not hear the phone when it rang. It was Lisa's soft voice that nudged her back to reality, back to the hard cruel world.

"It's for you, Blair. Line one."

"Did they give you a name?" Blair asked, looking at her assistant. She was a small woman, dainty, with long, straight taffy-colored hair that so many of the young ones seemed to have. But her features were fine, and she had exceptionally long-fingered hands and lovely cascading laughter.

Lisa nodded. "Yes, he did. Said his name was Worrell. Jack, I believe."

"Thanks." Blair smiled briefly, giving in to the relief that washed through her.

Once Lisa was gone, she lifted the receiver and said, "Hello, Jack."

"Well, how was it?" Worrell demanded, skipping the polite formalities.

"Everything went as smooth as glass," she lied. "But I'm glad to be back home."

"Mmm, I just wondered. Caleb came back acting like a bear with a sore paw."

Silence.

"Jack, if you're fishing, I'm not biting."

He sighed. "All right, Blair. It's just that I don't want anything standing in the way of this mission. If there's any problem between you and Caleb..."

"Nothing that I can't handle."

A pause. Then he asked, "Are you ready to make your move?"

"Yes. Today in fact."

"Have you told Caleb?"

A cloud settled over her face. "No. Actually I haven't. I haven't talked to him."

"Well, I'll tell him it's about to come down. We'll both be in touch."

The next thing Blair heard was a dial tone. Then without placing the receiver back on the hook, she glanced at the numbers scribbled on a pad in front of her and punched them out.

After a moment, she said, "Good morning. May I please speak to Mr. Tanner?"

Caleb did not bother to knock. Instead, he just barreled across the threshold leading into Jack Worrell's office. Even the secretary didn't try to stop him, merely winked as he sailed past.

"You wanted to see me?" Caleb asked without preamble, coming to a halt in front of his boss's massive desk.

Worrell looked up from the stack of papers strewn across his desk and reached for his pipe, all the while eyeing Caleb intently.

"Well, well," he drawled, "I can see nothing's changed. Still looking as though you've been run over by a Mack truck and acting like it, too." Worrell then commenced to calmly pack his pipe with the brand of tobacco that belonged exclusively to him.

Caleb sighed, holding on to his temper by a thread. "Dammit, Jack, surely you didn't call me in here just to have a counseling session," he said sharply.

Worrell grinned. "Nope, as a matter of fact, I didn't, but considering the mood you've been in since you got back from Denver, it wouldn't be a bad idea."

Caleb squirmed uncomfortably. He had no intention of letting Worrell, with a nose like a hound dog, know what had transpired between him and Blair—it was none of his business. Yet, Caleb felt the need to pacify him.

"That bad, huh?" he said.

"That bad."

"Well, let's just put it this way," Caleb said. "I've had a lot on my mind lately."

Worrell leaned back in his chair and puffed on his pipe as though life was a bowl of cherries. Caleb knew better. He knew that Worrell was fine-tuned to anything and everything going on—good, bad or indifferent. Caleb suspected he hadn't fooled him in the least.

He was right.

"Would I be safe in guessing Blair Browning for starters?" Worrell asked lightly.

Caleb frowned fiercely as he perched on the corner of Worrell's desk, but he remained silent.

"You're worried about her, aren't you?" Worrell pressed.

Caleb stood and quickly narrowed the distance to the coffeepot where he filled his cup generously, still not saying anything, resenting like hell Jack's careful digging.

"Well, if it's any consolation, I'm worried, too," Worrell announced, and none too casually, either.

Caleb spun around, only to slosh the hot coffee over his hand. "Hell!" he yelped, dropping the cup onto the counter. Then, with a dark scowl on his face, he nursed his scalded hand with his handkerchief. Had something happened to Blair that he didn't know about?

Worrell's lips twitched. "Maybe I should've given you a few days off and let you get yourself together, son. I don't think I've ever seen you this strung out."

"Dammit, Jack! Get off my case, will ya?" Caleb clenched his fists behind him and put ice into his voice. "Just cut the bullshit and tell me the latest on Blair."

The grin disappeared from Worrell's face as he became all business. "I just had word that the screws are tightening on Tanner and that he's coming apart under the strain. Time's running out."

"So? We already know that."

"True," Worrell admitted. "But what we didn't know is the pressure's obviously getting to him. Tanner was at a party last night, gambling and drinking, and after he'd had a sufficient amount to drink—" Worrell paused and clicked his tongue "—he blew his cool and started slapping around his female companion, and before they could pull him off she was a prime candidate for the emergency room."

Caleb's heart took a nosedive, but he managed to keep his voice even. "Prince of a fellow, isn't he?" he drawled, using his own brand of sarcasm.

"Let's just say," Worrell answered with a tired sigh, "that he ain't gonna win the American Legion award anytime soon."

"It's too much to hope the bastard spent the night in jail, isn't it?" Caleb asked, a hopeful note in his voice.

Worrell voiced an obscenity, effectively answering Caleb's question.

A silence settled over the room, with Caleb looking uncompromising and furious and Worrell looking pale and sorely agitated.

Caleb spoke at last. "We can't turn Blair loose on a maniac like that. What if he found out . . ."

Standing up, Worrell silenced Caleb with a wave of his hand. "It's too late, but even if it weren't, we have to go through with it. It's the only way."

A finger of ice trailed down Caleb's spine. "What do you mean it's too late?" he demanded, having heard nothing else Worrell said.

"That's what I called you into my office for, to tell you that she's made contact with Tanner and is going to have dinner with him this evening at his apartment."

Caleb's head came up and he tensed; he reminded Worrell of a big, powerful animal that had scented danger.

"Call it off!"

Worrell's glare was frozen. "Have you lost your mind? We can't do that. You're not thinking straight. That's the reason you trained her. She's the only chance we've got to nail that bastard."

Caleb made a hissing sound. "And what if he decides to work Blair over like he did that other woman?"

"That's not going to happen. I'm sure of it."

"Are you?" Caleb's tone was dangerous. "I don't think so, or you wouldn't have admitted that you were worried."

Caleb was standing now, and they faced one another in a silent battle of wills.

Worrell turned away, but his voice held strength. "All right, so I'm concerned. But I'm not going to abort the mission. The minute I got wind of the situation, I picked up the phone and called Blair. We'll both just have to hope you did your job and Blair can handle the creep."

Caleb felt his anger rise and his patience snap as he hunched across Worrell's desk, his hands splayed to hold his balance, so close that Worrell could see the tiny grooves bracketing his eyes.

They glared at each other for an extended moment. The animal comparison recurred to Worrell.

"Jack, did anyone ever tell you that you're a real sonofabitch?"

Leaving those words echoing around the room, Caleb pivoted on his heels and stalked out of the room.

Several minutes later, Caleb was closeted behind his desk in his own cubbyhole, still seething. He sank down in his chair and noted with dismay that his hands were shaking.

Hell, Hunt! Not only did you open your big mouth, but you shoved your foot in as well. Worrell would more than likely have his head on a platter, and he didn't much blame him. Worrell was right, he was strung out. Had been ever since he got back from the cabin. Blair Browning's haunting, elusive shadow was his constant companion. He simply couldn't get her out of his mind.

And now this. For once in his life he had no control over the situation. *But chrissakes, don't panic! She's a big girl. She knows the score. She can take care of herself. You're worrying needlessly. If he starts to lay a finger on her, she'll bolt. Won't she?*

He stood up and walked to the window. Yet, Tanner was a good-looking dude, a real charmer. What if... No! He would not, could not allow himself to think like that.

What was the matter with him, anyway? Hadn't he made a pact with himself to keep her at arm's length? To place under lock and key the time spent wrapped in her arms... stroking her breasts, teasing, sucking... the way she'd climaxed that first time...

"I'll survive," he whispered to himself, unaware that he was speaking aloud, unaware of his pain-ridden voice. "I'll survive."

But later he found himself digressing when he should have been concentrating on his work, thinking of Blair—the only woman who had touched something deep inside him.

By the time he left the office he felt as if he'd fought five rounds in the ring with Larry Holmes.

When Blair stepped out of the cab at San Francisco's most prestigious address, on top of Russian Hill, she knew she had never looked better. She was dressed in a designer original. The dress was a deep-peach color, made of shimmering iridescent silk organza that tied on one shoulder for a capelike effect.

It defined her high breasts, her small waistline and the curve of her hips in vibrant detail, swirling softly around her legs when she walked. With her hair piled atop her head and loose curls dangling around her neck and temples, she hoped she was a sight to draw men's eyes, preferably Paul Tanner's.

If only she felt as well, she'd be in top form. But, unfortunately, the butterflies were having a field day in her stomach.

The moment Tanner had come on the line and listened to her proposition about photographing his house for *Home Beautiful* magazine and had given his consent, she knew she had reached the point of no return. Especially after he'd asked her to have dinner with him the following evening. The invitation had been a godsend, allowing her a chance to move sooner than expected.

When she'd relayed her good fortune to Worrell, he'd been ecstatic. But then, several hours later, she'd learned that only the night before, Tanner had used a girl for a punching bag. Worrell had urged her to be extra careful.

Since then, she'd been dreading the evening more than ever. But she was determined to bury her fear behind a composed facade and do the job she had done so exceptionally well in the past. As "The Beauty," she had obtained her fair share of top-level secrets and had located high-security documents simply by using her beauty and intelligence to gain men's trust.

However, this time she felt none of that old exhilaration. Paul Tanner was special, she kept telling herself. Sooner or later the excitement of bringing him to justice was bound to surface. In the meantime, however, nothing was going to stop her from going straight for his jugular.

Now, as she squared her shoulders and walked toward the brightly lighted building, she glanced behind her briefly. The only thing that could add to her nervousness was to find

Caleb lurking in the shadows. Since she had made this appointment and passed the news on to Worrell, she'd been expecting that call from Caleb. It hadn't come and she was glad. She could not have coped.

She smiled and nodded at the uniformed doorman as she breezed through the door. Minutes later, she was riding the glass elevator to Tanner's penthouse. When the doors swished open, a carpeted hallway and white-paneled door confronted her.

It took only one soft knock before the door was pulled back and she was greeted by a serious-faced butler.

"Good evening, madame," he said politely.

Blair smiled and inclined her head, handing him her knit shawl.

The magnificent chandelier suspended overhead caught Blair's gaze straightaway. She had little time to observe the other amenities of the foyer, however. The glossy maple table and the antique mirror above received only the briefest of glances before she was escorted down a long hall. The thick carpet, serving as a springboard for her feet, finally spilled into a room illuminated by several lamps.

Blair was impressed by the grand scale and style of early San Francisco, reminiscent of a bygone era of elegance and old-world charm, that greeted her. Everything reeked of money, from the russet-colored sofas to the paintings on the walls, from the beautiful baby-grand piano that was proudly displayed in one corner to the spectacular view of the bay as seen from the floor-to-ceiling windows that lined one entire wall.

She was looking at one reason why Tanner was broke, Blair mused to herself. The upkeep of this place must take a fortune.

"It's a pleasure, Mrs. Browning. Welcome to my home."

Blair fixed a dazzling smile on her lips and watched as her host smoothly crossed the room, an answering smile on his face, though she noticed it never reached his eyes. They remained as cold as the north wind in January.

"The pleasure's all mine, Mr. Tanner," Blair responded softly, forcing herself not to cringe when his hand closed around hers. He was indeed charm personified. Everything about him was perfect—too perfect, Blair thought. There was no doubt that his gray pin-striped suit, shirt and tie had been tailored to fit his short, muscular frame. His eyes were on a level with hers.

"Let's dispense with the formalities, shall we?" he suggested with a deep laugh. "Call me Paul. And may I call you Blair? Such a beautiful name."

"Please do," Blair said lightly, smiling, trying not to notice the intimate way his eyes were sweeping up and down her slender body. Just the thought of his causing Josh's death sent fury drilling through her.

"What can I get you to drink?"

"A glass of white wine would be fine," she murmured.

He gave the order to the manservant, whose name she learned was Martin, before Tanner turned back to her.

She would have to be careful of Martin, she noted quickly. He seemed to be all ears.

"Come, let me introduce you to my other guests," Tanner was saying.

With another smile, Blair followed him to where a couple were lounging on one of the sofas, drinking and listening to the lulling stereo music that filtered the air.

The man stood up when they approached. "Joe and Marge Dalton, I'd like you to meet Blair Browning, a freelance photographer who's going to do an article with pictures of my house for..." He paused and looked at Blair as though asking for help.

She came to his rescue. *"Home Beautiful,"* she supplied in her most charming voice.

An odd light appeared in Tanner's eyes as his hand continued to rest in the small of her back. It was all she could do not to shrug it off and move as far away from him as possible.

"Ah, yes." He smiled. "I couldn't remember."

"Charmed, I'm sure," Joe Dalton said, pumping her hand for all it was worth. He was a tall, overweight man with silver hair and black-rimmed glasses. But he had a nice smile.

Marge Dalton smiled and her "hello" was soft and girlish to match her face. Joe Dalton had robbed the cradle, no doubt about it. Blair guessed her to be at least twenty years younger than her husband, but she was pretty, with short brown hair and vibrant green eyes.

After Martin served the drinks they sat down and visited, kicking around the most pertinent topics in the news, mainly the latest airline disaster. During the conversation, Blair learned that Dalton was a computer expert, that he owned his company and that his wife did nothing—except spend the money he made. She couldn't help but wonder if they knew their friend, Paul Tanner, was broke. Judging from their attitude, she thought not. But she could readily see why they didn't. Tanner certainly knew how to put on a good show.

Before they were served another round of drinks, Paul offered to show her around. That was what Blair had been waiting for, anxious to get her feel of the place, so that when the time came to make her move, she would be ready. The Daltons accompanied them, for which Blair was thankful. She was in no frame of mind to fight off Tanner's advances.

A short time later, dinner was served in a magnificent dining room adjacent to a state-of-the-art kitchen, and though the red snapper grilled in wine was delicious, Blair ate very little.

She was all too aware of Tanner's hot gaze on her, yet he kept the polite conversation flowing throughout the meal. Blair flashed him her most engaging smile, never losing sight of her purpose. Was he seeing her as an easy conquest? For the sake of the mission, she hoped so. For her sake, she hoped not. The thought of him touching her had all the makings of a nightmare.

"Tell me, Blair," Tanner demanded softly, for her ears alone, "do you find my home a subject worthy of your time and efforts?"

Blair batted her long lashes. "It's perfect," she gushed. "I can't wait to get started."

"I suppose you're used to being told that you're a beautiful woman," he whispered.

Playing along, Blair replied, "Well, it's always nice to hear it again, especially from someone like you."

"I'd like to see you again soon. Alone."

Something stiffened within her. "I'd . . . like that."

"I'll call you," he said and squeezed her hand, taking her acquiescence as a matter of course.

It was while they were enjoying after-dinner drinks that Blair got the opportunity to escape. Gracefully excusing herself, she made her way to the bathroom, where she leaned against the wall and took long, deep breaths.

The hour was growing late and she would be going home soon. It was now or never. It would be easy, she assured herself. Her target was the phone in his study, and it was next to the bathroom. She could slip in there without being seen from the family room.

Still, she hesitated. Would she be able to go through with it, after all? It had been so long. A tight band seemed to have formed around her ribs, making it almost impossible for her to move. She was reacting just as she had on her first mission.

"Quit stalling," she whispered to her reflection in the mirror. "You're wasting valuable time."

Getting inside the study was indeed easy. She had jumped the first hurdle, though she sagged against the wall for support and inhaled slowly, deeply, willing rigid muscles to relax.

Seconds later, she moved through the moonlit room like a phantom until she reached the desk.

Again her breath was coming in short, jagged pants. Her throat threatened to close.

With trembling fingers, she opened her purse and pulled out the tiny mechanical device. Then, not daring to breathe, she reached for the phone and, following Caleb's instruction to the letter, installed the bug in exactly the right place.

Once more, using the wall as a lifeline, she leaned against it, feeling the clammy sweat break out in pinpoints all over her body, and waited for the fear to subside.

It never did.

Even after she was home in her own bed an hour later, her heart was still palpitating, and the fear was a major force to be reckoned with.

"Relax," she ordered her cramped stomach, while she tossed and tumbled over the bed.

Soon after Blair got up and went to the bathroom, where she lost the entire contents of her stomach, heaved explosively up by her offended body....

Caleb was waiting for her at noon the following day.

The moment she walked out of her office building, Blair saw him. As she made her way toward the edge of the curb, the door on the right side of his car swung open.

"Get in," he ordered crisply.

Blair hesitated, trying to collect her wits about her. She hadn't seen him since that last day at the cabin when they'd made love....

"Blair!" This time his tone was colored with rough impatience.

She blinked as she came out of her trancelike state, and looked behind her. Cars were lined up and horns were going crazy.

Without wasting another second, Blair scrambled into the seat and slammed the door. After making sure she was safely buckled in, Caleb nosed the car forward, his eyes concentrating on the traffic in front of him.

Blair battled the anxiety, heavy on her chest, as she stole a glance in his direction, her eyes running over his craggy profile. Not only did he smell good, she thought, but he looked good as well. He was wearing brown slacks with a brown-and-white-striped shirt and was the epitome of the vibrant male.

A brittle silence hung over them as Caleb maneuvered the car out of the heavy traffic and onto the beach highway. How long they traveled in silence Blair did not know. She was staring out the window, still trying to come to grips with having Caleb next to her.

"Well, let's hear it," he said at length. "How did it go?"

She kept her face averted, noticing to her dismay that the outside world was becoming blurred. "Well, I . . . did what I was supposed to do."

"Any problems?"

"No," she answered noncommittally. *Other than the fact that I was scared to death.*

His face and voice sharpened. "Details, Blair. Give me the details!"

"Don't you dare yell at me," Blair cried, her emotions riding close to the skin, leaving her feeling open, exposed.

"Blair, for god's sakes, I didn't mean . . ."

"Oh, yes, you did," she countered, before he could get the rest of the words out of his mouth. Then, forcing a calm she was far from feeling, she went on to explain, in a halt-

ing voice. "After...after what seemed like hours of enduring Paul Tanner's brand of charm—" she almost choked on
the word "—putting up with his possessive hands, I was able
to get into his office and plant the bug in the telephone. End
of report. Satisfied?"

A string of savage oaths ripped through Caleb's lips as he
skidded onto the shoulder of the road. *No, I'm not satisfied!* he agonized silently. *Not as long as that bastard puts
his hands on you.* Just the thought of Tanner's touching her
made him want to commit murder. *Easy...easy. That's part
of her job....*

The silence stretched while the wind whistled and the
waves lashed against the rocks.

Caleb twisted around to face her, his back to the open
window, and stared, squelching the urge to pull her close
against his hard body. To do so would be suicidal and he
knew it.

But the image would not go away. He could almost feel
her bones melting against his, then a hand on her throat,
tilting her head back, his mouth...

Cut it out, Hunt! Face it, she can never belong to you.

Perfume. Her scent surrounded him, bringing him back
to reality. His eyes drank her in, this woman with glowing
skin and large golden eyes and a mouth so perfectly sculp-
tured. Perfect. All of her.

"I was there, you know, outside the building, watching
you go inside," he said softly. "You were beautiful."

Blair wanted to say something—anything that would dif-
fuse the tension between them, but all she could do was stare
at him and ache all the way down to her toes.

"Blair, please," he whispered thickly, "don't look at me
like that or..."

"Or what?"

In that instant Caleb's dream turned into sweet reality. He reached across and pulled her against him so suddenly that her hair came undone, some of it falling against his face.

His mouth tasted so sweet, the taste of tobacco on his tongue as it delicately probed the inside of her mouth. She couldn't breathe, and her arms were trapped so that she couldn't touch him as his mouth moved on hers, his lips smooth, his breathing sounding as painful as hers.

"Oh, Caleb," she groaned against his lips, feeling perfectly safe. Nothing could touch her except this man.

Then it was over as quickly as it had begun, shattering silently, like ice sliding down a windowpane.

"No!" He thrust her away, gasping. "I mean...I'm sorry. I promised I wouldn't. Oh, hell!—" he slammed his palm into the steering wheel "—I don't know what I mean!"

Her body had been so warm, he hadn't wanted the kiss to end. His hands itched to explore, probe, unlock and surprise her. There, in the middle of the day, in bright open daylight. Oh, God!

Blair closed her eyes, the blood thundering heavily in her temples. She didn't move, couldn't move; it was as though her insides were frozen. This was all so stupid, so *ludicrous*! Why had she let him touch her again, knowing that to do so would be sheer madness?

It wasn't as if she didn't know the score. She did. She knew she was only a passing fancy, a pleasant diversion, a little fling between assignments, an outlet for his lust.

Yet she was hopelessly addicted to the excitement that only his touch could bring....

"I'll take you back to the office," Caleb mumbled feverishly, starting the motor and yanking the car into gear.

The pain of rejection was sharp, like a stab wound. And once again, she was there—wrapped in deep despair where the earth shifted and she could not.

Chapter 8

She lifted the phone on the second ring.

"Blair. Paul Tanner."

Blair's hand flew to her throat as she sank against the pillow. "This is a surprise," she said.

"Were you asleep?"

"No, I've been awake for a while."

He chuckled. "Mmm, an early riser. I like that in a woman."

Blair felt her skin crawl at the low-toned suggestion in his voice, but she forced herself to say evenly, "I've been waiting to hear from you."

"I know," he said heavily, "but I've had a few... er...problems these past few days that have warranted all my attention." He chuckled again. "And I didn't need the distraction of a beautiful woman."

I just bet you didn't! "Well, when am I going to see you?" Her tone was as sweet as sugar. "You know I need to get started. I work on a deadline, or had you forgotten?"

she added, lying through her teeth. But all was fair in love and war. And this was definitely war.

"That's what I'm calling about. How would you like to start with my home in San Andreas this coming Thursday, day after tomorrow, and save photographing my penthouse till later?"

Blair didn't hesitate. "That's fine by me," she responded lightly, trying not to let her excitement show.

"Good. Of course, I want you to come as my special guest."

"Oh?"

"Actually, I'm throwing a weekend bash. I've invited several couples, business associates, friends, you know.... Anyway, it'll give you a chance to take all the pictures you want and at the same time—" he paused, his voice taking on a seductive note "—give us a chance to get to know each other better."

"I'll be looking forward to it," Blair said, forcing as much warmth into her words as she could muster.

"Would you like me to send my driver to pick you up?"

Blair's brain clicked fast. "No... no that won't be necessary. I'm not sure when I'll be able to leave the office. I'll drive myself. Thanks just the same."

"Be early, hon," he said in a conspiratorial tone. "Don't keep me waiting."

"I won't. Goodbye, Paul."

When she hung up the phone, her hand was trembling.

It had finally come. The anxiously awaited phone call from Tanner. It was five days since she'd had dinner with him and four days since she'd seen Caleb. Her pulse rate quickened. She'd begun to think she wasn't going to hear from Tanner, that he had decided to renege on the deal.

However, she had kept her impatience in check and had looked on the reprieve as a gift, putting her nose to the grindstone. She'd interviewed several new models for the style show and had worked with each of them on an individual basis. Then, Kyle had helped her improve her technique of placing the models in their best light. According to him, that was her one weakness. And without perfecting her use of light, she would never be as good as she wanted to be.

So the time had not been wasted and she had given a heartfelt thanks. When she'd agreed to take the bureau assignment, she'd been afraid her work would suffer, but so far she had managed to do both. So far...

But more important, the headfirst plunge into her job had been the panacea she needed to keep from thinking about Caleb. When he'd dropped her off at her office building, they'd been civil only because they'd had to, both still battling their own insecurities, their own tormenting thoughts. Caleb had demanded that she get in touch with him the minute she heard from Tanner and she'd said she would. That was that.

The strain on Blair was beginning to tell. She was afraid the dark circles under her eyes were becoming permanent. And she was still no closer to coming to terms with her turbulent relationship with Caleb.

If only his hands hadn't found her body's secrets.... If only her breasts didn't tingle with remembrance of the wet intimacy of his tongue.... If only...

Now, to add insult to injury, she had to call and check in with him. Blair lifted the receiver, knowing that if she didn't bite the bullet and call him now, she never would.

It rang several times before she heard the click of the receiver.

"Hunt speaking."

Just hearing his voice made Blair feel as if the floor had suddenly moved beneath her feet.

"Caleb... it's Blair."

Immediately she heard the change in his tone; it became less rough, or maybe that was her imagination. "Is anything wrong?"

She licked her lips. "No. I . . . I just got a call from Tanner."

"And?" His tone was sharp.

Blair could almost hear his brain working. He was the sharp-eared agent now.

"He's having a weekend party at his estate in San Andreas and he's invited me."

"A weekend party, huh? Sounds interesting."

"Is there anything special you want me to do before I go?"

Silence drummed through the line.

"Yeah. I want you to wangle me an invitation."

Though Caleb's response was quiet, he might as well have shouted. "What? I mean . . . why?" she stammered, feeling that old vulnerability rise up at the thought of being near him again.

He was noncommittal. "I just think it would be wise, that's all. How 'bout coming up with a way to get me in?"

"I'll do my best," Blair promised, still dazed from the sudden turn of events.

"Call me later," he said in his usual brusque manner and then hung up.

For the second time within minutes, Blair's hands shook. Oh, God, she didn't want to be around Caleb, not three days, not one day. Around him, her body overruled her brain, adding to her vulnerability, making her more susceptible to his potent charm.

To make matters worse, nothing had changed. She and Caleb were still worlds apart. He still thought of her as a spoiled, rich socialite, and she still saw him as a hard-nosed man who did not know the meaning of the word love.

So why continue down the primrose path, just asking for more heartache? *Because you have to, that's why. It's your job. Do what you have to do and then walk away.*

Then she thought of the softness of his lips....

"Stop it!" she cried aloud, pitching back the covers and bounding out of bed, determined to make the day count for something.

Other than chasing a rainbow that did not exist.

Thursday morning dawned bright and clear, and Blair noticed there was a light peculiar to the gorgeous day, soft hued and misty, like a watercolor. Like the weather, her emotions were mixed. One minute she was high, the next minute she was low.

Simmering underneath was a sense of excitement and anticipation that something positive was going to evolve out of the weekend. Was it possible that she could wrap up the assignment in one weekend sweep? The list of names; it was the key.

So far, the device she had planted in Tanner's phone at his penthouse had revealed nothing of importance. If he was keeping in touch with his Russian counterpart, it was not being done through Ma Bell. Blair was counting on the upcoming venture yielding much more fruit.

True to her word, she had figured out a way to get Caleb onto the premises. So she had called him and told him she had a plan. To her surprise, he'd laughed.

"What's so funny?" she demanded waspishly, though his deep-bellied laughter had shot through her like a dart, leaving her feeling shaky, unsettled.

"What'd you have in mind, sneaking me in as one of your models?"

"Don't be ridiculous," she retorted, not about to open that can of worms again. "I thought you could go as my assistant."

"Mmm, I guess I can handle that."

"You really think so?" she responded, her voice laced with a sticky-sweet sarcasm.

This time a chuckle rumbled through the lines. "Oh, yes, ma'am," he drawled, "but it just so happens that a friend of a friend weaseled me an invitation. He called and told Tanner I was a prospective buyer for a piece of real estate he's been trying to sell."

"Oh." Blair was piqued and it showed.

Another chuckle.

"Caleb, are you drunk?" she asked bluntly. Or was she just seeing another facet of this man's personality?

"Is that what you think, just because I'm being civil?"

His comment threw her off guard. "Well...I...," she floundered.

Again he'd laughed, and long after she had hung up the phone, she could still hear the sound. And for her own peace of mind, she liked him better when he was his old arrogant, obnoxious self.

That conversation had taken place the day before. Now, as she steered her car through the gates and up the circular drive of Tanner's San Andreas estate, she felt herself becoming uptight. Although she was not early, she suspected Caleb still had not arrived. She hoped not, as she wanted a chance to get oriented before facing him.

When she killed the motor and stepped out onto the graveled drive into the glaring sunlight, she was met by the housekeeper, who introduced herself as Alma.

"Welcome to Tanner House," she said formally, though a brief smile softened her otherwise harsh features. "Are you Mrs. Browning?"

Blair smiled while trying to smooth the wrinkles out of her silk pants outfit. "Yes, I am," she replied.

"Mr. Tanner's been waiting for you."

Blair caught a hint of reproof in the woman's manner that reminded her of her mother. It was only with an effort that she kept her smile intact.

"What about my car, my luggage?" Blair asked, stalling, dreading the moment when she would encounter Paul Tanner.

"Hampton will see to them," Alma said primly. "Don't worry."

Blair wasn't worried. She knew very well that her things would be taken care of—after all, she had moved in the same social circles as Tanner and still would if Sarah had her way—again it was just another ploy to prolong the moment when she'd have to endure Tanner's soft lips on her cheek and his hands on her arms.

She shivered in spite of the warmth of the day.

Then, stubbornly humoring herself another moment, Blair remarked conversationally, "It seems so peaceful here, so lovely."

"Yes, ma'am," Alma answered coolly.

Ignoring Alma's impatience, Blair stole a quick look around her. She had thought Paul's apartment was impressive, but Tanner House was far more imposing. Although the house was set splendidly among the tall trees, it was the grounds around it that claimed her attention. They were beautifully landscaped and manicured. From where she stood, she could see a row of guest cottages, their white paint glistening as they sat proudly in the distance. Next, her eyes took in the tennis court to her right, and almost beyond her vision was a swimming pool with all the amenities.

"If you're ready now, Mrs. Browning." The housekeeper's stilted nasal tone forced her back to the moment at hand.

"Of course," Blair said lightly.

"Mr. Tanner and his guests are out on the patio. He asked that you join him there."

Blair didn't reply, merely followed Alma into the house and through the foyer into a richly furnished den. Skylights flooded the room with light, allowing her to see the Italian marble hearth and the solid parquet floor. She quickly noted a red-oak-paneled library and a formal dining room adjoining the den, each offering a panoramic view of the grounds.

The entire back of the plush den was glass, and the wide French doors were open. From there she saw her host and his guests. The guests seemed to be a mixed bag. Some were graying, terribly fit and handsome men in their fifties and sixties, while others were quite a bit younger. The beautiful women, Blair noticed, followed a set style with their lithe bodies and pronounced high breasts, silky tans and beautifully kept hair. They all wore designer clothes of the type seen in the most exclusive shops, and they all looked as though they studied the same fashion magazines and had their hair done at the same salons.

Some were lounging on the gaily covered chairs on the patio, eating, drinking and listening to the music pouring from the speakers, while others were swimming in the pool.

Blair saw Paul Tanner make a beeline for her, one hand outstretched, the other holding a glass of champagne.

"Ah, Blair," he crooned, taking her hand and leaning over and kissing her cheeks. He then handed her the glass of bubbling liquid. "I was beginning to get worried, my dear."

She laughed back in her throat. "Remember, I'm a working girl."

"Well, you're here now, and that's all that matters," he whispered intimately.

"This is a fabulous place, a photographer's dream," Blair said quickly, her voice sounding scratchy, unlike her own. Tanner's arms felt like a cord around her. She took a large sip of the champagne and felt it burn all the way down to her stomach.

Tanner looked pleased. "I'm glad you approve." Then his eyes wandered beyond her shoulder and it was perhaps a minute before he spoke again. "I'd do anything to keep it."

Blair detected the hard, desperate note in his voice and thought, *You already have. You've sold yourself to the devil. And I'm going to see that you pay.*

None of those torrid emotions showed, however; instead, her face showed a puzzled concern. "There's no danger of losing it, is there?" she prodded innocently.

The hold on her arm tightened and Tanner laughed suddenly, the shadows disappearing. "Of course not." Then abruptly changing the subject, he added, "Come on, I want to introduce you around, before showing you to your room."

"Speaking of rooms," Blair said, "would it be possible for me to stay in one of those delightful cottages?" She wanted and needed the freedom of being as far away from this man as possible.

Tanner raised an eyebrow. "I hadn't thought about it, but yes, of course you can. I'll arrange for your luggage to be taken there."

Blair flashed him a brilliant smile. "Thank you."

"My pleasure," he said, steering her toward the rowdy crowd, refusing to relinquish her hand.

Tanner's arm was still locked around Blair's waist when Caleb stepped onto the outer edge of the patio. He stopped in his tracks, giving in to the hot rage that suddenly shot through him. Held captive by that blinding emotion, he was oblivious to everything around him, the loud music, the women, everything. Except Blair.

She filled his vision, looking stunning as usual, dressed in a three-piece salmon-colored outfit. Even with his untrained eye, he knew the clothes cost a fortune and couldn't have been more flattering. It brought out the unusual color of her hair and enhanced her complexion.

She looked good enough to eat. And he wanted to be the only one to sample her sweetness.

When he and Worrell had reached a joint decision that he should accompany Blair to the Tanner estate, he thought he had himself under control, even knowing that Tanner was making a play for Blair. But now, seeing Tanner's hands on her was more than he could stomach. *Dammit, she was his!*

Those words ricocheted in his brain like dynamite. Dear God, what kind of spell had she cast over him? She was lodged in both his heart and his mind and every breath he drew was filled with her. She had completely possessed him.

And the emptiness he would feel whenever he left her, would not be easily displaced. She was everything he wanted in a woman. He couldn't get enough of her, yet he knew he couldn't have her.

Suddenly a raucous giggle caused him to turn his head. A sultry blonde, with breasts to match her big mouth, sidled up to him. "Hey, handsome, you look lonesome." She giggled again. "Want a little company?"

"Some other time," Caleb muttered succinctly, before making tracks across the concrete toward Tanner, all the while fighting the urge to tear that sonofabitch limb from limb with his bare hands.

Blair was aware of Caleb's presence beside her before he said a word. He was suddenly too close to her even in the open air. She could smell the heated scent of his body; that, combined with his tangy cologne, made a lethal combination. She tried to control her rapidly accelerating heart.

"Excuse me for interrupting," Caleb said politely, his hand held out to Tanner, "but I'd like to introduce myself. The name's Smith. Randolph Smith."

Tanner hesitated a minute and then the light obviously dawned. "Ah, yes, Mr. Smith. You're the one who wants to purchase a large chunk of real estate."

Caleb laughed with just the right ingredients of caution and enthusiasm. "Well, let us hope so. That is, if we can come to terms."

"Oh, I'm sure that won't be a problem," Tanner answered shrewdly.

"I want to take this opportunity to thank you for the invitation." Caleb's eyes made a quick survey. "This is some place you have here."

"Thank you, and it's always a pleasure to entertain a prospective client. We'll have to make time between all the partying—" Tanner paused and winked boldly at Blair "—to talk business."

"I'll be looking forward to it," Caleb replied through clenched teeth.

Tanner then turned to Blair and, dropping formalities, said, "Randolph, this is Blair Browning from *Home Beautiful* magazine." He smiled and took the liberty of moving his arm from Blair's waist up to her shoulders, pulling her close against him.

Blair forced herself not to stiffen and turned toward Caleb. She almost gasped aloud; he looked like a volcano ready to erupt, but then he seemed to relax, to get hold of himself. When he spoke, his tone exuded a mocking warmth. "It's a pleasure, Mrs. Browning."

Tanner watched them closely. "Why don't you two visit for a moment while I go welcome some more of my guests?" Then, giving Blair's arm a brush, he strode off in the direction of his manservant, Martin, who was busy talking to another couple.

A suffocating silence hung in the balance.

Blair was reluctant to face Caleb again, but as though her eyes had a will of their own, she turned slowly toward him and was immediately ensnared by their dark brilliance. Her eyes clung to him.

Under the snug-fitting gray slacks and patterned shirt his muscles rippled as he shifted his weight from one foot to the other. He was such a large man, she couldn't imagine how he moved with such agility. Even now, the knit shirt strained against the powerful muscles in his chest and arms, and her stubborn mind insisted on wandering back to the day she'd touched them.

"How long have you been here?" Caleb asked, a flint edge to his voice.

Her gaze dragged unwillingly away from the dark column of his throat rising from the unbuttoned neckline. "Not long."

"Really?" he snorted, his tone sardonic. "Couldn't have proved it by me. Considering the way you two were so chummy..." His voice trailed into nothingness.

Red-hot fury surged through her. "What do you want me to do," she spat, "tell him to keep his hands to himself and blow the whole thing to smithereens?"

The tension could have been cut with a knife.

"Yes!" he hissed, only to suddenly backtrack. "No! Dammit you know I don't, only..." He faltered, unable to go on, caught unawares by her rounded breasts outlined beneath the thin material of her blouse. She didn't appear to be wearing a bra. Was it his imagination or could he see her honey-brown nipples...? He could almost hear his own sweat popping from his skin. In the soft folds of the material her slim body in its agitated state had never looked so womanly—yet so forbidden.

He cursed.

"Oh, Caleb," she cried, a spasm of pain quivering through her. "You know I have no choice."

The planes of his face were harshly drawn. "But do you have to act like you're enjoying it?"

She was never sure whether it was the champagne on an empty stomach or some little demon inside her that inspired her next statement, but the words were uttered, and nothing could bring them back. "If I didn't know better," she said hotly, "I'd think you were jealous!"

Long lashes narrowed his eyes. "Maybe I am."

His intensely spoken words knocked the breath from her, and the naked hunger in his face brought an uncontrollable trembling to her limbs. She hardly knew what to think about his terse statement. Being with Caleb was like riding a roller coaster—gut-wrenching anguish one minute and heady excitement the next. Where would it all end?

"Well, well, I see you two are getting along all right." Tanner's bold voice doused the moment between them as surely as if he'd splashed cold water in their faces.

Reluctantly, they both turned their attention to Tanner.

Tanner only had eyes for Blair. "If you'll excuse us, Smith, I promised to show Blair to her room." Then, as though it was both his right and privilege, he possessively placed his arm around Blair and urged her forward.

Blair didn't dare look at Caleb, for fear of what she'd see in his face. And even after she and Tanner had covered half the distance to one of the cottages, Blair could still feel Caleb's eyes boring into her back.

The remainder of the day and the following two passed in a blur for Blair. She made it a point to keep busy. It was easy, as Tanner House was a delight. Her camera was never still. Hours were spent snapping pictures of the five bedrooms, three with their own fireplaces, and the five bathrooms, also showplaces in their own right.

Huge plants and antiques dominated the main rooms, and the house reeked of an elegance that was hard to depict on film. But Blair worked doubly hard at it and, in spite of the cloud under which she worked, she felt that in the end it would prove to be some of her best work.

Comfort. It was perfected to an art. The cottage was like an elegant dollhouse and the service excellent.

But it was a bizarre situation and Blair longed for the weekend to come to an end. The endless music, the loud laughter, the drinking all grated on her nerves.

Of Caleb she saw very little. It was obvious he was making himself scarce, wanting to arouse no suspicions; he need not have bothered. There was no opportunity for them to carry on even the briefest of conversations. Tanner clung to her like a leech.

But each time she and Caleb were in the same room, which was often, Blair felt his eyes tracking her every movement. She made it a point, however, not to so much as glance in his direction, for fear of giving herself away, of revealing the desire to touch him whenever he was near. Yet, at the same time, she was forced to admit she liked having Caleb close, giving her an added confidence as she went about her duties with relative ease. In spite of Tanner, she had managed to place bugging devices in all the appropriate places.

Yet there were two majors areas where she had failed. She had been unsuccessful in getting any pertinent information out of Tanner, and she had not been able to get near his office and search it for the agents' names.

It wasn't as though Tanner didn't talk. Quite the contrary. It was just that what he said was of no relevance. He refused to discuss his business, and no matter how much probing and prodding she did, he remained uncommunicative. All he was interested in was trying to persuade Blair to go to bed with him.

In that endeavor he had failed miserably. Oh, but she had
played her part to the hilt—Worrell would have been proud
of her—laughing at his unfunny jokes, teasing him with her
smile, dazzling him with her clothes and her expertise with
a camera, while allowing him only a chaste kiss or two. But
never once did she drop her guard or let him make a dent in
the wall she had erected around herself. She loathed him and
it was all she could do to keep him from sensing it.

Failing, however, to rifle through his desk for the list of
the double agents preyed heavily on her mind. That was
when she had decided she had to see Caleb alone. But, as it
turned out, Caleb sought her out instead. His whispered,
"Meet me outside your cottage in fifteen minutes," had
been an unexpected gift.

Although it hadn't been easy, she had gotten away from
Tanner by pleading a headache and had met Caleb at the
appointed time. He'd been waiting for her, leaning against
a tree, the evening twilight casting him in a kind light. His
uneven features appeared less dominant, less rough....

"Let's walk," he'd said abruptly, thumping his cigarette
down and stepping on it as he met her halfway.

Glad to be out in the fresh air, away from the stale smoke
and the loud music, Blair hadn't argued.

"Knowing how adept at picking people's brains you are,
have you had any luck with Tanner?" she asked, looking up
and drinking in the sight of him. Did he get better looking
every time she saw him or was her mind merely blowing another fuse? she wondered. She swallowed against the con-
striction in her throat. Farther down the rabbit hole she
tumbled....

Caleb searched her eyes, those amber eyes that had the
power to turn him inside out. "No, I haven't. We talked, of
course, about the land deal, but I think he saw real quick
that I couldn't afford his price. So he clammed up like a

turtle. And I just talked to Worrell, and of course, he's anxious to know what you've come up with and so am I.''

Blair shied away from the disturbing sensuality of his gaze. "Nothing, I'm afraid," she said in a hushed tone, looking around.

This part of the estate was only partially open. The trees, together with the approaching darkness, provided them with adequate cover, granting them safety from watchful eyes. But the moon promised to be full, and already the woods were silver and black in the translucent light.

They walked in silence, not touching.

"Just as I figured, Tanner's a slick bastard," Caleb admitted at length. "Silent to the end. But then, he's the kind I like bringing to justice." Even in the gathering dusk, the satanic slant of his brows was very much in evidence and his eyes were as cutting as blades.

Blair swallowed against the uneasiness building inside her and didn't say a word.

"Time's running out, you know. You've got to get to his office."

Without looking at him, she spoke. "I know."

"Since tomorrow night's it, it'll have to be soon."

Blair felt the expected rise of fear slide down her spine. "Some way, somehow, I'll do it."

He stopped and they faced each other.

There was a pregnant silence and then he spoke again.

"You'll be careful, won't you?" he asked roughly, unnecessarily.

Blair tilted her head back and a wisp of hair swung accidentally against his cheek.

Caleb expelled his breath noisily.

They stood, as though helpless, immobile, while the sounds of night sang around them: the crickets chirped, the wind whistled through the trees, and still their eyes melted one into the other.

Blair smiled in the darkness, savoring his show of concern as a miser covets a penny.

"You can count on it," she whispered at last....

That had been the previous day. The tomorrow that Caleb had spoken of was here. The final bash was in full swing. Yet Blair hadn't had a moment in which to make her move. Again, Tanner was her constant shadow.

Blair's eyes scanned the room, as she nursed her mounting frustration. She saw Tanner making his way back to her with a drink in each hand.

She watched as Dalton, the man she had met at his penthouse, stopped him. Shortly, Tanner approached her with an apologetic grin on his face.

"My dear, would you mind very much if I played a game of chess?" he asked. Then, without warning, he leaned over and grazed her cheek with his lips. "We'll have plenty of time together later," he added in a whisper.

Blair could barely contain her excitement, though she doubted her free time would last long, as no one seemed sober enough to play even one match successfully. "By all means play," she cooed. "I can always entertain myself."

She waited until Tanner ambled off and then she moved, knowing she had to make every precious moment count.

Hoping that Caleb was watching her, she squared her shoulders and quietly slipped from the room.

No one stopped her.

When she stepped into the office a few seconds later, she paused to smile with grim satisfaction. *So far so good.*

Stinging rivulets of perspiration saturated her forehead. It was as if she'd run ten miles and still her task was undone.

Then, on unsteady legs, Blair crossed rapidly to the desk and switched on the lamp. Once she sank down on Tanner's plush chair, though, her nervousness vanished and her confidence returned. She quickly searched through the top drawers.

Zilch.

Blair gritted her teeth, moving to the bottom right-hand drawer.

Bingo. It was locked. Something important? Had to be.

Quickly she opened the middle drawer again and searched for a key. No key.

She hesitated only a moment, then unsnapped her evening bag and rummaged through it until she found her nail file.

After thrusting the file into the tiny slot and picking and twisting, she smelled success. She could almost taste it. The adrenaline was flowing.

Then, without warning, the door opened.

Chapter 9

Blair's heart gave a series of hyper beats, as if it were lurching in her chest. The dread that overcame her was like paralysis. She didn't dare shake or move. For a split second, she sat motionless.

Tanner.

She could almost feel his eyes.

She flung her head up and around.

Lady Luck was smiling on her.

She stared wild-eyed at the figure in the doorway while going limp as a willow on the inside. Her lips felt cracked; she wet them quickly with her tongue.

"Oops, sorry," a young woman said, giggling uncontrollably, using the doorjamb to hold her up. A loud hiccup followed another giggle. "I . . . I thought this was, er, the potty."

Blair was just able to force the words through her lips. She swallowed. "It's . . . two doors down on your left."

"Thanks," came the reply, punctuated by still another hiccup and giggle. The woman closed the door.

Blair fell limp against the back of the chair. *Breathe deeply,* she pleaded with herself. *Make your heart stop racing. Think about Caleb—no, don't think about him or you'll start crying. Just breathe!*

After taking her own advice, Blair felt her head clear, enabling her to move. It was then with the quickness of lightning that she opened the bottom drawer and went through it.

Strike two. Empty—except for real estate papers. One more strike and she would be out. She was trembling like a leaf in a wind storm.

There was nothing left to do now but get up and stumble toward the door and pray that she made it.

The door seemed miles away, but once there, she opened it and closed it behind her, a groan of relief pouring from her lips like water.

Caleb despised having had to pressure Blair. To his way of thinking, it could only do one thing and that was increase the danger factor—for her. And when that happened, the best-laid plans had a tendency to unravel, come apart at the seams. He had seen it happen too many times.

He just hoped it wouldn't happen that night. But he was prepared, as always, feeling his .25 automatic rub against his ankle, strapped in a holster. A quick draw with an ankle holster was difficult, but it was better than nothing.

Suddenly he looked down at his hands. He was shaking. If Worrell could see him now, he'd never let him live it down. But the thought of Blair getting hurt...

He shut his eyes for a second and drew deeply on his cigarette. However, before he could reopen them, Blair's face popped up on the back of his eyelids. Where was she? It was getting late and he was getting worried. His lashes flew up as he tried to isolate his emotions, ridiculing himself for being such a soft touch where Blair was concerned.

It was then that he saw her. Caleb felt the muscles of his face grow taut, tug downward, and he straightened, every bone in his body jumping to attention. Blair was standing in the doorway, having come from the direction of Tanner's study. Caleb waited and watched.

She looked as if she had just seen the devil himself. He didn't move, only swore as he saw her pause, seemingly to regroup, to compose her features. His eyes then tracked her as she walked jerkily through the drunken, boisterous crowd and out the French doors.

Caleb forced himself to stay put. He couldn't follow her, not yet; it would be too obvious. While he waited, unanswered questions circled his brain. What went wrong? Had she found the list of names and Josh's had been crossed out? Or worse, had that snoop Martin walked in on her, catching her red-handed? If the latter, why hadn't he alerted Tanner? There was still time for that, Caleb cautioned himself, though Tanner was still playing chess and had not been approached.

His uneasiness spread while sweat oozed out of every pore in his body. He didn't know how much longer he could stay there before charging after her. He forced himself to remain stationary, his only consolation being that Tanner was under his watchful eye and if he made one move toward that door, he would stop him.

One way or the other.

Blair was still trembling all over.

It took every bit of energy she could muster just to close the cottage door behind her. She sagged against it, battling the nausea that threatened to overwhelm her.

Sobs racked her body and she did nothing to dam their cleansing flow. But they did not bring the relief to her battered senses that she sought, so she began pacing the floor, her sobs having downgraded to hot, salty tears.

What if that had been Tanner at the door? Or Martin, instead of that inebriated young woman? That didn't bear thinking about. But she had to, because next time— How much longer could she keep this up? she screamed silently.

Tap-tap. The sound curtailed her pacing. Her feet froze. She heard it again. The rapping floated into her mind, finally penetrating. Someone was at the door! *Oh, dear Lord!*

"Blair, it's me, Caleb."

She was having trouble winding the key that would make her talk.

"Blair, let me in."

"It's . . . it's open," she whispered, her voice sounding faint, faraway.

Caleb's roughly spoken curse reached Blair's ears through the door. Then it was thrust open and his big body lumbered across the threshold.

Blair stood reed-straight in the center of the room, making no effort to check the liquid flowing from her eyes.

Caleb, too, stood still as though suddenly nailed to the spot, fear clutching his insides like a vise, his eyes taking in Blair's pale, stricken face bathed in tears. He longed to sweep her into his arms, to hold her tight against the cruelties of the world.

At the same time, though, he felt hot anger rise up in him at everyone, including himself, who had brought her pain. The strength of his emotions frightened him. He was totally out of his depth, but he couldn't back off. Not while that look of suffering was in Blair's eyes, and not while he wanted her, wanted her in any way he could have her.

Yet, fear of her reaction held him stationary. He waited for her to cry out, to demand that he get out, that he leave her alone. But she said nothing. She just stood rooted to the spot, battling against the panic that turned her entire body to stone, immobilizing her.

"God, Blair," he whispered harshly, "what happened?"

After a moment, Blair found her voice, and swiped at the tears with the back of her hand. "I . . . I was going through his desk when the door opened and . . ." She faltered.

Although Caleb felt as if a hammer was pounding his insides, he didn't rush her. "Take your time," he said gently.

The words spilled from her lips, "I just knew it was . . . Tanner. But it was a drunk looking for the bathroom. Oh, Caleb, I was so scared."

She began to sob uncontrollably, while involuntarily lifting a hand to him—incapable of doing more.

But that was enough. Caleb closed the distance between them like someone in a dream, enfolding her in his arms. A cry ripped through his chest and tore from his mouth as he hid his face in her hair, letting the cushion of his body absorb her shock.

"It's okay, it's okay," he whispered, rocking her in his arms. "Shh, don't cry. It's behind you now."

"Oh, Caleb," she cried, her tears dampening his neck.

His sole intention was to bring comfort, to stop her from shaking. But when her body pressed into his, the thin layers of silk outlining the curves and hollows he'd touched with his hands and mouth, it was more than he could take.

A groan splintered the air as comfort turned into a burning desire. Wordlessly, he pushed her away just enough to peer down into her eyes. They were raised to his, her eyelashes sparkling with tears; they reminded him of heavy drops of dew clinging to flower petals in the dawn of early morning.

Their eyes held for an interminable moment before his lips lowered to meet the parted sweetness of hers.

He was lost.

One kiss did not suffice, did nothing to quench his thirst. It made him yearn for more. And he took what was so freely offered, his tongue sweetly embedding itself in the hot cavity of her mouth.

They clung to each other as though their very lives depended on it. When they came up for air, Caleb swept her up in his arms, carried her into the adjoining room and laid her gently on the bed.

"Blair, Blair," he whispered incoherently, against her lips, "you're like a fever in my blood. I can't get enough of you."

"Oh, yes, yes," she whispered in turn.

He had lowered himself beside her, the mattress creaking under his weight, and was raining tiny kisses on her face. "Tell me it's the same for you," he rasped. "Two perfectly sane people who touch each other and go crazy."

"Yes, oh, yes," she repeated deliriously.

"Never. I'll never let anyone hurt you again."

Blair could only nod, the lump in her throat so large she couldn't speak.

Caleb brought his mouth back to hers, tasting the sweetness of her responses, lying beside her, holding her against him, savoring the increasing heat of her body, the swelling of her flesh beneath his hands.

Blair lay helpless, as though swallowed up by his eyes and his unasked question. Her own eyes relayed their silent message.

Without taking his gaze off her, Caleb rolled to his feet and began removing his clothes, item by item. The sky was without flaw, allowing the bright moon into the room. His naked body turned silver.

Blair gasped with the desire that arrowed through her. Suddenly the moment was devoid of all reality; Caleb was the only thing real to her. She needed him, needed him as she needed air to breathe. And she wanted him. Would it be that wrong to steal this one evening, postpone the inevitable for a while longer? she thought fleetingly.

When his hands touched her body again, Blair had her answer. Feeling helpless as a kitten, she let him disrobe her and, like him, her body fell privileged to the same bright moon, which turned her to silver.

Blair matched his hot gaze boldly, facing his eyes as they touched her breasts, her face, her knees, her breasts again. His need matched hers; she knew he was excited, anxious. Yet she wasn't frightened, though she was sure she was about to say and do things that would later shock her. She didn't feel she could trust her instincts. She was too willing to be trusting. As before, he only wanted to love her body, she told herself, it didn't mean he wanted to love *her*.

But that didn't matter. Not now. Just feeling his arms around her, their bodies joined as one, was all that mattered.

He kissed her lips, then stroked her face, shaping it beneath his hands, going on to do the same to her breasts, her highs, her buttocks, whispering, "You make me crazy," over and over, "you make me crazy."

"Hold me, love me," she cried softly.

"Yes, oh yes."

His mouth melted her bones, creating an ache deep inside her, before leaving to find a breast. She arched closer, thinking, *He knows, he knows what he's doing to me*. His lips, his tongue, his teeth, ever so lightly, were devoted to that breast.

She moaned against the heat rising in her throat, that darting spasm in her chest, and clutched at him. His hand moved between her thighs and she closed her legs to hold him there, moving against him. His mouth moved to her other breast while his finger circled, circled.

It was wonderful. It was fantastic, moving with and against the feeling. On and on and on it went until he tightened his arm around her. Suddenly her body took off in a series of violent contractions, leaving her gasping.

"Good?" he asked, hugging her.

"Mmm," she murmured, then added, her eyes glazed with tenderness, "it's your turn now."

Blair lay on top, kissing him, deeply, searchingly, feeling his stirring heat in response. With a moan, she slid down the length of his body, leaving kisses strewn across his shoulders and chest, his belly. She then settled down beside him so she could watch his face when she did this, see the pleasure softening his features, hear his rattled breathing as her hands and mouth performed their magic.

Then he turned fractionally, his hand moving up over her thighs, and together, as interlocking scissors they cut precisely and ever so gently into each other's bodies, creating something potent, yet fragile as a porcelain rose.

With him buried deep inside her, there was no time to think about any of it, for she was once more riding frantically with the pleasure. He was taking her all the way through. Start to finish. No games. No promises. All the way to the end.

Still, finally, she held him in her arms thinking she'd never let him go, just keep him there forever, heavy on her body, holding her safe and protected.

"Still good?" he whispered, his face in her neck, nipping at her soft skin.

"I can't talk," she murmured.

His deep chuckle was the last thing she remembered before falling into a deep, drugged sleep.

Caleb moved ever so slightly, twisting his head to gaze at the clock on the table next to Blair. The digital numbers registered three o'clock. He longed for a cigarette, but fear of waking Blair kept him from reaching for one.

However, he did manage to ease an arm above his head without disturbing the sleeping figure beside him. He could feel the steady rise and fall of her chest, even though her back was to him, and could also feel her buttocks against his leg.

He cast another glance in her direction, pleased that she was sleeping like a satisfied tigress. He smiled to himself, and though he was exhausted he felt good. He felt triumphant, yet humble. And he felt fear.

It was in that moment the truth hit him with all the power of a blow to his stomach. Suddenly a deep tremor slid down the length of his torso. He had to force himself not to shudder visibly. *He was in love with her!* Damn! Did that mean he had to go through it all again—the pain, the frustration? He didn't want to go through it again. He didn't want to form any permanent attachments. He was a loner and liked it that way. *But that was before you lost your fool head!* an inner voice taunted.

As though he had to prove that it wasn't all a crazy dream, he lifted his hand to touch her, only to have it fall by his side. He moaned silently, gazing at her hair shining in the moonlight, several strands flying away against the headboard like dark cobwebs.

He couldn't stand it any longer; he had to touch her. Reaching over, he very gently pushed her hair back over her shoulder. Her shoulder was so smooth, so round.

Oh, God I do love you. All of you. Everything. The day she came running from the woods, he'd stormed out of the cabin wanting to pick her up if she fell, scared to death she would fall, not wanting her to hurt herself, and then the laughter...

He'd loved her then, only he hadn't wanted to admit it. Still, he didn't want to admit it, but now, after what they had shared, he had no choice. He couldn't run from the truth any longer. And it wasn't just sex. It was that, too, of course. But it went much deeper—home, family, the whole bit. That scared the hell out of him, because he knew it would never become a reality. She did not love *him*. That was the bottom line.

But someone needed to take care of her. Maybe someone needed to take care of *him*. He didn't know. He honestly didn't know. He had never been so confused or torn in his life. Never.

Suddenly he couldn't stand his thoughts another moment. He gritted his teeth, willing himself to go back to sleep.

When he finally closed his eyes, he wasn't surprised to find his face wet with tears.

Blair stirred and rolled over. And when she made contact with a muscled leg, her eyes opened. Caleb was looking at her. Then, like the gush of a waterfall, it all came rushing down on her: Tanner's office, the fear, Caleb's comforting arms, their heady night of passion...

She blinked several times, her mind circling frantically, testing her emotions. Was she sorry? No. Even though he still did not love her nor she him, she was not sorry. Nor did she feel any shame. He affected her like no other, made her feel like a woman, and she was selfish enough to take what the moment offered and run with it.

She stretched, a long, lazy stretch.

Caleb sat up, using one arm as a prop and stared at her with lazy indulgence, while giving in to the intense relief that washed through him. He had half expected her to bolt like a wounded deer when she opened her eyes. Thank God, she hadn't. He didn't think he could have borne it.

"What are you thinking?" he asked, taking the liberty of dropping his arm across her waist, feeling the soft skin of her stomach bunch beneath it.

Blair tilted her head toward him and smiled. "How I wish tomorrow would never come." There was a tenderness in her look, a confession of a kind.

Caleb's heart raced out of control. "Which means you're glad of today, this minute?"

Blair reached out and touched his face. "Yes," she whispered simply.

In the bluish light of the early dawn, his eyes gleamed into hers. He almost didn't trust his hearing. Yet, a peace and empathy hovered between them that had not been present before, and he knew she felt it the same as he.

Forever barred, forever close.

The truth lay in their silence, not in what they had just said to each other. Caleb wanted to speak; he was a man on the brink about to plunge: to confess his love. She must know, he thought. Still, his insecurities held him fatally back. Doubt of her? Doubt of himself? Fear of rejection? Fear of response? He didn't know which was the culprit, maybe all of them. But one thing he did know, fear had a lock on his tongue and wouldn't let go.

Warm breath caressed his ear as Blair leaned closer and whispered, "Make love to me, please." Then she slid slightly away, letting her hand trail down the length of his body before reversing to his side, her hands and mouth cool.

Caleb still had the same nagging sensation that none of it was real, merely part of a fantastic dream—being in bed with Blair, her body touching his. But it *was* real, achingly and wonderfully real.

"Oh, Blair...oh, yes!" He ceased to think, his thoughts having been effectively scattered by her potent mouth, her tender hands and the sight of her, as she gave him the profoundest of pleasures.

Suddenly unable to stand the heat of her passion a moment longer, he reached for her, eased her on top and down, feeling her surprise, delighting in it, in her, in both their enormous appetites....

Later, holding her cradled against his chest, caressing her hair, smoothing it, he asked, "What's the best way for you?"

"Inside you mean?" Her tone was muffled.

He nodded.

"On...top."

"Is it good?"

"It's wonderful."

"Why aren't you shy about this?"

"I always have been...until now, that is."

He had to pause, think about that.

"Caleb?"

He almost squeezed the breath from her. "That's a hell of a thing to tell me," he said, laughing. "If that's the case, I'll keep you locked up in here for the next thirty years."

Blair laughed, pulling away. "Think we could get away with it?"

"Mmm, never know till you try."

She laughed again. "Are you thirsty? I am?"

"Hadn't thought about it, but now that you mentioned it, sounds good. Why?"

"There's a bottle of wine in the fridge. I'll get it."

"No, let me."

He walked unself-consciously out of the bedroom, returning with a glass in each hand, and smiled as he handed one to her.

They eased themselves back down onto the bed and faced each other.

"If anyone told me I'd be doing this, I'd have called them a damn liar."

"Same here," she responded softly.

"Is that the same as saying you're sorry?"

There was a long silence and she felt his gaze almost physically. His eyes wandered over her slowly, and again she asked herself what there was about him that turned her into a completely different person. He had the same instantaneous effect on her as the most potent of wines. She felt drunk on him already.

"No," she whispered at last. "I'm not sorry."

His face cleared and his lips curled into his rare smile. "We're crazy, you know."

She laughed, taking a sip of her wine. "I know."

Her eyes sparkled when she laughed, her lips parted and he saw the perfect teeth, her tongue darting between the rows, teasing him. He couldn't take his eyes off her mouth.

Suddenly Blair was aware of her thumping heart and the thickness in her throat. When he looked at her like that she forgot the mission, the danger, the craziness of the moment. She forgot everything but him....

Neither one knew who made the first move, but it didn't matter. Blair knew she would be lost if he touched her.

He did.

And she was.

Her sleep was deep. She didn't want to wake up. Why didn't whoever was trying to wake her up go away? *Go away!* she pleaded silently. She was so tired....

The sound persisted. Louder this time.

It's just your imagination; go back to sleep.

The doorknob rattled. Blair flinched against the grating sound. She lifted her head off the pillow, not fully awake.

Then suddenly, silently, she felt Caleb tense beside her. She rolled over and stared at him, her eyes wide and questioning.

"Say something," he mouthed.

Blair licked her dry lips. "Who... who is it?" she asked in a small voice.

"Paul." The voice was gruff.

Welcome to the real world! Blair held her breath, panic rushing up the back of her throat like bile. She clutched at Caleb's bare leg, still touching hers.

"Stall him," Caleb mouthed again, while edging to the far side of the bed and easing himself into a sitting position. His eyes darted to the patio door in the middle of the bedroom/sitting room combination, before turning back to Blair.

"Just . . . a moment," she stammered, her tone high and cracked.

She was standing now, having found a robe, and was in the process of tying the sash around her waist, stalling, giving Caleb time to button his pants and shirt.

"Dammit, Blair, what's taking you so long?" Again the doorknob shook.

Blair's eyes sought Caleb's. He was now standing only a hairbreadth away. He leaned down and whispered, "Get rid of him. I'll be outside." His eyes reminded her of chips of ice, and the snub-nosed automatic shone menacingly in his hand.

Following a quick brush of her lips, he moved across the room with the quickness of a panther.

Somehow Blair made her wobbly legs carry her to the door, though she was positive she would hyperventilate before the ordeal was all over. *He knows. What are you going to say when he confronts you?* Then, remembering that Caleb was only a heartbeat away, she yanked open the door.

Tanner's face bore a distinct stamp of hostility as well as bloodshot eyes and a heavy beard. His clothes were mussed up, his tie askew. It was obvious from his ill-kept appearance that he hadn't been to bed.

"I don't like to be kept waiting," he said.

Blair kept her cool, though her bones had all the substance of Jell-O. "Sorry, but did it ever occur to you that I might still be in bed?"

"That's what I was hoping," he whispered, stepping closer.

His alcoholic breath was like a slap in the face. Blair forced herself not to back away, keeping her stance in the doorway.

"How 'bout a little company?" Tanner said with a leer.

Again she panicked. It was obvious that Tanner wasn't aware of his invasion of her privacy. All he was interested in at the moment was getting her into bed. But there was no way she could let him past the door. If Tanner so much as laid a finger on her, she shuddered to think what Caleb would do. It didn't bear a second thought.

Thinking fast, Blair cajoled, "Of course, I'd like your company. Only I was thinking more like joining you for breakfast, first, and then later...who knows...?" The invitation was left hanging in the balance.

Tanner cocked his head sideways and Blair could almost see the wheels turning in his head. Was he going for it? Had she convinced him to back off?

Blair held her breath and waited.

"All right, breakfast it is," he said with resigned acceptance. "Give me thirty minutes to get cleaned up."

After shutting the door Blair couldn't move. She remained stiff as a board, glued to the floor. Then she remembered.

Caleb!

Was he still outside?

Fueled by her need to see him, she ran toward the patio door and looked outside.

Caleb's back was all she saw. He was following Tanner.

She wanted to cry. She wanted to scream. She did neither. She just stood there and gave in to the pain and despair that washed through her.

Chapter 10

Jack Worrell sat down, only to suddenly make a face when the springs in his chair squeaked loudly.

"Dammit," he grumbled, "you'd think that as long as I've been around here, I'd be able to get a piece of furniture that didn't talk back to me."

"Ah, come on, Jack, you wouldn't know what to do with a new chair," Caleb said.

Worrell's frown deepened. "Well, I sure as hell would like to find out."

Caleb smiled outright this time. "Just think of it like this, it keeps you company when you're in here all alone slaving over those boring reports."

Worrell's scowl shifted into a grin. "How in the hell did we manage to get off on this ridiculous subject, anyway?"

"Just goes to show you, we'll do anything to take the pressure off this job."

"I know what you mean, boy," Worrell said, his face matching the seriousness of Caleb's. "I know what you mean."

For a moment they stared at each other in silence, their minds running parallel, both knowing that even though their job was far from glamorous, they were addicted to it and wouldn't be worth a damn doing anything else.

However, there were times when Caleb needed to chuck it all and head for his cabin and become a hermit. This was one of those times.

Swallowing an expletive, Caleb jerked his head around and strode to the window and looked out, though nothing of the outside world registered on his tired brain. He hadn't seen or heard from Blair since they had come back from Tanner's, and that had been three days before. To him, it seemed like a lifetime.

"Since I haven't read your entire report yet, you want to tell me about it?" Worrell asked.

Caleb tensed. "There's not much to tell," he said in a clipped tone, keeping his back to Worrell. "That's the sad part."

"How so?"

Caleb faced Worrell, his lips drawn in a pencil-thin line. "The whole weekend was a damned fiasco, that's what it was!"

"I disagree. From what I have read, you—"

"To hell with the report," Caleb cut in roughly. "Nothing was accomplished. Tanner spent the entire time trying to get Blair into bed."

There was a brief silence before Worrell spoke.

"Caleb, is there something between you and Blair that I ought to know about?" Although Worrell's words were casually spoken, Caleb wasn't fooled. Each syllable was coated with steel.

Hell, yes, there's something between us, at least on my behalf. I've fallen in love. But that's my problem and has nothing to do with my work. So butt out, Jack!

"Not a thing," Caleb said.

Worrell gave him a hard stare, then demanded gruffly, "Go on with the details."

"As I was saying," Caleb said, his expression revealing nothing, "it was a waste of time. I couldn't get a thing out of Tanner except the price of land, and Blair didn't fare any better with her questioning. When she finally did make a move, she came up empty-handed." Caleb paused with a sigh. "And to make it worse, she got the scare of her life. Some drunken idiotic woman came in while she was searching his drawer and she thought it was Tanner."

Caleb fell silent, then started pacing in front of the desk like a restless lion in a cage.

"Hell," Worrell said, "sounds like nothing went right for Blair, but we had to cover all the bases, anyway."

Caleb's eyes pinned Worrell's for a moment. "I just wish she could have gotten her hands on those operatives' names. Tanner's bound to have them written down somewhere, or else on microfilm. If Blair had managed to get her hands on that list, he'd be severely crippled and we'd have half of our battle won."

Another silence followed his tirade, though Caleb kept up his pacing.

Finally Worrell spoke. "Have you talked to Blair since you've been back?"

It wasn't so much what Worrell said that sent a shiver of alarm up Caleb's spine, but the way Worrell said it. "No." He was eye to eye with Worrell now, his voice guarded. "Actually, I haven't seen her to talk since the day before we left." He paused. "I thought . . . we needed a little breathing space," he added lamely.

"I see," Worrell said quietly.

"No, Jack, you don't see," Caleb answered tightly.

Worrell's head popped up. "What's that supposed to mean?"

Careful, he's sniffing like a bloodhound again. "Nothing whatsoever," Caleb lied.

That assurance seemed to mollify Worrell. His features lost their pinched look. But it was a moment before he spoke.

"I thought about letting Blair off the hook. She's close to the breaking point."

Caleb showed no emotion, not even so much as a tiny flinch, though he felt a jangled shock in his solar plexus. If that happened, he would have no reason to see her ever again. *Dear God, not to see her... not to touch her...* He couldn't bear that loss. Not now. Maybe not ever.

"When did you talk to her?" Caleb's voice was so hoarse and constricted he could barely talk.

"Yesterday afternoon. We had a very short and very unpleasant conversation."

Caleb's face was white and the muscles in his jaw were tense. "So, did you?"

Sighing Worrell answered, "No... no, I didn't offer her a way out."

Caleb's pent-up nerves relaxed, though he damned himself for being selfish, knowing that Blair would be better off bailing out of this mess before she did get hurt. But wasn't it his job to see that no harm came to her? Tanner was his piece of meat; he could more than meet the challenge. After all, he loved her, more than life itself. It could be no other way.

"But I was tempted, mind you," Worrell was saying. "She looked so vulnerable...." Suddenly he pounded his desk with a fist, his bushy eyebrows jumping in unison. "It's times like this when I—"

"When you wish you could retire. Right?"

"You hit the nail on the head."

"Why don't you, then?"

"I just might do that."

"Ah, shit, you know better than that, Worrell."

"Don't be too sure, my man," Worrell said with a shake of his head.

"Huh, that'll be the day."

Worrell rooted around in his chair. It squeaked again. "Ever thought about a desk job, yourself?"

Yes, many times, since meeting Blair. But it will never work, because Blair and I will never work. "Nope, can't say that I have."

"Well, think about it."

Caleb's brows slanted up sharply. "You serious?"

"Hell, yes, I'm serious."

Pushing a hand through his hair, Worrell sighed again. "Many more weeks like this one, and I'll show you just how serious." He paused and then said abruptly, "I know you're bound to have something else to do, so get the hell out of here and do it."

Caleb, used to Worrell's sudden changes of mood, took no offense. He merely nodded and made his way toward the door.

But when his hand touched the knob, Worrell added, "Blair will be in touch when she gets ready to make her next move."

Caleb nodded again before walking out and closing the door behind him. His feet were sluggish as he strode toward his office. His mind, however, was not. It was churning. Jack Worrell quit the agency? Impossible? He, Caleb Hunt, fill his shoes? Also impossible. Yet gut instinct told him that Jack had not been teasing. And, just suppose he was serious—could he fill Jack's chair? If so, would that make him more respectable in Blair's eyes? Hogwash! *You, most of all, Hunt, should know that fairy tales don't come true.*

Still, it was food for thought.

Blair awoke with the feeling that something was wrong. It was. Her head was banging like a sledgehammer. For a minute she lay still in hopes the excruciating pain would subside. It didn't, so she tossed back the sheet and very gingerly got out of bed and padded to the bathroom. After dashing her face with cold water, she reached in the medicine cabinet, groped for the bottle of aspirin and swallowed two of them.

Her headache was from tension, she knew. If only Worrell had offered her a way out. But would she have taken it? she wondered. She honestly didn't know. She hoped she wouldn't have, though when she'd gone to see Worrell immediately after her return from Tanner House, she'd been awfully strung out. It had always been easier to let others make her decisions for her, namely her mother, and that flaw in her character was still very much in evidence. That was why she wanted to see this through. Anyway, she hedged, she had given her word....

Too, it seemed as if fate had played a big part. Just as she'd gotten back from talking to Worrell, the phone had rung. Afraid it would be Caleb and not wanting to talk to him just yet, she'd contemplated not answering it. But in the end, she'd lifted the receiver. Tanner's smooth voice had met her cool hello. He had asked her to have dinner with him and she'd accepted.

From then on, she hadn't seen any light at the end of that long dark tunnel.

Thinking now that a shower might help to buffer the pain, Blair turned on the water as hot as she could stand it and climbed behind the curtain. Moments later, her skin tingling, she dried off and then gazed in the mirror. She looked a mess. If she was going to keep her luncheon date with her mother and uncle, she was going to have her work cut out for her.

She frowned and spoke to her reflection. "If you don't watch it, old girl, someone is going to mistake those bags under your eyes for your cheeks."

Then, refusing to dally a second longer, she slapped on her makeup. In no time, Blair looked as composed as ever in a cool, silk print dress with cap sleeves and open cowl neck, and a pair of beige sandals.

Later, as she turned onto the tree-lined street where the restaurant, MacArthur's Park, was located, she found that her head no longer throbbed with the same dreaded intensity.

She had just turned off the motor when she looked up and saw a big dark-haired man get out of a car two yards in front of her.

Caleb!

"Oh, no," she whispered, blinking rapidly.

Then the man turned. Blair slumped against the seat, feeling like a balloon that had suddenly been punctured; the air drained out of her lungs slowly. It was not Caleb. A likeness, but not Caleb.

Blair remained where she was, using the seat as a prop. Her turbulent insides refused to calm down. She had purposely not thought about Caleb, knowing that to do so would merely add to the boiling turmoil within. Instead, she had plunged into her work, yearning for a normal life-style again.

When thoughts of Caleb rose to the forefront of her mind, she pushed them away. Only now she found she could no longer do that. Thinking she saw him had blown her self-restraint to smithereens. He had invaded her heart; it was almost as though he were sitting beside her. She ached to touch him.

Suddenly Blair clutched at the steering wheel and, to her dismay, a tear trickled down her cheek. She opened her purse and pulled out a tissue and gently patted her cheeks. It wouldn't do for her mother to see her in such a state.

Though she controlled the tears, she was powerless to shut off her mind. Why couldn't she let him go? Love did not enter into what they shared, she told herself for the thousandth time. Caleb was merely a passing fancy in her life with no future in the offing. When the assignment was finished, they would be finished.

She knew this, had known it all along.

So why did the thought of losing Caleb make her feel all withered and dried up inside like an uprooted weed?

They were watching for her.

Thomas stood up when Blair approached the table, a grin spread across his face. "Hello, dear heart," he said, kissing her soundly on the face, pulling out a chair for her.

"Hi, yourself," Blair murmured, clinging to his hand a moment longer than necessary. Then she stepped over and met her mother's upturned cheek with her lips.

"How are you, Mother?" she asked more formally than she intended.

"I'm better now that you seem to be through with your galavanting around for a while, anyway."

Blair took her seat, ignoring the petulant ring to Sarah's voice.

"Would you care for a glass of wine before we eat?" Thomas asked as the waitress hovered nearby.

"I'd love one," Blair responded enthusiastically.

Thomas gave the order, and after the waitress disappeared he turned to Blair, that ever present twinkle in his eyes. "Well, what have you been up to lately?"

"Working most, Unc," Blair said with a smile.

Sarah sniffed. "Huh, I wouldn't call running off to a weekend party, working," she chimed in sharply.

"Now, Sarah," Thomas cut in, throwing her a mild warning look, "let her be."

Blair could see that her mother longed to make a scratching comeback, but surprisingly, she did not. Instead, Sarah met Thomas's eyes and Blair was positive she saw something pass between them.

It was after that exchange that her mother seemed to relent. Either way, though, Blair remained unruffled, having made up her mind that Sarah was not going to upset her.

"Have you forgotten, Mother, that I went to take pictures of the house for *Home Beautiful*?"

A smile suddenly touched Sarah's lips, softening her features. In fact, Blair had never seen her look better. Younger, more at ease. Love in bloom? She knew then, beyond a shadow of a doubt, that her mother and Thomas were in love. Hallelujah!

"Well, go on," Sarah encouraged, "tell us about the house, the pictures, everything."

Blair couldn't believe her ears, but she certainly wasn't going to look a gift horse in the mouth. "There's not much to tell really," she began, only to stop when the waitress appeared with their drinks and to take their orders.

Once the orders were given, Thomas turned back to Blair. "Before we hear about your trip, I just want to say I'm glad you're going to eat something. From the looks of you, a gentle breeze would blow you away."

"I couldn't agree more," Sarah said, her face all tensed up again.

Blair cut her eyes at Thomas. "Thanks, Unc. Remind me to do you a favor sometime."

Thomas looked sheepish. "I did open a can of worms, didn't I?"

"That you did."

"All right, you two," Sarah exclaimed, "I give up. If you want to be a bag of bones, daughter, then so be it."

"But a beautiful bag of bones," Thomas countered with a grin.

There was a difference in her uncle, too, Blair noticed, observing him closely. Although his charm was always infectious, there was an added sparkle to it now. Yes, she decided, something was definitely going on between those two, and she couldn't have been happier.

Now, maybe Sarah would stay off her back, Blair thought, quit living her life through hers. Or was she being too optimistic too soon?

Thomas spoke again. "Well, we're all ears."

The luncheon hour passed by in a pleasant haze. On several occasions, Blair even had her mother laughing. The food was delicious, and for the first time since returning from Tanner House Blair felt herself relax.

Then her mother asked, "Did Kyle go with you?"

Blair imagined she felt a prick, like a tiny thorn embedded under her skin. She had a feeling she knew what was coming next.

"No, Mother, Kyle did not go with me," Blair said dully, sending Sarah a resentful glance. *So much for optimism.*

A loaded silence followed.

Then, Sarah demanded bluntly, "Who's the man you've been seeing?"

Blair turned her head sharply, her eyes accusing. "What do you mean, who's the man I've been seeing?" Her words mimicked Sarah's to the T.

Stiffening, Sarah answered, "Several of my friends have reported seeing you with a strange man. He was seen picking you up in front of your office.

Though she felt sick, Blair's eyes flashed fire. "Don't interfere this time, Mother, I'm warning you."

"Blair—" Sarah started to inject, but Blair cut her off, leaning across the table, glaring.

"Make no mistake, some of you has rubbed off on me, Mother. I can be just as stubborn and bullheaded as you. And if I decide I want another man, or any man for that matter, there won't be a thing you can do about it. So hands off! Understand?"

And with that ultimatum Blair stood up, snatched up her purse and swept out of the restaurant, leaving Sarah Stephens's mouth gaping open in astonishment.

Caleb arrived at work the following morning looking poorly, and feeling so, too. He wasted no time in going to his office and shutting the door behind him. After thankfully collecting a cup of coffee that his secretary had brewed, he settled down at his desk and opened up the folder in front of him.

The words were a bunch of gobbledygook.

He slammed the folder shut and stared into space. He hadn't been able to rid his mind of the seed that Worrell had planted there. He knew it would never become a reality, his taking Worrell's place, yet the seed continued to germinate.

Unconsciously Caleb gave his head a vigorous shake. He knew he was good at his job, but he saw himself as a field agent, not a pencil pusher.

"That's just not for you," he told himself aloud.

Then he drummed his fingers on the desk as a vision of Blair flashed through his mind. He also had a vision of the loneliness he would feel when Blair was no longer part of his daily routine, no distractions or excitement to make him forget. *You're going off the deep end, man!*

The phone rang. As though reaching for his salvation, he answered it on the first ring.

Blair's voice said, "Caleb."

It seemed difficult to get air in. "How are you?" Caleb finally asked.

"Okay," Blair said. "And you?" Her voice was small.

"Functional. Sort of."

"Caleb..."

"Yes."

Tension flowed like an electrical current through the line.

"I'm...I'm sure you're aware that I'm having dinner with Tanner tomorrow evening."

He set his coffee cup down on the desk. He could feel himself beginning to shrink on the inside. He didn't know if he could stand the thought of Tanner slobbering over her again.

"Yes. You'll be careful, won't you?"

A tiny shudder ripped through Blair. "Of course. Will I see you soon?" Blair asked, her voice barely there. The question slipped from her before she had time to censor it. It emerged by itself, from the chaos he was creating within her.

His sigh was long and tortured. "That goes without saying."

A heavy silence filtered through the line.

"Goodbye, Caleb."

"Goodbye."

After he hung up, Caleb got to his feet and crossed to the window, feeling tired beyond his years. It was raining. Below him, some of the wet flower petals on the sidewalk washed into the gutter.

And the rain kept coming.

Blair could feel Tanner's hot breath as his face hovered near hers. She knew he wanted to kiss her and she had to fight the urge to move her head out of harm's way. But to do so would jeopardize everything. Instead, she held herself rigid, determined to see the charade through to the bitter end.

When she'd taken a taxi to his penthouse thirty minutes before and stepped out at the canopied entrance, she had felt a spurt of the old excitement. Finally. There had been the same great tension and the clawing fear just before she had committed herself.

It was as though she had been inside her body and outside, calmly observing herself. The mood of recklessness had taken over—after all, this was to be her last hurrah.

Now, fear had overtaken the reckless boldness, she realized suddenly. Her legs trembled under her and her heart was flying around like a loose bird, hammering to get out. She folded her arms over her chest as if to keep it close, and stared at Tanner.

"Ah, come on now, Blair darling, loosen up," Caleb whispered, closing in on her, reaching out and pulling her tight against his hard chest. "I refuse to be deprived of your luscious mouth a moment longer," he added huskily.

When his lips touched hers, Blair felt revulsion gurgle in her throat. She wanted to scream; instead she held herself erect and took the punishment his lips were dishing out. It was as if Tanner was hell-bent on breaking down the barrier she had built around herself, and if it took physical force to do it, then so be it.

"Paul, no," she pleaded after a moment, pushing at his chest. "You're . . . you're hurting me."

There was a fierce light in Tanner's eyes as he stared directly into hers. "Baby, baby, you're going to have to loosen up if we're going to make any progress."

Blair forced herself to smile and stepped out of his arms. "Well, the evening's still young," she said lightly, her voice full of false promise.

Tanner smiled without warmth. "Ah, yes, it is, isn't it?"

Beyond Tanner's shoulder, Blair spotted Martin standing in the doorway.

Tanner, following the direction of Blair's eyes, turned around.

Martin inclined his head. "Dinner is served, sir."

"Thank you, Martin."

Much to Blair's surprise, dinner was tolerable. Tanner couldn't have been more charming or have worked harder at putting her at ease. They discussed not only the article and the pictures—she had brought copies of them with her—but they also discussed the president's proposed tax reform and other current events. Blair did everything she could to make Tanner talk. She fed his ego, flirted, but when she tried to get him to talk about himself, he froze up and carefully changed the subject.

By the time Blair had eaten a portion of her prime rib and salad, she was beginning to feel that old sense of frustration claw at her insides. She was getting nowhere fast.

Tanner pushed away from the table and stood up, moving to hold out her chair. They adjourned to the den in silence. Once there, Tanner walked to the bar and began mixing their after-dinner drinks.

Make your move. Now. Once she had searched his office, she could plead a headache, anything that would obtain her freedom. She had no intention of letting him touch her again.

"If you'll excuse me, I'd like to go powder my nose," she said huskily to his back.

His hands stilled and he turned. "Take your time, my dear. I have to speak to Martin a moment, anyway."

Was there an edge to his voice, a certain glint in his eye that hadn't been present until now? No, she readily assured herself. It was simply paranoia raising its ugly head.

Blair skirted past the bathroom and made her way down the hall into Tanner's office. She didn't hesitate, as time was still her most precious commodity.

She closed the door softly behind her. Then, drawing the small flashlight out of her purse, she surefootedly crossed to the desk.

In what seemed like only a twinkling of an eye, she searched every drawer in his desk.

Nothing.

She clenched her teeth.

Then suddenly an idea came to her. She'd have to do the next best thing. Just as she reached for the stapler, her hand suddenly paused in midair.

Had the doorknob turned?

Paranoia again?

She listened.

Her heart was beating in her chest like a running hare.

There was no other sound.

There was nothing.

Relief.

Then reflexes took over. She dug in her purse again, this time yanking out a tiny microphone and screwdriver, and quickly disassembled the stapler. After placing the instrument inside and putting the stapler back together, she set it on the desk exactly where it'd been.

Knowing she could not afford to tarry another second, she stood up and raced to the door.

Seconds later she was rounding the corner into the den when she heard voices coming from down the hall, near the front door. She halted in her tracks and listened, but she couldn't make out what was being said. The voices were low, muffled. Who was it? Obviously it was someone Tanner didn't want her to see.

Her adrenaline started to flow again. Could it be his Russian connection? It was possible. She had to get closer. Then, just as she unlocked her legs, she heard a door slam.

She panicked.

Hurriedly she crossed into the den and immediately switched her mind back on another track—how to escape Tanner's amorous attentions. If only Caleb... *Forget it, Blair, it's not in the cards!*

Then Tanner came into the room. His face was ashen. "Something's come up that needs my attention." He made no effort to smile. "I'm afraid we're going to have to call an early end to the evening. I'll have Martin see you to a cab."

Blair's knees almost buckled with relief.

Saved.

Caleb was in agony. He had seen Blair when she got out of the taxi and went into the building. She had looked ravishing in a backless dress that glittered like diamonds when she walked. Just to look at her had caused a tightening in his loins.

He had kept his eyes glued to the building ever since. And waited.

After shifting his cramped muscles to another position, he looked again at the building and decided he was getting too old, too breakable for the game. With that thought, he reached out and banged his hand against the steering wheel. The action served no purpose. His stomach still felt as if he'd swallowed a load of gravel.

What were they doing? Untold horrors tiptoed across his mind with vengeful slowness. Was Tanner kissing her now? Or was he taking her clothes off, item by item, smelling the magnolia-sweet scent of her, tasting the warm velvet of her skin...?

Cut it out! Stop torturing yourself this way! She's doing her job. Accept it.

He could not. Knowing that she was with Tanner was like a boil festering inside him, ready to erupt at any moment, spewing its poison all over the place.

Impatiently he pulled out another cigarette, a new pack, the second in two hours. He glanced down at his watch, the glare from the lighter enabling him to see the time.

Only nine o'clock.

Time was creeping by at a snail's pace.

Inhaling deeply on the cigarette, he experimented with keeping his mind blank. It usually worked, but at that moment it wasn't easy. If he wasn't careful he'd start to think again, and if he thought of *things* again, then his stomach would hurt again.

He slouched in the seat.

And then he saw her. He shot to an upright position and watched. She was alone, getting into a cab. He took a breath. She was safe.

The panic eased out of him, only to be replaced by loneliness. A special kind, as if a hole had been cut in his chest and it had fallen out.

It was shaping up to be a helluva long night.

Chapter 11

Paul Tanner's heart knocked violently. He felt panic in every part of his body. Sweat was collecting around his shirt collar.

"Wringing your hands like an enraged child won't solve the problem."

Tanner swiveled around to face his lackey, Martin, his eyes sharp as daggers. "That's easy for you to say," he hissed. "You're not the one taking the risks." His voice was getting hoarse. The level of it had dropped.

Martin pushed his middle-size frame away from the bar, where he'd been leaning on an elbow, watching his boss pitch his little fit. His watered-down blue eyes peered coldly at Tanner.

"Oh, I'm taking risks, all right," he said with deadly calm. "And don't you forget it."

"Don't worry, you'll get your share of the loot," Tanner said with a sneer, "and the way things are looking, you'll get your share of the pen, too."

His nostrils flaring outward, Martin stalked closer. "You'll see to that, won't you?"

Tanner stood his ground without flinching. "You bet I will."

They glared at each other, while a grim silence filled the room, neither wanting to be the first to back down.

"Dammit, Martin," Tanner exploded after a moment, "why are we bickering? God knows, we need to stick together if we're going to pull this deal off."

Some of the tension seemed to drain from Martin, though his eyes remained hard as nails. "Do you think that Browning woman has caused it to go sour?"

Tanner's lips slanted cruelly. "That little bitch. You can't imagine how badly I wanted to wrap my hands around her throat and choke the very life out of her."

"She didn't find anything, did she?"

"Hell no, it's all up here." Tanner paused and pointed to his right temple. "But the fact that she played me for a fool is grounds enough to waste her."

"Not to mention all those bugging devices that we had to rip out of all the phones and lamps." It was obvious that Martin was enjoying adding insult to injury. Sooner or later he was determined to say, I told you so.

Tanner stared at him and the lines from his nose to the corners of his mouth were deep. There was a small tic in his eyelid. "That too," he spat harshly.

Martin started to open his mouth.

"Don't you dare say I told you so," Tanner said, cutting him off. "I thought that bitch was legit, that she was exactly what she said, a photographer from the magazine." He began pacing the floor, the sweat now pouring down his face. "When I opened that door and saw her going through my desk . . ." He left his sentence unfinished, drawing out a handkerchief and mopping his face. His fingers were shaking.

"Hey, man, just say the word and I'll blow her away like a midsummer dandelion."

Tanner stopped his pacing. "Dammit, don't you understand that if she's on to us, then others are right behind?" He squeezed out his words like dust through a clogged filter.

Martin paled.

"You finally get the picture, huh? Not so funny now, is it?" Tanner asked.

Martin shifted his eyes. "FBI?"

"More than likely."

"Well, if the broad didn't find anything to report, no names and nothing from the bugs, then what makes you think we can't still pull it off?"

Tanner threw him a dark look. "Time, you idiot, time. If we don't move soon, it'll be too late. The FBI'll be swarming over us like a buzzard over a carcass."

"What about Guzenko? Can we still trust him?"

Tanner made a sound like a boxer taking a blow to the chest. "We sure as hell better can. That's why he came here tonight, to say they'd pay me the kind of bread I wanted, only they're still stalling on the exchange date."

"You smell a rat?"

"Yeah. But I got 'em by the you know what and they know it."

This time it was Martin's lips that twisted cruelly. "And just think, that Browning dame came within inches of screwing it up royally. If she'd heard you and that Russian talking..."

"That's right. When I saw her coming down the hall, after I'd caught her snooping and Guzenko was at the door, I nearly had a heart attack right there on the spot. I practically broke the Russian's nose, closing the door in his face."

Martin laughed without pleasure.

Then Tanner crossed to the bar, jerked a bottle of whiskey off the shelf and mixed himself a double on the rocks. He took two healthy swigs before turning to Martin again.

"You thinking what I'm thinking?"

"Yeah, boss, I am." Martin's grin was satanical. "The Browning woman?"

"You're right on target, my friend. Find out everything you can about her."

"And then?"

"I'll tell you what I want you to do."

Blair was sitting on the side of the bed trying to shake herself awake when the phone jangled beside her. Automatically, she lifted the receiver and said, "Hello."

"It's Saturday, isn't it?"

The receiver almost slipped from her hand when she heard the deep voice.

"Yes, it is." Her mouth felt devoid of moisture.

"Are you all right?"

"Yes," she said again.

"Anything to report?"

"A lot," she said. "Though nothing of importance," she hastened to add. She couldn't put her finger on it, but she detected a difference in Caleb this morning. He sounded less tense, more at ease. *Warm.* Was that the adjective she was searching for?

"No list of names?"

"No."

"He didn't... I mean...?" Caleb stopped short of finishing the question and cleared his throat. "That bastard didn't..." Still he struggled.

Blair felt her heart turn over, knowing what he was trying to say. "No...no, he didn't," she whispered.

She was positive she could feel his relief vibrate through the phone line.

"Thank God," Caleb said, and then changed the subject. "How 'bout throwing on some clothes and going with me to the races."

Flabbergasted, Blair could say nothing.

A chuckle answered her. "Don't gasp, just say yes."

"You mean now? Today?"

"I mean now. Today. This minute."

"But . . . I'm still in bed."

A silence fell and seemed to magnify.

After a short interval, Caleb spoke, his voice sounding rusty. "How long then will it take you to, uh . . . dress?"

Blair paused before speaking and then said, "Caleb, are you sure? I mean . . ." She was completely and thoroughly flustered.

"Hey, no dark shadows," he pleaded. "Not today. Okay?"

Blair smiled, only to ask herself if she would ever understand Caleb Hunt? *Not in a million years,* a little voice taunted.

"Blair?"

"Give me an hour," she murmured huskily.

"Yes, we really *are* going to the races," he mimicked, his intense gaze robbing her of her next breath, while the naked hunger in his face brought an uncontrollable trembling to her knees. She was glad she was sitting down.

They were in Caleb's car, in front of her condominium with the windows down. The day promised to be lovely. The fog had lifted and the sky was virtually cloudless. Blair felt as excited as a kid with a new toy.

Later, she knew, she would question the sanity of that minute, that hour, that day. Heartache was the name of their game. But, for now, she was going to go with her heart instead of her head and delight in just being with Caleb.

She felt his eyes on her and the scent of his warm body was intoxicating her senses to the exclusion of all else.

"You look beautiful," he said, his Adam's apple working furiously.

And she did. She was dressed in a cap-sleeved gold blouse and pleated, beige-and-gold-striped pants in a nubby-textured cotton. Her hair was brushed away from her face and caressed her shoulders like a silk curtain. Caleb ached to touch her, though he dared not, knowing the thread of civility between them was so fragile that one wrong move, one wrong word and it would shatter like a plate-glass window struck by a bullet.

"Thank you." She examined him, trying not to gape at the brown hollow of his throat, visible above the open neckline of his shirt. There was a faint moisture on his skin that was magnified by the sunlight, and she had the craziest impulse to run the tips of her fingers across his chest and taste their plunder on her tongue.

Unaware that her feelings showed in her face, she was shocked out of her daydreams by Caleb saying thickly, "Please...you're doing it again. Don't look at me like that."

The raspy tone of his voice feathered down her spine, leaving her breathless. "I'm...I'm sorry," she mumbled, unable to remove her gaze from his face, her eyes clinging to the revealing lines of weariness that etched shadows in the bone structure of his cheeks. But she wasn't sorry. She could never tire of looking at him. Or touching him.

"Oh, Blair," he muttered weakly, "haven't you figured out what you do to me yet?"

Then, before she could answer, he reached across the seat and pulled her toward him. "If I don't do this, I don't think I can last another second."

His mouth touched hers, warm and tender. She sat still, afraid that if she moved he might go away. He kissed her slowly, sweetly, shaping the contours of her mouth to exactly match his. The world went silent around her. There was only the thumping of her own heart, and maybe his, she wasn't sure. A private world, theirs, full of sweet sensations and longings.

He had never kissed her quite like that. Her body trembled against him and she felt his arms tightening around her back. The tip of his tongue touched the corners of her mouth and her heart jumped crazily.

Then, without warning, he seemed to lose control. He was no longer gentle. His hands slipped down to her hips and pressed her intimately against him. His lips were now full of urgency and fire. The blood rushed to her head and she clung to him dizzily, thoroughly shaken by the feelings he could unleash in her. From her throat came a low, wordless sound.

Caleb twisted free and, breathing hard, clenched his hands around the steering wheel.

Blair shifted back to her side, her heart thumping wildly.

"Damn!" Caleb ground out. "At this rate we're not even going to get away from the curb."

"Not to mention the show we put on for the neighbors," she added in a tight-strung voice.

Their eyes tangled then, and Blair felt her face grow hot with embarrassment.

He looked at her for another moment, a low, rumbling laughter shaking his chest. Then he pulled away from the curb and threaded the car into the flow of traffic.

Once they were cruising on the freeway, heading toward the Oakland Bay Bridge and the racetracks, Caleb glanced at her and said, "Tell me about last night."

Blair sighed and stared out the window, a portion of her mind wandering at will, thinking inanely that the few clouds dotting the sky looked exactly like giant cotton balls.

"Hey, look at me," he demanded softly.

"Do I have to?"

"Yes."

She faced him. "I didn't find a thing." Her tone held disgust.

"But you said you had a lot to report. Remember?"

Blair chewed on her lower lip. "It's probably nothing," she said.

"Why don't you let me be the judge of that?"

Blair didn't want to talk about last night; she wanted nothing evil or sinister—and Tanner fit both those adjectives—to mar the day. Yet she knew the only reason she was with Caleb was because of Tanner. But, for a moment, she had purposely let it slip her mind that she and Caleb weren't just another happy couple out for a Saturday's outing. Suddenly she felt a stinging sensation at the back of her eyelids and deliberately shut off that avenue of thought.

"Blair." He was waiting.

Having mastered her emotions as best she could, Blair turned and said, "I made it to his office without a hitch, only to come up empty-handed." She paused and breathed deeply.

"Go on."

Her voice was toneless. "Although I know now that it was just my imagination playing another trick on me, I thought I heard something or someone at the door. But when I raised my head, there was nothing."

"Are you sure?" Caleb asked, his face ashen.

A tiny frown wrinkled her brow. "As sure as I can be. Of course my head was down while I was digging through the papers."

"Then what did you do?"

She leaned back and clasped her hands behind her head. The position showed off her perfect breasts. "I grabbed the stapler, bugged it and then got out of there."

Caleb massaged the bridge of his nose and there was a slight curve to his mouth, almost a smile. "The stapler, huh? Never would've thought of that in a million years."

She threw him a furtive glance. "Rather stupid, wasn't it?"

He shrugged. "Can't tell. Anything at this point is worth a try."

"There's something else, too," Blair said, moving closer.

He caught a whiff of her perfume and instantly rebelled against the tightening in his groin.

"When I started back to the den I heard muffled voices."

"Whose?" The word shot out of his mouth like a bullet.

"I don't know, that's just it." Frustration tempered her voice. "But someone was at the door and the second Tanner got wind of me coming around the corner, he slammed it. And right then and there, he called a halt to the evening."

"I'd give my eyeteeth to know who it was."

"Think it might have been his Russian contact?"

"I'd be willing to bet my life on it."

"Well, as I said, I couldn't see a thing, though it was obvious that whoever it was, it shook up Tanner. He was as white as a sheet when he followed me into the den."

"And to think I scrutinized everyone who walked through the door of that building and I still missed him."

Her face wrinkled into a frown. "You were there?"

"You're damned right I was there."

"But I didn't see you."

He smiled. "You weren't supposed to. If you had, I wouldn't have been doing my job."

"But—but—" she stammered.

"Close your mouth and quit stammering," he ordered with another brief smile, then shrugged. "After all, that's part of my job."

"I understand that, but what good were you outside the building while I was inside? There's quite a distance in between."

"You're right," Caleb agreed, a harsh strain to his voice, "and if you hadn't come out when you did or shortly thereafter, I probably would have come in after you."

He spoke so matter-of-factly that at first Blair thought he was teasing her, but she should have known better. The Caleb Hunt she knew didn't tease. A man of few words, he said what he meant and meant what he said. But to her way of thinking, his standing guard outside, worried about her, went above and beyond the call of duty.

When she held her silence, Caleb spoke again, his voice deep and unsteady. "Sometimes I worry about you so much that I can barely breathe."

She turned and stared at him, feeling vertigo. He was not looking at her. He was staring straight ahead, a muscle in his cheek bunching. This second confession was even more overwhelming than the other one. Why did he have to say that to her? Here. Now. Blair felt as if her mind might simply split from the sudden, swelling pressures on her brain.

"I...I don't want you to worry," she stammered, her voice sounding dry, out of use. She coughed lightly.

"Hey," he said softly, reaching over and placing a hand on her knee, "don't close up on me."

A wobbly smile crossed her lips. "Sorry. I guess my mind just shorted out for a minute." A finger was tracing up and down her leg. She felt it touch a responsive chord deep within her.

Caleb's hand eased back to the steering wheel. "That's understandable," he said, measuring his words, "especially after what we've put you through."

A frown furrowed her soft brow. "And I don't have a thing to show for it, either," she responded bitterly. "If only I could have gotten my hands on that list." She wadded her hands into a ball. "Or could've seen who Tanner was talking to. Just anything!"

His face gentled. "Come on, you're being too hard on yourself," Caleb admonished softly. "Those bugs you planted are still the key. Just like I told Jack, getting our hands on the names would be great, but we couldn't arrest him until we catch Tanner exchanging them for money. You know that."

"I know, but still it's frustrating as heck," she said in a choked voice, turning her back to him, feeling suddenly as though the light had gone out of her day and hating herself for allowing that to happen.

A short, strained silence followed.

"Have you lost interest in going to the races?" Caleb finally asked, his low, grating voice splitting the silence.

Blair swung around. He was looking at her, his gaze like a soft insistent touch.

A tremor ran through her. "You want the truth?"

"I wouldn't have asked otherwise."

Simple enough. "Yes, I have. How about you?"

"Me, too."

"Any ideas?"

As long as I'm with you it doesn't matter what we do or where we go. "None. Do you?"

"Yeah. A couple, in fact." Caleb was facing straight ahead and again that same willful strand of hair was dangling across his forehead. As before, she itched to reach over and push it back in place. She did not. Instead, she threaded her hands like a rope and simply stared at his profile, wondering how she was going to cope when this big man was no longer part of her everyday existence.

Suddenly Caleb slanted her a sidelong glance. "Wanna take a vote?"

"What are the choices?"

A benign smile hovered around his lips. "Well," he drawled, shifting to another position, "we can go to the redwood forest and walk off our frustrations. Or we can go to the beach and walk off our frustrations."

"How about both?"

He laughed. "You're on."

Their day together was filled with the stuff dreams are made of. The moment Blair had called his hand on his crazy suggestions, he had swerved the car off the freeway at the next exit and, following a U-turn under the bridge, he'd headed back toward the forest. Though she had been there numerous times, she never tired of the magnificent beauty of the trees. This day was no exception.

Once they pulled off the highway short of the entrance into the forest, she experienced that same feeling of awe. It was as if someone had closed the last window in a house. The silence was vast.

They strolled through the grounds, looking at and touching the huge trunks and then staring up at the heavens, listening to the howl of the wind and the thrashing of the interlocked branches.

Each giant trunk they stood in front of seemed to loom above them, threatening, as if poised to fall any moment. Many had twisted roots like huge bumps around the base, while others rose tall and sleek.

From there they had driven the short distance to a deserted stretch of beach, but not before stopping and purchasing bread, cheese, wine and fresh cherries. After strolling along the beach, talking little, they had sprawled on the grass and shared the food.

There were long silences in which they'd moved about each other, occupied with their various thoughts. And Blair had soon learned that silences didn't necessarily require filling. It wasn't mandatory that she grope around looking for words to toss into the gaps.

But then later, under her tender prodding, he had opened up and told of his childhood, refusing, however, to dwell on the hard times and the loneliness of those years, instead calling to mind the few good times he remembered.

The pain had been there just beneath the surface, and she had longed to ease it somehow. But the words had jammed in her heart. Too, she had known better than to give him sympathy, so she had bitten her tongue and held her silence.

It had been one of the few glimpses that Blair had gotten of the man behind the mask. It had touched her soul, for she, too, had known what it meant to be alone—and lonely.

Yet, the light moments had far outweighed the serious ones, and though he hadn't touched her, an electric awareness had sparked between them just waiting to be ignited.

It was after they were full and lazy from the wine and food, the sound of the waves cresting in the distance, that Blair had sensed he wanted to touch her. But he'd turned away and the moment was lost, never to be recaptured.

Now, as they stood at the door of her apartment, the day drawn to a close, they suddenly didn't know what to say.

With the door open behind her, Blair opened her mouth to say thanks for the day, but found she wasn't capable of speech. She wanted him to go, yet longed for him to stay.

Blair's stomach knotted while their eyes locked, and that same mysterious current rendered them motionless.

"Aren't you going to invite me in?" he asked, the low tone of his voice holding a ragged edge of pain.

Still she was silent. A feeling, warm and fragile, spiraled upward and again her throat closed.

"Blair...?" A vein pulsed in his right temple.

"I..." Suddenly, foolish tears welled up in her eyes and with a muttered groan, Caleb backed her into the apartment and slammed the door behind them.

She just kept staring at him.

"Oh, Blair, what have we gotten ourselves into?" His voice ground out, scraping over the pain. "We...you and I..." After a moment, he, too, stopped trying to talk and just looked at her.

Blair just knew she was drowning in the dark. And that was when she knew. *I love him,* she thought, stunned. *I love him. But, dear God, I didn't mean to. I didn't mean to....*

"Oh, Caleb...hold me."

His arms were around her in a rush, spreading himself about her like a protective shell. His mouth found hers with hungry urgency and her lips parted under his impatience. He had lost control; he had to touch her, everywhere. Of their own free will, her arms looped his neck, her fingers sliding into the hair at his nape, her tongue mating with his.

Finally, after all the days and nights of pretense, Blair had come full circle, realizing that she needed his arms around her to survive. She loved him, she loved him, her heart sang. All the previous objections melted, like her bones.

She sank into him, feeling the sharp bones of his pelvis, the rigid muscles of his thighs against hers, the demand of his body, rising.

His body communicated with her. The silent man, the locked and barred man, was suddenly wide open. And she bestowed on him all the soft and loving silence he needed, letting her body speak alone to him, and he heard. They moved together like courting butterflies.

He carried her to the bed and unwrapped her like an unexpected gift. His mouth drifted over her breasts; his tongue searched her neck and belly; his hands finally slipped between her thighs, long, narrow fingers searching deep in the flooding warmth.

To him, she was a flower, her mouth and legs, petals, opening wide. Her own hands moved insistently, eager to possess and discover, as if it was the first time all over again. The hard planes of his back, his spine, the heavy satin of his

stomach all reveled in the touch of her fingers as they
roamed deliciously over him. And the heart of him that
pushed past her moving palm was impatient, fevered, om-
nipotent with its promise.

Blair guided his body into her own and locked him within
her, lifting her hips to meet his thrust with a thrust. And
then again, until surrender. He ran wild inside her, a velvet
hammer pounding, driving deep.

At last their cries were heard in the darkness, bringing a
sigh of release from both of them.

The rays from the moon painted them as they finally lay
silent, almost afraid to believe the doors were open between them at last.

Before dawn, while Blair slept softly against his shoulder, the pain from his arms going to sleep awakened Caleb.
It felt as if tiny hot needles were piercing his skin. He lay
still, enduring it, not wanting to disturb her.

Suddenly life seemed so simple. All those roads, all those
turns and curves, and this was where he was headed all
along. Only he hadn't known.

"Blair," he whispered. She didn't stir, but a faint smile
shadowed her lips. Caleb lit a cigarette and leaned back
against the headboard. His watch showed nearly six. Daylight was just over the horizon.

How did you knock down my defenses, Blair? he asked
silently. *How did you manage to get inside me? It can't
work, you know. I'm no good for you. We're no good for
each other.*

Violently he stubbed out the cigarette until it shredded in
the ashtray, as he gave in to the fear that rumbled through
him.

Why couldn't he just savor the moment? Just feel? Go
with it, his mind told him. He couldn't. For he was fearful
that what he had from her was stolen, not freely given.

But whatever she felt for him, he was not about to name it, or even identify it. Neither did he want it labeled or defined. He would simply take whatever she had to offer and stash it in his heart, and once she was gone from his life, the memories would warm his heart and his empty bed.

But could he survive without her?

He had no choice.

It was just another dead-end street.

Just another missed turn.

Blair stirred, and with her eyes still closed she flung out a leg and felt for Caleb. Nothing. Her eyes fluttered open. The bed was empty. Scrambling to a sitting position, she scanned the room. Then she heard the water running. Blair eased back against the pillow. If he had left, she didn't think she could have stood it.

A smile brought the color back to her cheeks. *I'm in love.* She couldn't believe it, but it was true. *Now that you've faced it, what are you going to do about it?*

Her smile disappeared. Then another truth hit her with a punch: *Even though their bodies had found harmony, nothing else had. Caleb did not return her love.*

Blair whimpered and closed her eyes. Hadn't he made it plain what he thought about her social status and her money? About her? And what about their personalities, their goals in life? Weren't they still in total conflict? When they were together, it was indeed like satin rubbing against granite. *Except when we touch.* Then it was like satin against silk—perfectly compatible.

Slowly Blair smiled again. That was the way she was going to remember the magical time in his arms. She would take the moment and squeeze the most out of it.

And tomorrow be hanged.

With her naked body hidden in the folds of a negligee, Blair paused just inside the bathroom door. Caleb was standing at the sink, nothing but a towel draped around his middle. He saw her in the mirror and turned around.

At first they looked in each other's eyes, caught in a peaceful, easy moment that only morning brings.

Then she smiled.

His breath shortened.

Blair moved farther into the room and perched on the side of the tub. "Do you mind if I watch you shave?"

"I'd like the company," Caleb muttered indistinctly, trying to keep his eyes intent on the task at hand, as if shaving required his full concentration. But, as if straying of their own accord, his eyes had followed her slender body from the door to the tub. Through the flimsy garment he could see her flat stomach and her firm high breasts. He felt himself grow hard again as he attacked his face with the razor.

Blair was fascinated with the ease between her and Caleb. In the years she'd been married to Josh, she'd never shared this intimacy with him. Never cared to. Witnessing the entire process, the cup of coffee near his hand, the burning cigarette in the nearby ashtray, watching his hands as he lathered his face before carefully shaving, made her believe that they were a normal couple in love.

Everything about him entranced her. His skin, even the scars that marred it, were pleasing to her touch, the fine line of hair that dissected his belly, running down to his groin...

The sound of the water splashing on his face jarred her out of her trancelike state.

"Want another cup of coffee?" she asked unsteadily, when he cast the face towel aside.

His eyes seemed to devour her. "No thanks."

"Are you hungry?" she asked, her breathing sounding decidedly shallow.

"Only for you."

Their hands met and linked like the most intricate of Chinese puzzles.

"Oh, God," Caleb whispered, "should we be happy now?"

"Yes," she said, smiling. "Yes, definitely."

He laughed outright and let go of her hand. "Last one back to the bed has to cook breakfast!"

As they dived for the bed, Blair's squealed, "You cheated!" was lost against his lips.

And then there was silence.

Chapter 12

Life was indeed filled with promise.

That night of love set the precedent for the following days. Blair coveted each moment spent with Caleb, refusing to question the sanity of what she was doing or why. She had never been happier and was satisfied with what she had.

The only cloud on her otherwise bright horizon was a crazy fear that Tanner would show up out of the clear blue on her doorstep. Blair thought it uncanny that she hadn't seen or heard from him since that last night at his penthouse.

She found it hard to curb her anxieties. Every time the doorbell rang unexpectedly at home, or the phone jangled at work, she went into a mild panic. However, he made no move to harm her or see her. Nor had he made any move toward meeting his Russian contact. It was a wait-and-see game for all of them.

In the meantime, Blair worked at the office, concentrating on the show that was only a few weeks away. There was so much to be done: temperamental models to be dealt with, clothes to be selected and fitted, decorations to be chosen. She wanted everything to be perfect, as this project would be a "make it or break it" situation for her.

If the show turned out to be the success she envisioned, then she would indeed have launched her career as a photographer, and on her own to boot—no help from the family name or her mother's influence.

Yet, as important as that was to her, it did not take the place of Caleb. He had an exclusive on her nights. There were times, however, when in spite of her promise not to question tomorrow, she found herself doing just that. For Caleb had yet to utter words of love.

But then, how could she condemn him for being noncommittal? She couldn't bring herself to tell him she loved him, either. It was the fear of rejection that kept her mute. He was unaware of her feelings, she was sure of that. On occasion, though, she caught him looking at her in a curiously speculative way, and her heart missed a beat at the possibility he might suspect her secret.

So she guarded it well and simply enjoyed the strong, silent man whose bark she had learned was far worse than his bite. She had accepted him for what he was and loved him in spite of it. But the crux of the matter was, could *he* accept *her* for what she was?

During the evenings they shared, she began to believe it was possible, as he seemed interested in everything about her. It was nothing for him to suddenly put down the book he was reading—she'd been astounded when she learned he loved to read—and slip her robe off her shoulders, leaning on his elbows examining the size and shape of her breasts and nipples, the surface of her belly, the length of her thighs.

"You're perfect," he'd say in that low, grating voice that had the power to turn her bones to liquid.

For the time being that was enough, sharing what little of himself he allowed her to share. She found herself savoring those moments when they were together.

This afternoon followed that same pattern. She had just received a phone call at the office from Caleb, saying that he was at her condo. He had been out of town for the past two days, having been subpoenaed to testify on a former case. His huskily spoken, "Hurry," was still ringing in her ear when she breezed by her assistant's desk and said, "I'm on my way home. Caleb's there. If anything important comes up, you know where I'll be."

Lisa smiled knowingly. Her words, "Have a good time," followed Blair out the door.

With her head still in the clouds, Blair crossed the street to the parking lot and got into her car. After buckling her seat belt, she shoved the key into the ignition and the engine purred instantly to life.

It wasn't until after she had turned onto a side street and was slowing down for the upcoming intersection that she had the first inkling that all was not right.

Blair touched her foot to the brake. Nothing happened. Her heart lurched. Cars whizzed past her.

Don't panic, Blair. Simply try again.

She pressed harder. Still nothing. Panic time. Forcing herself to take deep breaths, she buried her foot into the brake petal and pumped frantically. It was no use—she had no brakes.

She jerked her head up. The intersection was upon her and the light was a glaring red. Cars were lined up, waiting. She trembled violently.

What to do?

She was on an incline; her speed was building. She felt panic in every part of her body. Her teeth were clenched and nausea burned her stomach.

Whipping her head to the right she checked the street—all clear. Then suddenly her mind cleared as well. The ditch. That was her only alternative.

Reflexes took over.

In that split second before she reached the intersection, she swerved and nosed the car toward the ditch. Brakes squealed to the side of her, behind her. Someone shouted.

Oblivious to it all, Blair concentrated on the grassy embankment in front of her. It looked like Mount Everest.

She was in trouble and she knew it. Yet she was helpless. Her muscles were too exhausted, her lungs too paralyzed with fear, and the human will too weak to even cry. Instead, she yearned to surrender, to lie down on the seat. Anything to stop the fear of motion.

Suddenly the car slewed across the gravel and jackknifed. When the impact came, there was no time to move.

Blair screamed a soundless scream. No one heard.

A lightning pain cracked through her skull and everything went black.

It was night when she came to and a tender spot throbbed just over her right eye. Blair moaned, afraid to open her eyes. Where was she anyway? She moaned again and her eyes opened slowly. Nothing looked familiar. The smell, she'd know it anywhere. The hospital. She was in the hospital.

Josh! Not Josh! Please...help him! Oh, please, don't let him die! Not like this. They told her they could put him back together. But didn't those doctors know that Humpty-Dumpty couldn't be put back together again?

"No!" she cried.

"Shh, it's all right. You were dreaming," a soothing voice answered, the sound caressing her ear like the gentle wind of spring.

Blair opened her eyes and tried to focus. She blinked several times before she obtained the desired results. The face bending over her finally fleshed out.

"Caleb. . ." The word was a groan. She lifted her hand.

He folded his large one around it. "Shh," he repeated gently. "It's all right."

"What . . . what happened?"

Panic drilled through him. "Don't you remember?"

"Yes. . . and no."

Some of the tension seemed to ebb from him.

Clinging to his hand, Blair whispered, "I remember the brakes. . . . When I pressed them . . . there was nothing and then . . . there was this grassy hill . . . so big . . . and then nothing."

Caleb was visibly trembling now, his eyes filled with unsurpassed emotion, as he remembered how she looked when he had arrived at the hospital: her face waxen, blood matted on her forehead from where she creamed the steering wheel. . . .

Struggling for control, Caleb said softly, "Just the fact that you can remember something is enough for now."

"When . . . can I go home?" Her voice was groggy, unclear.

"Here, here, you're rushing things, aren't you? You're still in emergency. The doctor wants to move you to a room and keep you overnight." He paused. "Thanks to your seat belt, you came out of it with only a minor concussion and bruises." His voice was harsh, as if the words had been clawed from his throat.

Her brows puckered. "I still want to go home."

"We'll see," he said, humoring her. "But I don't think that's a good idea. Why don't you follow the doctor's orders for now and see what happens?"

Blair was beginning to feel drowsy, but she fought it, wanting to stay awake. "How...do you know about the accident?"

Caleb hid his pain. "The police called your office and your assistant . . . called me."

"Caleb...it wasn't just a mechanical failure, was it?" His face swam before her eyes.

Seeing her droopy eyelids, Caleb whispered, "You just rest and we'll talk later."

Unable to stand the clamor inside her head, Blair's eyes drifted shut, her lashes spreading across her pale cheeks like fans.

It was only after Blair had drifted off into a deep sleep that Caleb moved. He stood up and tenderly untangled their fingers. But when he turned and stalked to the door and jerked it open, his face was a mask, tight and pale.

And there was murder in his eyes.

"Don't you think it's time we stopped playing this game of cat and mouse?"

"I don't know what you mean."

"Oh, yes, Sarah, I think you do. The days of pretending are over."

Sarah Stephens pushed herself up off the couch and walked to the fireplace. She placed her hand against the mantel as though for support and turned and stared into the sharp gray eyes of Thomas Stephens.

"You know I love you," he said softly. "In fact, I can't remember a time when I haven't loved you."

Sarah knew he spoke the truth. She had known for years how Thomas felt about her, but she had ignored it, choosing to use him and his love, unmercifully at times, for her own selfish needs.

She ached for both of them, fearing it was too late. At this point in her life, Sarah wasn't sure she was capable of sharing herself, or her life, with anyone. Anyone other than Blair, that is. She thought she was too jaded, too shriveled up on the inside.

Yet when Thomas had held her in his arms—was it only a few weeks ago? it seemed like a lifetime—she had felt a warmth spread through her equal to nothing she had ever experienced. She had felt loved. And though she hated to admit it, she had yearned for more.

Her marriage to Warren Stephens had been a farce. There was never any tenderness between them, only sex. Even those times were few and far between. And when her husband had come into her room, he had always used her violently. The last time he had done so, she had told him she'd kill him if he ever touched her again.

From that moment on, she had vowed never to let any man use her again. She had simply placed her emotions on ice. Her whole life was then devoted to her daughter. And when Warren died, that did not change.

Now this man, who truly was a gentleman in every sense of the word, was trying to defrost her emotions, wanted to make her feel again. She shuddered inwardly. Was it possible? Or was he asking too much? she wondered. Perhaps, more importantly, was she capable of giving?

"Sarah, we have to talk."

Thomas's solemnly spoken words penetrated Sarah's fragmented mind. She gave a start. "I know."

With a muted groan, Thomas closed the distance between them and for only the second time since he'd known her, he pulled her gently into his arms and placed his cheek against hers.

Sarah stiffened in his arms.

"Oh, Sarah, Sarah, my love, you need me, just as I need you. I know that even if you don't."

In spite of herself, Sarah felt her resistance melt. She tilted her head and looked into Thomas's face. His heart was shining in his eyes.

"Oh, Thomas," she cried, "why do you still want me after all this time?"

His lips curved crookedly. "How 'bout if I told you I was just a lecherous old man."

Without meaning to, Sarah laughed, giving him a gentle push. "That's a lie and you know it. Anyway, there must have been a multitude of women...." The sentence trailed off, but the point was made.

Cupping her chin between his fingers, Thomas tenderly forced her to meet his eyes. "Yes, there've been other women, but contrary to what you think, there've only been a few."

"It...it doesn't matter."

"No, it doesn't, because you're the only one I've ever loved." With a groan, he pressed his lips to hers, forcing hers open to accept the hunger of his. "Oh, Sarah, don't make me wait any longer," he pleaded desperately. "Marry me."

"There are things you...you don't know." Her voice was strained.

"It's Warren, isn't it?" Thomas let her go and lifted his shoulders in a gesture of defeat. "He hurt you, didn't he?"

Sarah's eyes were very wide. "Did he tell you that?"

"No," Thomas assured her quietly. "He didn't have to. I knew my brother." He reached out and ran a finger down her still-unlined cheek. "You have nothing to fear from me. I'm as different from Warren as daylight and dark."

"Oh, Thomas," she wailed, diving into his arms once again. "I know what you say is true, only..."

Thomas cradled her close. "Only what, my love?"

"Only I need more time. There's...Blair."

"Sarah, my sweet, sweet Sarah," Thomas said, exhaling deeply, "we've been over this a thousand times. Blair doesn't need a nursemaid."

"But she needs me. Look at the mess she's already made of her life."

"Dammit, that's just the point. It's *her* life."

Sarah's chin wobbled and she pulled away. "She's...she's all I've had for so long."

You've had me, only you were too stubborn to admit it. A regretful sigh passed between his lips. "You've got to let her go, both for your sake and hers." He reached for her hand. "You don't even realize how different you become when you're around Blair. Your personality changes completely, and not for the better," he added gently.

"But..."

Thomas placed a finger across her lips, effectively silencing her. "There are no buts about it. Let Blair have her own life and we'll have ours. I can make you happy, I know I can."

"Please, Thomas, I need...I must have more time."

He frowned. "How much more?"

"Soon. I promise I'll give you an answer soon."

He tucked a strand of hair behind her ear, his fingers lingering. "Well, I guess I'll have to be content with that for now. But please, don't keep me waiting too long."

Suddenly the phone rang, startling them both. They froze.

Then Thomas laughed, feeling as though he had a new lease on life. "Want me to answer it?"

Sarah smiled. "Please."

The room was quiet as he lifted the receiver and listened on the line. With each passing second his face lost a little more of its color. Then he muttered tersely, "We'll be right there."

"Thomas?" Sarah dug her nails into his arm.

"It's Blair. There's been an accident."

"That sonofabitch tried to kill her!"

Caleb's anger cut into Worrell's consciousness like a double-edged sword. "Why don't you calm down and tell me what this is all about. I've been out of the office for a while and I don't know the latest development." Worrell shuffled the papers out of his way and gave the hostile man in front of him his undivided attention.

"Calm down, my ass!" Caleb roared, leaning across the desk, his face becoming eye level with Worrell. "Just tell me how in the hell I'm supposed to calm down when Blair's lying in the hospital with a concussion and multiple bruises."

This time Worrell turned deathly white. "Dammit to hell, what happened?"

There was a moment of silence as both men fought to get control of their emotions. They were both standing now, both breathing heavily.

Caleb couldn't block out of his mind the image of Blair's inert body, looking like death itself lying on that stretcher. *If anything had happened to her...* A blistering curse escaped from his lips and he felt his temper flare again, glad of an excuse to release the tension pent up inside.

"Tanner tampered with her brakes, that's what!" Caleb said at last. "And Blair's car rammed into an embankment and, if she hadn't been wearing her seat belt, she'd be a statistic right now!"

"How the hell could Tanner be responsible? He didn't even know she was on to him." Worrell's eyes suddenly narrowed into tiny slits. "Or did he? Was there something I was supposed to know and wasn't told? When Blair turned in her report, there was nothing out of the ordinary in it."

When Caleb didn't answer, Worrell charged from behind his desk. "Caleb!"

Caleb's anger had enlarged to such an extent that the heat of it was working its way up from the pit of his stomach, spreading along his back and shoulders and down his arm. He could feel his face getting hot.

"Not that I was aware of at the time," he answered dully.

"What the hell kind of answer is that?"

"Blair thought that she heard something while she was going through Tanner's desk in his penthouse," Caleb explained, his voice sounding tired now. "But when he looked up there was no one there."

"Tanner was there. Why that sneaky, low-life—"

"That's putting it mildly," Caleb said, the anger seeping out of him like air out of a punctured tire. And right on the heels of the anger came the pain. Because Blair had been so sure it was just a case of nerves, he hadn't followed up on it himself. Mistake number one. Then he had failed to tell Worrell of her suspicions. Mistake number two. Both could have been fatal to Blair.

If only he'd stuck to his promise not to get involved, never mix business with pleasure. If only he hadn't taken leave of his senses and fallen in love with her, his judgment would not have been colored. If only. . .

"We'll get him," Worrell said at length, though he didn't sound nearly as confident as before.

Caleb ignored him. "It's my fault. I should've suspected that he might be on to her." His voice bore testimony to the pain that was twisting his guts into knots.

"That's hogwash and you know it. The one thing we don't need is for you to start wallowing in self-pity. Blair knew the score when she went into this."

Caleb didn't believe for a minute that part of it wasn't his fault, but he knew Worrell was right. It was not the time to whip himself mentally. There would be time for that later. Protecting Blair from any more attempts on her life took precedence over everything else.

"She's through, Jack. I don't want her going anywhere near that slimeball again, except maybe when she has to testify against him in court."

If Worrell thought it odd that Caleb had changed his attitude about Blair, that he seemed unprofessionally concerned about her, that he had never known him to behave in quite this manner, he kept his thoughts to himself and his mouth shut. For now.

"Provided he makes it to court, that is," Caleb was saying.

Worrell was cramming tobacco into the huge bowl of his pipe. His hands stopped in midair. He glared at Caleb.

"You make one more move that's not by the book, Hunt, I swear I'll pull you off this case faster than a cat can lick its butt. Is that clear? We'll bring Tanner down by the book."

The room grew as quiet as an empty church.

A vein ticked in Caleb's temple.

"Well, what's it going to be?"

"You know I'll play it your way," Caleb growled.

Relaxing, Worrell began puffing his pipe full steam ahead. Then, through the smoke, his gaze zeroed in on Caleb once again. "Now, back to Blair. You're right, she is finished. I told her that before she ever went back to Tanner's place. But that doesn't solve our present problem."

"Jack, I want her to have round-the-clock protection."

Worrell's expression was openly curious now, but his tone was bland. "That goes without saying."

"Thanks."

Silence.

"Well, I guess I'd better get back to the hospital," Caleb said suddenly, shifting uncomfortably under Worrell's piercing eyes.

"Caleb, is there something else you're not telling me? You and Mrs. Browning—" he stressed the Mrs. "—aren't by any chance . . . ?"

Caleb scoffed. "Whatever gave you that idea?" *Dear Lord, was he wearing his heart on his sleeve for the world to see?*

"The way you're acting," Worrell said bluntly.

Caleb allowed himself a slight sneer. "Blair Browning and I are from two different worlds and nothing will ever change that."

Worrell didn't say anything. There wasn't anything to say.

Finally, Caleb said, "I hate feeling like my hands are tied behind me."

Abruptly, Worrell shoved back his chair and got up. "Don't worry, we'll get him. If Tanner's after Blair, then he's running scared. He must think she's found something. Right?"

"Either that or he's out to get her for making a fool of him."

Worrell moved his pipe from one side of his mouth to the other. "If he'd only make final contact with the KGB agent. I'm sure with all the bugs Blair planted we're..." He paused in midsentence, looking as though he'd just seen a ghost.

"That's right, boss," Caleb cut in. "Since Tanner caught Blair snooping, then he's bound to have debugged the premises."

"Godalmighty!" Worrell bellowed. "I should've thought of that first off." He bit down so hard on his pipe stem that Caleb expected to hear it crack under the pressure. Then Worrell sagged heavily against the back of his chair. "Retirement's looking better every day." And then, speaking more to himself than to Caleb, he added, "That two-timer's got one up on us. We're back to square one."

"Maybe not."

"What do you mean?" Worrell snapped.

Caleb almost smiled. "I forgot to tell you. Blair bugged Tanner's stapler that sits by the phone. I betcha he didn't find that one."

Worrell jumped up, his eyes flashing. "Hot damn!"

Caleb grinned fleetingly.

"When he makes a move, and I expect it'll be soon, we'll be there," Worrell vowed.

"You can count on that," Caleb said, his voice as sharp as a razor. "You can count on that."

When Blair opened her eyes a second time, she was again in strange surroundings. And again she wasn't alone.

She saw her mother first. Sarah was sitting beside the bed in a straight-backed chair, her hands clenched in her lap, her eyes closed, a frown pinching her features. Then a shuffling sound from another part of the room drew Blair's attention. Thomas was standing by the window, his back to her, his shoulders hunched.

"Mother?"

Sarah's eyes opened and she immediately stood up and leaned over the bed. "For heaven's sake, Blair, you gave us the scare of our lives."

Careful, Blair. Careful that you don't tell too much. Stalling for time to organize her thoughts, she answered with a question. "What . . . what did the doctor tell you?" Her voice was as scratchy as sandpaper.

Thomas had moved to stand beside Sarah and was smiling down at her. "Hello, sweetheart," he whispered before Sarah could speak again. He took Blair's hand in his.

Sarah's tone was sharp. "I tried to talk to the doctor, if you can call him that. For a little or nothing, I'd have put that upstart in his place. All he would tell me was that you were in an accident and that you were lucky to have come through it with only a slight concussion and bruises."

Blair shifted and a whimper followed. "Well, I don't feel very lucky," she groaned. "Every time I move, I feel like my bones are grinding together."

Thomas's pressure on her hand increased. "How did it happen?"

"I...I couldn't stop," Blair answered. "My...my brakes failed."

"Oh, no," Sarah whispered. "This reminds me so much of that cloak-and-dagger stuff that went on when you worked for the FBI." She spit the word out as if it was some dread disease. "If I didn't know better, I'd think you were involved with them again." She paused. "You're not, are you?"

If possible, Blair's face turned whiter. Only by averting her eyes was she able to hide the truth. "Oh, Mother, please," she wailed.

"For goodness sake, Blair, talk to me!"

"Sarah, not now," Thomas cut in, a rough edge to his voice that even Sarah couldn't ignore.

Sarah threw him a venomous look; she didn't say another word.

Blair closed her eyes, hoping to ward off another bout of dizziness that was threatening to suck her under like quicksand. Her mother was to blame. Would there ever come a time, she wondered, when she wouldn't let Sarah run roughshod over her? Oh, she'd made great strides toward winning her independence, but obviously she still had a way to go yet. Sarah was still in there pitching.

When she opened her eyes again, her mother was saying, "This is the best suite the hospital had to offer. I insisted that if you were going to be kept overnight you be moved here. When I told that doctor you were a Stephens, and that our money had built a wing of this hospital, you should have seen the change that came over him."

Blair was mortified. "Mother, you didn't?"

Taken aback, Sarah answered petulantly, "Of course, I did. I wanted you to have the very best of care. I thought you'd be pleased."

Blair bit down on her lip to keep from shouting her frustration. But in the long run, she knew it would do no good. When Sarah Stephens was in one of her moods, nothing could stop her. Anyway, Blair simply wasn't geared up for battle. Not today, not when there was a much more pressing problem weighing her down. *Someone had just tried to kill her!*

The numbness she had prayed would last was swept away like mist, and a dull aching rolled in like the tide. In an effort to escape her thoughts, Blair fumbled for the automatic gadget that controlled the bed and punched it. Almost immediately she was in an upright position. Her eyes turned to Thomas.

"Thanks for coming, Uncle Thomas, and for bringing Mother." Blair's weak smile included Sarah. "I don't want you to worry, I'm going to be just fine. In fact, I'm sure I'll be able to go home tomorrow."

Thomas returned her smile. "I'll be here to take you home," he said sincerely. "All you have to do is say the word."

"I know and thank you." Blair patted his arms. "You're a dear."

Sarah spoke up, breaking into the tender moment. "Why don't I call Kyle? I'm sure you would rather have his company this evening than ours."

Her breathing faltered a moment, then Blair said, "No, please don't. I don't want to see Kyle just yet." *Only Caleb,* she amended silently, closing her eyes, knowing that the time had come to do battle.

"Of course, you want to see Kyle," Sarah countered. "He'll never forgive either of us if we don't call him. And I certainly don't want you to be alone. I . . ."

"Blair."

At the sound of the strange voice, Sarah choked down the remainder of her sentence and craned her neck. Thomas followed suit, casting his eyes in the same direction.

There was no need for Blair to open her eyes to know who was standing in the doorway. Her heart leaped.

Indeed, when her eyes fluttered open, Caleb stood against the doorjamb like an avenging angel. Looking completely disheveled in dark pants and a white shirt with the top buttons loose, he stared into the silence.

Blair felt suddenly as though there was a suffocating lack of air in the room. As always, Caleb's nearness was a potent distraction, and at the moment it was even more so.

Caleb's black eyes were fixed on her mother. They were hard and unyielding, glittering with a savage brilliance. His mouth was compressed and the lines that Blair had noticed occasionally bracketing his nose in time of stress were evident.

"Mother...Uncle Thomas," Blair said, slicing into the silence "I'd like you to meet Caleb Hunt...a friend. Caleb, Sarah and Thomas Stephens."

Sarah stared at him with chilled distaste.

Sauntering into the room, Caleb nodded toward Sarah and said, "Ma'am."

Blair heard both the sarcasm and the contempt packed together in that one word, and knew what it was costing him to be civil to her mother, especially in the light of her hostile reaction. She stood like a regal queen, looking down her nose at a servant. For the first time ever, Blair had the urge to slap her mother.

Caleb held out his hand to Thomas. "Sir."

"It's a pleasure, Mr. Hunt," Thomas said cordially.

Then, ignoring both of them, Caleb turned his eyes on Blair. "How do you feel?" he asked softly.

"Better. Much better."

"Good."

For a long heartbeat, their eyes held.

Thomas coughed discreetly. "Blair, honey, we'll be going now and let you visit with, er, your friend." He wrapped his hand around Sarah's arm. "If you need anything, just call."

Sarah shook her head adamantly. "No, I'm not ready," she said.

"Mother, please," Blair whispered. "I'm fine, really I am. I'll talk to you later, I promise."

Sarah's eyes seesawed back and forth between Blair and Caleb, giving both of them a frosty look. "All right," she said ungraciously. "If that's the way you want it." Then she leaned over and pecked Blair on the cheek.

As soon as she straightened, Thomas steered her toward the door. Then he paused and turned around and winked. "Take care, sweetheart."

The instant the door closed behind them, Blair's eyes sought Caleb's.

His face was bleak. "Is your mother always that uptight, or was it just me?"

"Pay no attention. That's . . . just mother," Blair said, fighting back her feeling of weakness.

Caleb's mouth clamped into a thin line before he turned his back to her. "I doubt that," he said bitterly. "Seems like she took one look at me and knew that I was completely out of her class. And yours," he added quietly.

Blair leaned back and watched his eyes as they roamed the room, his expression telling her better than words what was going through his mind. He reminded her of a little boy who had just stuck his hand in the cookie jar only to come up empty-handed. In that moment, she almost hated her mother. And she had never loved him more.

"Caleb," she whispered to his back.

The silence stretched into minutes.

Finally, without turning, he asked, "Who is Kyle?"

Chapter 13

Blair's mouth opened and closed wordlessly. Her min
grappled to switch tracks.

Caleb had turned and was looking at her now.

The blinds on the windows were parted and the late
afternoon sunlight still had enough punch to flood the roor
with light. From her position, Blair had no problem read
ing the expression on Caleb's face. It was ominous.

The silence deepened.

"How...how did you know about him?" she stam
mered at last, her eyes mesmerized by the way the muscle
bunched in his shoulders. *Why, Caleb?* she agonized s
lently. *Why do you care who Kyle is? You don't love me; yo
only want me.* And desire was no substitute for love.

Caleb shook his head disgustedly. "Your mother, that
how," he said.

The light dawned on her. He had been standing in th
doorway much longer than she'd thought. "He's just
friend," she murmured.

"Didn't sound like it from the way your mother talked."

"Well, Mother would like our relationship to be more than it is," Blair said tiredly. "And so would Kyle, for that matter, but he's a dear friend and no more." She paused with a sigh. "He taught me everything I know about photography and without him I wouldn't be where I am today, careerwise."

Suddenly, Blair felt drained. She hadn't been up to this verbal skirmish, and together with the long speech and the emotional upheaval of the past few hours, it had finally taken its toll. She was both mentally and physically exhausted. And there wasn't a place on her body that didn't ache. Tears pricked behind her eyelids and she wanted to scream at Caleb to say something.

Realizing that it wouldn't take much more for her to get on a crying jag, she shifted her gaze away from Caleb.

All she wanted was for him to hold her. Was that asking too much?

Caleb stood like a statue, calling himself every foul name he could think of and then some. What the hell was the matter with him for thinking about something so unimportant at a time like this? he ranted silently. He had nearly lost her today, and here he was feeding on his damned jealousies. And for what? If she married the man it was none of his business. He had no control over her. Never had. Never would.

Oh, for a while he'd entertained his fantasies and let his imagination run wild, thinking they just might have a chance for a lasting relationship, but then, something always came along and shattered that illusion, just as it had now. Her mother had certainly jerked him upright and forced him to face reality. Yet it still rankled, especially now that Blair had come to mean more to him than life itself.

The abyss was at his feet again, and he felt tempted to just give up and let himself fall into it.

Then, with a muttered curse at his self-indulgent musings, he stepped closer to the bed. "Blair," he began tentatively, seeing her body quiver.

No answer.

Her face was as white as the hospital gown she still wore, and the arm that was out from under the sheet looked as frail as a long stem on a rose, as did her hand, with the purple veins protruding through the alabaster skin. And her back... Oh, God... A groan tore through him as his eyes clung to the tender flesh that was exposed, the gown failing to cover it adequately. He could almost smell and taste that scented skin....

Tension churned in his stomach. His throat felt tight. He didn't even know if he was capable of speaking again. "B-Blair, are you in pain?" he whispered.

Blair rolled over and stared up into his gaunt, tight features. Her heart turned over at the agony mirrored there. Suddenly she felt as sorry for him as she did for herself. A smile broke through her tears.

"No...not really. My body just feels...like it's been used as a punching bag, that's all."

Blair was rewarded with an answering smile, though it was a long time in coming. It was almost as if he'd forgotten how.

Caleb inched forward, encouraged, his legs finally making contact with the side of the bed. "I'm glad you didn't make a fuss about going home," he said huskily, held spellbound by the way the tears sparkled like dewdrops on the tips of her eyelashes.

Blair couldn't quite meet his eyes. "I wanted to, but felt...I'd be better off here."

Caleb's gut gave a brutal twist. "Once you thought about it, you were afraid to go home, weren't you?" he asked.

"Yes," she said simply, keeping a tight rein on her emotions.

Tanner, you scum. You'll pay for this. I promise you.

"You don't ever have to be again," he said gently. "From now on, you'll have round-the-clock protection."

She tried to smile. "I kinda figured that."

"We'll get Tanner. You know that, too, don't you?"

She nodded mutely, unable to stop the tears from making a scalding track down her throat.

Their eyes closed the distance and locked.

"Blair, please...don't cry." His voice sounded barely human.

She held out her arms and whispered, "Hold me."

Needing no second invitation, Caleb lowered himself carefully onto the side of the bed, feeling it give under his weight, and folded her trembling body within the strong confines of his arms.

"Oh, Caleb." His name was a sigh on her lips.

His mind spun in giddy circles that collided head-on as he buried his face into her neck. She smelled of tears and springtime. To hold her was like holding a basket of flowers.

And for the moment, it was enough just to hold her and listen to the beat of her heart against his. Then, unexpectedly, Blair turned her head, and silently, hungrily, their lips meshed. While Caleb drank deeply from the sweetness offered, he fought to maintain his control, feeling liquid and adrift.

After a long time, he pulled back and peered down into her upturned face, barely visible now in the fading light. A smile toyed with his lips. "What happens if we get caught like this?"

Blair frowned, her senses still drugged from the aftermath of his kisses. But then the question soaked in. "Oh, I hadn't thought of that," she said, her eyes darting toward the door.

"If I were a betting man, I'd say they'd kick me out on my you know what."

"You're probably right."

His head sank lower. "Think I should move?"

"Do you want to?"

"No."

Blair shrugged. "Then don't."

"You're willing to take a chance?"

"I want you to stay with me, hold me."

His eyebrows raised. "On the bed?"

"On the bed."

"What if we get caught?"

"We'll just get caught."

Caleb threaded her silken curls through his fingers and muttered indistinctly, "You're on."

"There was never a doubt in my mind," Blair whispered, nestling her head against Caleb's chest, feeling as though nothing could ever hurt her again.

Seconds later, the only sound in the room was the motorized purring of the bed as it shifted back to its level position.

Ah, God, Caleb thought, closing his eyes, to reach heaven, one must go through hell.

The spring morning was clean and cool and bright. Caleb stopped at a McDonald's and bought a large cup of coffee and an Egg McMuffin. It was early. People were scurrying to work, as if they were all late. After he had finished his breakfast, he dropped his empty cup in the nearest trash container and strolled outside.

As he pulled the car into gear, his thoughts turned to Blair—not that they ever left her for long—her face coming between him and the windshield. Memories of the past evening suddenly painted a half smile across his lips. He still found it inconceivable that they hadn't been caught flagrantly breaking hospital rules. But no sharp-tongued nurse in a white uniform had come charging into the room the entire time he had lain beside Blair.

It was only after she had fallen into a deep sleep that he had unwound his body from the pulsing softness of hers and eased off the bed. He had stared down at her for the longest time, thinking that he was becoming a bigger fool over her with each day that passed.

Then, abruptly, he'd turned on his heel and left the room, only to go home and immediately take out his frustrations under a cold shower.

He'd considered going by the hospital first thing that morning, but changed his mind, as it was too early, and anyway, he knew Blair was well guarded. She was in safe hands and for the moment that was all that mattered.

Yet knowing that something had to be done about Tanner, he parked his car and quickly made his way into the bureau's office building. It was just after eight o'clock. He stopped by Worrell's office first. His boss looked as though he'd been there for hours. His sleeves were rolled up, his tie loosened at the neck. There was a half-empty container of coffee on his desk.

When Caleb came in, Worrell raised his head.

"Morning," Caleb said, thinking that even with his tie askew and his sleeves rolled up, Worrell looked, as he always did, brand-new. What was left of his sandy hair was freshly cut and his face was clean-shaven. His shirt was freshly laundered, crisp with starch. His beige slacks and brown blazer were unwrinkled.

Caleb couldn't imagine the office without him. Well, no doubt he wouldn't have to, he told himself. He felt certain that Worrell had been talking just to hear his head rattle; he wasn't leaving the bureau.

"Where the devil have you been?" Worrell demanded roughly.

Caleb shrugged. "Stopped and got some coffee. Why?"

Worrell crossed to the coffee bar and refilled his own cup. "You stopped for more than coffee, because I've been ringing your phone off the hook for the past hour."

Caleb tensed but kept his voice even, afraid to hope. "Something up?"

"Would you believe it if I told you that we hit the jackpot?" Worrell asked when he was back behind his desk, his eyes alight.

Doubling his fist, Caleb pounded it into the palm of his other hand. "Tanner, I take it?"

"None other." Worrell was grinning now, from ear to ear. He drank more coffee.

"Hot damn!" Caleb shouted, using Worrell's favorite expression. "Details, details, give me the details."

"It's just as we figured. Tanner made the call from his penthouse and we picked up the conversation clear as a bell. The second I got the word, I started huntin' for you."

Caleb was too excited to sit down. "It was the stapler, wasn't it? Blair will be happy to know that she came through, after all. She was feeling like she hadn't contributed anything toward bringing Tanner down."

At the mention of Blair, Worrell's face lost a bit of it animation. "How is she? Damn, everything's been so hectic around here that I haven't had time to check on her. She *is* all right?"

Caleb's face was sober as he answered. "Was last night. Other than being sore, she's fine, except mentally..." He didn't finish the sentence, but he didn't have to.

"Mentally, she's not so hot," Worrell added, finishing for him. "Right?"

"That's about the size of it. Otherwise she wouldn't have agreed to spend the night in the hospital."

Worrell smiled fondly. "She's a stubborn woman; I know that for a fact. However, I'm glad she stayed, especially since Tanner's making his move."

"When's it coming down?" Caleb asked eagerly, plopping down on the edge of Worrell's massive desk and reaching into his pocket for a cigarette.

"Today at Golden Gate Park. Two o'clock."

"Damn, that's soon," Caleb muttered, jumping up, unable to sit still another second.

"That's what I said, only worse," Worrell countered with a grin. Then it disappeared, his features becoming stiff. "But we'll be ready, you can count on that. I've already put the ball in motion."

"Tanner's mine, Jack." Caleb's tone was dangerously low, almost a growl.

A muscle twitched in Worrell's jaw. "I haven't changed my mind about going by the book."

"I gave you my word, didn't I?" Caleb said hotly, the cords in his neck knotting.

Worrell seemed satisfied. "Sit down then," he said, "and let's get our heads together on how you're going to handle this little 'hammer and sickle' party."

"There's not but one way to do it," Caleb challenged, paying no heed to Worrell's directive. He began prowling the office like a caged tiger. "We gotta wire it, sound it and gift wrap it for the good old Justice Department."

"Dammit, will you put your rear in a chair? I can't keep up with you and think at the same time."

With an exasperated sigh, Caleb sank his large frame into the government-issue plastic and chrome chair and pinned Worrell with his dark eyes. "We won't be allowed one mistake, you know. If this is going to be done by the book, we have to make sure the case will stand up in any liberal judge's court, without any holes for the rat to escape."

"This is your baby, Caleb. You call the shots."

"I won't let you down."

"Then let's get down to brass tacks."

Caleb leaned forward. "I'm all ears."

Caleb spoke softly into the small walkie-talkie resting snugly in his shirt pocket.

"Come in, Deavers. How's it lookin'?" Caleb asked, his eyes scanning the area where he and several other agents were staked out waiting for Tanner and the Russian to show. He was ready. Unconsciously, he felt for the Smith & Wesson Chief's Special clipped onto his belt just in back of his right pants pocket; the butt caused only a modest break in the line of his lightweight Windbreaker.

From his position under a huge shade tree, Caleb could see the knoll, dotted with hedges, where the big-lens camera was nestled among them. Even with his trained eyes it could not be detected, he was sure of that, or at least not from where he stood. And if Tanner had no reason to suspect there was anything amiss, he wouldn't be looking.

"Deavers, you asleep?" Caleb asked again. This time his tone was brisk.

"Er...no sir, nothing yet," the agent finally answered. "How 'bout yourself?"

"Nothing on this end, either," Caleb said, glancing down at his watch. Only one-thirty. He swore. As far as he was concerned watching a clock was the same as watching grass grow.

"Ah, but I have something to report," another voice cut in.

Suddenly static rattled in Caleb's ear. He delved in his pocket and shifted the "device." A clean silence met his efforts. He picked up the voice again.

"There's a girl and boy, or at least I think it's a boy—nowadays you need a program to tell—they're playing kissy face right in my line of vision."

"Is that you, Spaight?" Caleb demanded, his voice dripping with ice.

"Yes, sir!"

"How 'bout cutting the crap and doing your job?"

"Yes sir," Spaight said again, the humor gone from his voice.

"Are you certain that camera's ready to roll?"

"Just checked it," Spaight answered. "Everything's in great shape on this end."

"It had better be," Caleb warned, his tone unchanged. Then, addressing the entire crew he added, "Remember, gentlemen, to close in on my order only. No Lone Ranger stuff. Understand? We want them on film and very much alive."

After each man had once again acknowledged his order, Caleb braced himself against the huge trunk of the tree and smoked a cigarette, wanting to give the impression that he was out for a Saturday afternoon of pleasure in the park. He was dressed casually in jeans and a knit shirt. A pair of jogging shoes and white socks completed his outfit.

His men were dressed in similar garb so that none of them would stand out among the gaily clad tourists or residents who thronged the park on this gorgeous May afternoon.

Caleb tilted his head. Not a cloud to mar the beauty of the sky. The only thing visible to his naked eye was a plane, and it was so tiny it could have been a toy. When he lowered his head, his nostrils picked up the heady scent of the flowers growing throughout the area.

Suddenly his thoughts switched to Blair, sending a shaft of longing through him. He was sure she was at home by now, being pampered and petted by her family, her mind a long way from Caleb Hunt. And when Tanner was in the slammer, she'd have even less reason to think . . .

Knock it off, Hunt!

Shaking himself mentally, he checked his watch again. He tensed, noticing that both the hands had hit their target. It was two o'clock.

"Caleb."

He stood erect, his stomach muscles going haywire. "See something, Deavers?"

"Sure 'nough. Black limo with gray top is rounding the corner at the south entrance to the park. Windows black. Number of passengers unknown. Repeat. Number of passengers unknown."

"Don't take your eyes off the limo, Deavers," Caleb ordered. "Spaight, stand by to roll film. I'm shifting location."

Then, like a streak of lightning, Caleb tore off across the expanse of grass that separated him from the south entrance. Once there he moved into position behind a clump of trees, not three yards from the camera. He nodded to Spaight and his backup.

Deavers spoke again. "Caleb, Tanner's been sighted getting out of the car. He's wearing a navy-blue suit and white shirt."

"I read you loud and clear. I've got him in my vision now. Everybody stand by."

Caleb watched as Tanner calmly stood by the side of the car and looked around. Then he turned and dipped his head back into the vehicle. After speaking to the driver he slammed the door and began walking toward the path that angled in front of a large spewing fountain.

Caleb's heart pounded.

When Tanner reached the fountain, he stopped and again looked around. Then he crossed to a narrow bench almost directly in front of the water and sat down. He was alone.

Caleb mopped the sweat from his brow with a handkerchief. Still he watched. And waited.

"Caleb." It was Worrell.

"Yeah, Chief?"

"Everything under control?"

"Right on target."

Static scrambled the line, then it cleared. Caleb smiled to himself, thinking that Worrell wouldn't hesitate to step in if he thought Caleb was bungling it.

Tanner hadn't moved.

"Hunt, this is Deavers. Short baldheaded man with briefcase is heading in your direction."

Caleb shifted, his adrenaline stirring. The Russian.

"Suspect sighted," Caleb said at last, his eyes glued to the scene unfolding before him like a well-organized play.

The man sporting the case was indeed short and overweight to boot, Caleb thought, as the man sat warily on the opposite end of the park bench from Tanner. Neither man looked at the other, but from where Caleb stood, he could see their lips moving as they stared into the distance, seemingly unconcerned.

Caleb spoke again. "Both pigeons on the ground and gathering."

Silence.

Then he looked on as the Russian left an attaché case on the bench and walked a few yards away, ostensibly to feed a pigeon from the small bag of popcorn he produced from a pocket.

There! An envelope! Caleb's breath came in jagged spurts.

Tanner picked up the briefcase and left the envelope lying on the bench as he stood up. The Russian, as if on cue, returned to the bench and retrieved the envelope, putting it into a suitcoat pocket. Both men stood together and exchanged a few words.

Bingo!

Caleb stepped forward, the taste of victory sweet on his lips.

"Move it. Now!" Caleb ordered, already advancing toward Tanner.

That was when it happened.

Tanner turned, blinked as though something was in his eye and then stared, a look of sheer terror on his face.

In what seemed like an eternity, but in reality was only a second, Caleb followed his eyes.

The camera. Tanner had seen the camera. The glint of the sun had flashed it like a neon sign.

Dammit to hell! Caleb's heart almost banged out of his chest.

Just as Caleb moved, Tanner shouted something to the Russian. They both turned and started running.

Caleb bolted. "Stop the Russian," he shouted. "Tanner's mine!" Out of the corner of his eye, he saw the Russian plow chest-first into Deavers. One down.

Caleb's feet thundered across the ground while his eyes tracked Tanner's fleeting back. Then Tanner turned and looked over his shoulder. Not smart. It slowed him down. Caleb took advantage of the momentary lapse and lunged for his ankles.

The ground rose up to meet Tanner.

For a moment Tanner was stunned, but by the time Caleb surged to his feet, Tanner was up also. Still Caleb had the edge.

"You bastard," Tanner cried. "You don't have a chance."

Caleb hit him with a left hook. Tanner went rattling back against a tree, his knees buckled and he sagged without falling. Then, like a bull, Tanner dived headfirst for Caleb's stomach. But he was too slow. Caleb leaned away, then drove another left into Tanner's stomach. Tanner blocked it and pounded him in the solar plexus. But there was not as much steam behind the blow as there should have been, and Caleb was inside now, up against him. He had weight on Tanner and was stronger.

Forcefully Caleb rammed him against the tree and hit him in the stomach with both fists. Tanner grunted but didn' give up. He shoved himself away from the tree and lunged at Caleb, only to move into a straight left, which stopped him cold.

Panting, Caleb grabbed Tanner by the hair of his head and yanked his neck back, hearing it snap. Tanner hollered. Then, with his free hand, Caleb reached for his gun and pointed the barrel at the little indentation in Tanner's upper lip, right below the tip of his nose. A kind of pressure was building in Caleb, and he saw everything indistinctly.

Wild-eyed, Tanner stared down at the gun barrel. Caleb could smell his fear.

"Still think I don't have a chance, you bastard?"

Tanner said nothing.

"Caleb! Damn you. By the book!"

Worrell. He's right. You're not worth dirtying my hands on, you scum.

Caleb shook his head. Holding Tanner with his left hand, he reholstered his pistol, fighting to maintain his professionalism, only to then turn and pop a roundhouse right to Tanner's jaw. *To hell with the book!*

Tanner's eyes rolled in their sockets, showing the whites as he dropped to the ground—and stayed there.

"You have the right to remain silent. . . ."

Where was Caleb?

Blair could not imagine why she hadn't heard from him. Deep down she thought she knew the answer to that question. He was more than likely scared, just as she was. When he'd held her and kissed her—had it been only last night?— she had felt close to him, really close to him for the first time since he'd invaded her life. And she had been confident, also for the first time, that it could work between them. When he'd lowered his big body beside her onto the bed and wrapped his arms around her, she'd felt love.

Or had she merely been chasing that elusive rainbow again? she wondered. She hoped not. She loved him so very much and wanted desperately to convince him of that.

She vowed to do just that as soon as the mess with Tanner was over and she could lay that part of her life to rest. Josh would be vindicated and she could go to Caleb with the scars completely healed.

They would have a wonderful life together, she thought. She could see it now. He would continue with his work, of course, albeit she hoped that one day he'd see his way clear to giving up working in the field. And she would continue with her work until it came time to have a baby. A baby. Caleb's baby. What a joy that would be.

Now, as she fidgeted around her apartment, waiting, wondering with sugarplums dancing in her head, she asked herself again, where was he?

Blair was so sure he would have checked on her by now. Her mother, instead of Thomas, had brought her home from the hospital that morning. She had expected Caleb to follow. Because of that, she hadn't let her mother badger her into going home with her.

"I can take care of myself," she'd told Sarah.

"Oh, Blair," Sarah had wailed. "You're in no shape to stay by yourself."

Blair remained adamant. "Yes, I am. I know you mean well, but I'd rather be here. I can rest better," she added.

Sarah's expression turned cold. "It doesn't by any chance have anything to do with that man—" her lips curled around the word "—who was at the hospital, does it?"

"No," Blair lied. "It doesn't."

They had stared at each other for a minute and then Sarah had backed down.

"All right," she said peevishly, her tone bearing out the fact that she didn't believe a word that Blair said. "Have it your own way then. Call me if you need me."

Once Sarah left Blair had tried to sleep, but she hadn't been able to. Her mind had been too full of Caleb. She was too sore to do anything except creep around like an old woman, and the hours had dragged interminably by.

What if he didn't come? What if she had misjudged what they had shared? *Don't*, she scolded herself severely. *He's busy. After all, he has more to do than just cater to you.* Knowing Caleb, he was more than likely trying to garner new evidence against Tanner.

Worrell. Worrell would know where Caleb was. On the spur of the moment, Blair decided to call him. She crossed to the phone and was about to lift the receiver when the doorbell rang.

Caleb?

She rushed to the door, wincing against the pain that darted through her, and she yanked it open.

It was Caleb.

They stood in silence for a bone-jarring moment and then she stammered, "Come... come in."

"I hope you don't make a habit of opening the door without first asking who's there."

Blair's eyes fell beneath his piercing gaze. "Stupid of me, wasn't it?" she asked.

He nodded, shutting the door behind him.

Blair stepped back, her eyes lovingly followed the hollow line of his cheek, the angle of his dark hair. He looked worn out. There were lines across his forehead, more pronounced than usual, and he had a bruise on his right cheekbone. A lump rose in her throat and fear quickened her heartbeat. Something had happened.

Voicing her fear, Blair whispered, "Why the bruise?" Then, without thinking, she reached out and gently stroked the purplish-blue spot.

Caleb groaned and trapped her hand against his cheek while his eyes devoured her.

"Does that have to do with Tanner?" she murmured.

"You hit the nail on the head."

"I was about to call Jack and tell him not to count me out when . . . when the doorbell rang."

A slow excited grin spread across his face. Blair stood transfixed, feeling as if she was seeing sunlight through a passing storm.

"No need," he drawled jubilantly.

Blair's eyes glowed. "You mean what I think you mean?"

"Yep." His grin was dazzling.

"Oh, Caleb," she cried, hurling herself into his arms, oblivious to the groan of her muscles. "I can't believe it! I can't believe it."

He hugged her close. "Well, believe it. That bastard'll never hurt you or anyone else again. When we get through with him, they'll throw the key to his cell away. And we have you to thank for it all."

She pulled back enough to look up at him. "Me?"

"Remember the stapler?" Blair nodded. "Well, that's the one bug he didn't find, and this morning he made the call to his KGB contact and arrangements were made. We were waiting."

Again Blair touched his bruise. His skin was warm to the touch. "Compliments of Tanner?" she asked huskily.

"Afraid so." He smiled. "But I'm happy to say he's the one that came out on the short end of the stick." His smile broadened into another grin. "In fact, he had one helluva time just picking himself up off the ground."

Blair dived into his arms again. "All I can say is, thank God it's over."

"I couldn't wait to get to you," Caleb said, his voice low, guttural, the rhythmic thud of his heartbeat matching hers.

It's our time now, Blair cried silently. She waited to hear those words from him, her heart almost singing.

But there was only a crystal stillness in the room as Caleb rocked her in his arms, the gentle curves of her body touching him on all levels. He seemed to have gone deep inside his own silence.

Suddenly Blair broke away and gazed up at him, her eyes filled with unanswered questions.

Caleb stared at her for a long, aching moment. "What now?" he whispered in a strangled voice.

The words simply flew from Blair's lips. "We could get married?"

Caleb's harsh intake of breath echoed around the room. The seconds, the minutes ticked by.

His voice, when he finally spoke, seemed barely connected to him; it seemed to ease out of somewhere deep and remote. "Yes, we could," he said. "But we both know it wouldn't work. Don't we?"

Like bricks, the words dropped into the silence.

It was the worst moment of Blair's life. Her entire lifetime seemed to have been condensed into the past few days with Caleb, and it seemed now as though she had always loved this man who had suddenly shattered all her hopes and dreams.

Tears clogged her throat, rendering her speechless. *Oh, Caleb, it would work, only you don't love me, have never loved me. It's because I'm rich and you're not. Oh, how you flaunt your pride like a badge of courage. Please don't do this to me, to us.*

At last she tried to speak. "Caleb, I…" Unable to go any further, she turned her back, unwilling for him to see how deeply he had hurt her.

That was the straw that broke the camel's back. He felt himself wither and die on the inside. *No!* he screamed inwardly. *Don't shut me out. Tell me it will work, that nothing else matters except that we love each other.* But she did neither; she just kept her back to him while the silence hummed around them.

His hands, normally steady, were trembling like a drunkard's as reality struck him that final blow. There was no use kidding himself any longer. She didn't think he was good enough for her, would never be good enough for her, and the sooner he got the hell out of her life the better off they both would be.

Pivoting on his heel, Caleb stamped to the door.

Blair heard the unexpected movement and whirled, tears saturating her face.

"Caleb." The word seemed to have been ripped from her heart. She couldn't let him go, not like this, never to see him again.

He gripped the doorknob and turned, looking as though he might break. He radiated tension and hurt. But he remained silent.

Courage drained from her. She could not, would not beg him to love her. "Friends?" she whispered irrationally. "Couldn't we . . . be friends?"

You were never my friend; you were my dream. "Never," he groaned before yanking open the door and disappearing through it.

When it closed behind him, Blair fell down, crying, her legs folding under her at the knees. She sank to the floor like a penitent in prayer.

Chapter 14

"God, Blair, you look like death itself."

"Thanks, Jack," Blair said wryly, leaning against the door, feeling off balance from the unexpected visit. And even more shocking was the cluster of violets he held in his hand.

Worrell looked uncomfortable, as though he'd spouted off his mouth where he shouldn't have. "Here," he said, thrusting the bouquet at her. "Nothing much. Just a token of my appreciation as well as the agency's," he added brusquely.

Blair's fingers curled around the cellophaned stems. "Why, thank you," she murmured, burying her face in the fragrant petals.

Then, remembering her manners, Blair said a trifle breathlessly, "Please, come in and sit down. I'm dripping some coffee. It'll be ready in a minute."

"Mmm. Smells good."

Blair gestured for him to join her on the multicolored couch that sat prominently amid tall urns of plants.

"Nice," Worrell commented, sitting down, his eyes scanning the room, taking in the books that brightened the bookcases on either side of the fireplace, the white wicker furniture and glass-topped tables. "Somehow, this looks like you."

"I'll take that as a compliment," Blair replied sincerely, perching on the edge of the cushion, one ear listening for the coffeepot in the nearby kitchen. Then she said, "I certainly wasn't expecting to see you on my doorstep this time of the morning." She smiled with her lips only, though it served to loosen the anxiety on her face. "My mother, yes, but never you."

Worrell was clearly puzzled. "Oh?"

"She's getting married tomorrow night, to my uncle," Blair said by way of explanation. "And she's had me running around like mad helping her with the arrangements for the wedding." Blair knew she was rattling on, but if she didn't talk she would start thinking and to think, she knew, would be fatal. Seeing Worrell reminded her painfully of Caleb, and she felt that hole in her heart expand.

"Is that why you look like you've been sick?" Worrell asked, staring at her strangely.

Blair fought to regroup, countering with a question of her own. "Do I look that bad?"

"You look that bad."

Abruptly Blair stood up, afraid of his close scrutiny.

"It's not your mother's upcoming wedding that's made those circles under your eyes and knocked ten pounds off your bones."

It wasn't a question, but a statement, and because he spoke the truth, Blair had no comeback. The fact that she had chosen to slip into a pair of old jeans and a skimpy cotton shirt made her gauntness more pronounced, but as this was Saturday, she thought she'd earned the right to be comfortable. How was she to know she was going to have a visitor? Luckily, she had put on her makeup. Without it, she did look ill.

"Excuse me and I'll get our coffee," she murmured, escaping to the kitchen, where she took two coffee cups out of the cabinet with unsteady hands and a heavy heart. Why had he come? She felt certain there was something behind his uncharacteristic visit and she had a feeling she knew what it was. After filling the cups, Blair carried them back into the family room.

They sipped on the hot liquid in silence, and Blair had the urge to demand that he say what he came to say and go away before she asked him about... Caleb. She was hurting. Memories were crowding in on her, suffocating her, and she just wanted to be left alone to wallow in her misery, preferring to nurse her wounds in private. Even Thomas's warm and loving solicitude had been unsuccessful in drawing her out of the cocoon she had spun around herself.

Worrell set his cup down, the noise shaking her out of her reverie. "That hit the spot. Thanks."

Blair nodded, continuing to sip on hers.

Worrell shifted to the edge of the couch, his eyes piercing. "What I came for, other than to say thanks for coming to our rescue, was to tell you that Tanner has confessed and that it won't be necessary for you to testify."

"That's a relief," Blair responded softly.

Adding to the somber mood, Worrell sighed. "I thought you'd also like to know that Josh's name was definitely on the list that Tanner turned over to the KGB." He paused, as though to gauge her reaction before going on. "So now that the swine responsible is behind bars, you can put this all behind you and make a new life for yourself."

Not without Caleb, Blair cried silently, brokenly. But outwardly she remained stoically calm, unwilling to share her pain at Josh's needless death and her yearning for Caleb.

"Was anyone else implicated in his scheme?" she asked, changing the subject, while thinking it was odd that she hadn't thought to ask Caleb that question when he'd told her of Tanner's arrest. But when she'd learned that Tanner had gotten his comeuppance, she hadn't been concerned with anything other than Caleb and herself.

"You bet," Worrell drawled. "A man by the name of Martin Neal, Tanner's right-hand man, was arrested. And of course, the Russian agent. They were both nabbed the same time as Tanner. In fact, the Russian ran straight into the arms of one of our men in his bid to escape."

"Sounds like everything's tied up in a neat little package," she said.

Worrell scratched his chin. "Well, the wheels of justice are usually mighty slow grinding, but not this time," he said. "Day after tomorrow Tanner's to be sentenced."

"I hope they put him under the cell."

Worrell chuckled, lightening the mood. "That's almost verbatim what Caleb said."

Hearing his name spoken aloud, Blair recoiled as though she'd been struck.

Her reaction didn't escape Worrell's sharp eyes. "Blair," he began, "I don't quite know how to say this, and you can tell me to mind my own business in a New York minute if you're of a mind to, but I know there's something between you and Caleb and if I can . . ."

"No, please, Jack, don't say any more," she pleaded, pain attacking her from every angle. "There's nothing . . . I mean . . ." Her words became garbled; she couldn't go on.

"Sorry," Worrell said gruffly, standing up, damning himself for his lack of tact. "First Caleb, now you," he mumbled under his breath, his eyes searching hers. "Just remember, if you need a friend..." he finished awkwardly.

Blair stood up and kissed him on the cheek. "Thanks for caring," she whispered, "but this is something I have to handle alone."

Worrell squeezed her on the shoulder and said, "I'll see myself out."

Dry-eyed, Blair sat down on the couch again and let her head fall back against the cushion. She was opting for a life of loneliness without Caleb, she knew. But the prospect did not dismay her.

Which was a pity.

The wedding was beautiful.

The Stephens mansion was aglow with candlelight and the champagne was flowing. The upper crust of San Francisco society—the beautiful people—were very much in evidence.

Blair was oblivious to all of this as she stood beside her mother while the vows were exchanged, a lump in her throat the size of a goose egg. She blinked back the tears and smiled tremulously as the last "I do" was repeated in front of the tall, redheaded minister.

Blair had never seen her mother look more beautiful or Thomas handsomer; they truly made a striking couple. Had it been just the week before that they had told her they were getting married? She had met them for dinner at Fisherman's Wharf to celebrate.

The news had delighted her, convinced as she was that her mother's marrying Thomas would turn out to be just exactly what the doctor ordered. Sarah had long needed a purpose in her life besides her daughter and money. Now she had that purpose.

"You may kiss the bride, sir," the minister was saying, following the moment of hushed silence.

Thomas obliged and pandemonium broke out. Bride, groom, best man and Blair were all besieged with hearty congratulations, rowdy grins and healthy slaps on the back.

Finally Blair pushed her way out of the throng, only to run straight into the arms of Kyle Palmer.

"Whoops!" he exclaimed, holding her at arm's length, his blue eyes twinkling down into hers. "I'd say you barely got out of there with your life."

Laughing, Blair tugged at the seams of her peach-colored suit, making an effort to piece herself back together. "I'd say you were right. Whew! Talk about a mob scene."

They both turned and looked, and still the people were closed around the newlyweds and cameras were popping like fireworks on the Fourth of July.

"It's great to have friends like that," Kyle pointed out after a moment.

"You're right, it is," Blair agreed. "But just think how long Mother and Uncle Thomas have lived here."

"How about finding a quiet corner while I get us a glass of that bubbly stuff that's floating around?"

Blair smiled her thanks and said, "I'll be out on the deck."

The evening air was cool and crisp and did wonders to revive Blair after the smoky, clogged atmosphere indoors.

Lowering herself onto the cushioned glider, she took several breaths deep into her lungs and was no longer feeling light-headed when Kyle appeared with the drinks.

He handed a glass to her and then sat down. They drank in silence for a while, content to listen to the music of the night creatures. They were flaunting their tunes as though determined to rival the strains of music floating from inside the house.

Kyle finally met her eyes. "Haven't seen much of you lately."

Blair flushed guiltily. "I've . . . been busy."

"With the show?"

"Yes, and other projects as well," she hedged.

Kyle's breath came out a sigh. "If there's anything I can do to make it go smoother, you'll let me know, won't you?"

"Oh, Kyle, you've more than done your part. If it doesn't fly now, I'll have no one to blame but myself."

"Well, the offer still stands, but I know everything will go just fine."

"Thanks for the confidence, but I don't know how I'll ever repay you as it is."

He leaned sideways. "You could marry me."

"Yes." Blair nodded, not lifting her face to look at him, "That's true, I could, but it would be a disaster."

"Because you don't love me. Right?"

"That's right," she agreed, her voice gentle.

His mouth was grim. "Well, I've always known that. I guess that's why I started seeing someone else." The last sentence was rushed out, as though if he didn't say it quickly, he wouldn't say it at all.

Blair stared at him, her lips slightly parted. "I think that's wonderful." And she meant it, too.

"Do you? Do you really?" He didn't sound hurt.

Blair found his hand and pressed it. "You deserve so much more than I'm capable of giving. Go for it," she added in a whisper, "and be happy."

He stood up. "I'll always be your best friend, you know."

"I know."

After Kyle left, Blair was alone for only a few minutes before Thomas came striding through the doorway. He spotted her instantly.

"Your mother and I were wondering where you were." He frowned and eased down beside her. "Kyle told me where you were hiding."

Blair didn't answer. Instead, she scooted over toward him and placed a hand on his clean-shaven cheek. "Welcome aboard, Dad," she whispered, blinking back the unshed tears.

Thomas slipped his arms around her shoulders and held her close for a long moment. "Thanks, daughter," he said, his voice tight with emotion.

They sat quietly, content just to glide back and forth in the swing, savoring the moment of closeness.

Then Thomas said, "We're worried about you."

Stiffening, Blair pulled away, feeling suddenly chilled. "Oh?" Her tone was cautious.

"It's that man, Caleb Hunt. He's to blame for your depression. Isn't he?"

Blair saw no reason to deny it. "Yes."

"I was afraid of that. I knew that day in the hospital you were involved with him. The way you two looked at each other was a dead giveaway."

"Well, it doesn't matter now," she said in a shaken voice. "It's over."

"You still love him?"

"Yes, but he doesn't love me. You see, he's of the old school, thinks of himself as being from the wrong side of the tracks, that he doesn't belong in my social class...."

"I know all about him," Thomas interrupted softly, as though unable to bear the pain in her voice.

"You know? But...how?" Blair asked, confused.

"Your mother had him investigated. We know all about him."

Blair jumped up, venting the rage boiling within her. "How dare she do that to me!"

"Because she loves you, that's why."

"Don't give me that!" Blair ground out. "She did it because she can't stand not to be in control of my life and you know it. But why she did it is beside the point. As far as I'm concerned there's no excuse!" Her voice kept climbing several octaves.

"Maybe not to you, but to her it was valid," Thomas said calmly, countering her hysteria.

"What else did Mother find out on her witch-hunt?"

Thomas hesitated. "Well...after checking Caleb out, Sarah decided you were probably involved with the FBI again." Blair felt his eyes on her in the muted light. "Care to comment on that?"

"Afraid not."

"I didn't think you would," Thomas said heavily.

"Whose side are you on, anyway?" Blair asked abruptly, swinging around to face him. Her mother must never know she had done this special assignment, she told herself. Although she might suspect, she had no proof and that was the way Blair intended to keep it.

"I know how all this must look to you," Thomas reasoned, "but we both love you and hate like hell to see you hurt again."

Suddenly, the fight drained out of Blair. "Well, it's a moot point anyway. It's all over and, as I said before, he doesn't love me and that's that." She inhaled a long trembling gasp.

"If that's the case, then you have no choice but to rebound and go on with your life," Thomas argued gently.

Blair was stunned. "That's easy for you to say. You're not the one hurting."

Thomas stood up and faced her, then tipped her chin up, the moonlight flickering across her pale features. "No, it's not easy for me to say. I've been in your shoes. But you're a fighter, Blair Browning. And I'm betting on you this time, too. Think about it."

With those words he turned and walked off.

Blair stayed still. Her face hurt, her head ached and her stomach felt bottomless. She was nearly dizzy with fear.

Thomas was right, she knew. But what if she couldn't close the gap in her life that Caleb, with his piercing but honest eyes, his rough but gentle hands, his firm but tender lips, had created? What if Thomas was wrong and she couldn't put Humpty-Dumpty back together again?

What then?

Blair was still asking herself that same question during the weeks following the wedding. Though she was trying to put her life back on track, it was an uphill battle. The only thing that kept her sane was the fashion show. It had been a huge success and had buoyed her spirits considerably. She had received more recognition than she had ever thought possible. Several newspapers ran articles on the show, profiling her as well. Business began pouring in.

But nothing took the place of Caleb. Her thoughts were overrun with him. She dreamed of his hands on her body, the way he made her feel when he was buried tight inside her....

Why couldn't she let him go? It was over. Why couldn't she get that through her thick skull? She had been nothing to him but a fun roll in the hay and that was all. Yet her heart kept denying that, telling her there'd been more, much more.

She guessed that was why she couldn't let go, thinking that maybe if she'd just said one more word, things might have worked out differently. But then she'd turn on herself, shutting that thought down, knowing it would only add to her agony and heartache.

So one day drifted into another and with it came the struggle to begin life anew.

This evening was no exception. As she stepped out of the bathroom at her mother's house after reapplying her lipstick, she made her way into the den where Sarah, Thomas and she were to have after-dinner drinks.

The day before the newlyweds had returned from their honeymoon cruise and insisted Blair join them for dinner

When she'd walked into the house two hours previous, she was astounded at how good they both looked. There was even a warmness to her mother that had never been there before. And every time Thomas looked at Sarah, it was as though he could eat her with a spoon.

"We were beginning to wonder what happened to you," Sarah said when Blair waltzed into the room and sat down.

Blair smiled vaguely, not having completely forgiven Sarah for prying into her business. But some things were better left unsaid and she'd decided to let bygones be bygones. "I guess I'm just too full to hurry."

"What'll you have to drink?" Thomas chimed in, standing by the bar.

Thinking a moment, Blair finally answered, "Mmm, nothing right now. There's just no room to put it."

Thomas chuckled. "I know what you mean. I'm pretty full myself. But if you change your mind, don't hesitate to holler, and I'll fix you one of my mean brews."

Blair laughed. "I won't," she said, turning toward her mother. Sarah was staring at her.

Blair's heart took a dive, instantly recognizing the expression on her mother's face. *Oh, please, don't start anything. Not now. I'm simply not up to it. Can't you see my heart is breaking?*

"Blair."

"Yes, Mother," Blair answered, resigned.

"You can't keep on going this way." Sarah paused and looked at Thomas as though to garner his support. He came and sat down beside her, handing her a drink. "You tell her, Thomas. Tell her how awful she looks."

Blair winced.

"Have you looked at yourself in the mirror lately, Blair?"

"Just a moment ago," Blair quipped, trying to make light of the situation.

Sarah took offense. "I assure you, this is no laughing matter."

"Mother..." Blair began, rising to her feet.

"Don't you 'mother' me in that tone of voice," Sarah cried. "What I can't understand is how you can carry on over a man who's not good enough for you, who—"

Blair began to shake. "Mother," she repeated, "I suggest you quit while you're ahead." This was Caleb she was talking about. No one had the right to criticize him but her! The shaking intensified, loosening everything within her.

Sarah paid no heed to Blair's warning. She was now standing in front of Blair, blocking the path to the door. "He'll never be good enough for you, either socially or monetarily. Why can't you see that?"

"Don't you think you're being a tad hard on her?" Thomas put in, turning to his wife, trying to calm the ruffled waters between the two people he loved most in the world. "She loves him, Sarah," he added quietly, as though that explained everything.

"Rubbish! I don't believe that for a minute. Not my daughter and some.... danger-seeking renegade."

Blair's face was white with rage. "Oh, no..." She could barely speak. The shaking had moved up to her throat and seemed to be choking her.

Making the most of Blair's inability to speak, Sarah continued, "You're a *Stephens*! And for heaven's sake, don' ever forget it."

Something inside Blair snapped. She swayed on her feet It was in that moment that she saw herself through Caleb' eyes, and she didn't like what she saw. *Caleb's right. You ar haughty and proud. But most of all, you're a coward. Wher faced with something you can't handle, you run for cover— afraid to take a chance.*

After opening her eyes in the midst of the thundering si lence, Blair pushed herself up to full height. "The Stephen name doesn't mean a damn to me! I'd gladly give up my name and every penny that goes with it just to feel Caleb's arms around me.''

She turned then and walked calmly out of the room. Once outside, Blair fell exhausted against the door. She had done it! For the first time, she'd taken charge of her life. It felt good. Scary, but good.

And in order for that life to count for something, she knew she had to go to Caleb. She had to tell him she loved him, no matter what the outcome.

Her breath was coming in short spurts and her eyes were stinging as if she would cry.

But there were no tears.

The second Sarah heard the door slam she turned to her husband, her face crumpled in anguish.

"Oh, God, Thomas, I've really done it this time, haven't I?" she cried, tears beginning to stream down her face. "Oh, God," she said again, "why can't I learn to keep my mouth shut? Do you think Blair will ever forgive me?" she added on a sob.

Thomas hugged her close, staring over her head toward the door. "Somehow I think she will, my love," he comforted. "You probably did her the biggest favor of her life; you made her look into her heart and face the truth."

Chapter 15

Thanks, but no thanks."

"I'm going to pretend I didn't hear that," Jack Worre[ll] responded laconically, staring at Caleb through the haze of smoke that Caleb's cigarette had created.

Caleb threw his boss a hard look. They were in the coffe[e] bar on the top floor of the FBI building long after workin[g] hours. Suddenly, the small room seemed to lack air. Cale[b] ambled to the window and raised it slightly. Fresh air im[-]mediately filtered into the room. Then Caleb thumped hi[s] half-smoked cigarette through the opening.

He didn't want to think. About anything. He hadn't bee[n] able to think since he'd walked out on Blair. Instead, he r[e-]alized he'd been concentrating on balancing a dull ache. [If] he was careful, he could keep the ache from turning int[o] despair.

With his back to Worrell he said, "I still can't believ[e] you're serious about stepping down. I thought you were ju[st] full of hot air."

"Well, you were wrong," Worrell said with emphasis. "And I've recommended you for my job."

Caleb felt flattered, no doubt about that. And a few weeks before, he might have jumped at the chance, but not now. He was washed out, both emotionally and physically. Again Blair touched his mind. He flinched.

"You love her, don't you?"

Caleb grunted as if he'd been hit.

When he remained mute, Worrell continued, a faint edge to his voice. "How the hell the two of you ever got together is beyond me." He shook his head. "Why, you're as different as champagne and beer."

Pivoting on his heel, Caleb faced Worrell, feeling as though his insides were being put through a paper shredder.

"That's one of the many reasons why it won't work," he pointed out savagely.

"And Blair's the reason you won't take the job?"

"Partly."

Worrell was watching him. "She loves you, too, you know."

"You're wrong." Caleb's voice was hoarse. More coffee, that was what he needed, he told himself. Something to relax his larynx. Yet he didn't move.

"It's killing you, isn't it?"

"I love her," Caleb said simply.

Worrell got up and trudged over and stood beside Caleb at the window. He looked out. "Empty."

Caleb didn't pretend not to understand.

"That's the way the rest of your life's going to be if you don't swallow that damn pride and go to her."

Caleb turned and slammed his open palm on the bar top. "Don't you understand, I can't! She's everything I'm not. Even if I took this job, the interest on just one of her C.D.'s probably more than I'd make in a year."

"Baloney. And you think that matters?"

"It matters."

"Only to you, dammit, only to you," Worrell exploded. "And that chip on your shoulder is growing bigger by the day."

"Do...you really think there's a chance?" Caleb's breath shook as he dragged it in.

"You won't know till you try."

The muscles in Caleb's jaw moved slightly.

"Well, what the devil are you waiting for?" Worrell demanded.

What *was* he waiting for? Caleb asked himself. Blair haunted him day and night. He had dreams that she came to him in the night and slid her body over his, opening her thighs in silence to take him inside herself. He awakened from those dreams with what felt like an ache in his arms from having striven so hard to contain her within them.

He loved her. Wasn't worth a damn without her. So what if she took what was left of his heart and cut it to pieces? Nothing could be as bad as the empty feeling that threatened to consume him.

Worrell snorted rudely. "Dammit, go for it!"

A broad grin suddenly split Caleb's lips. "I owe you one, you old sonofagun!"

Great day in the morning! Worrell thought, grinning into space. Some things do change, after all.

When Blair rounded the corner, she saw his car.

Then she saw him, leaning against the white pillar on his porch.

Panicking, she stomped on the brake and came to a screeching halt in the middle of the street. Thank goodness it was deserted, she thought, her head spinning.

What was he doing camped on her doorstep? What did it mean? Could it be possible that he, too, had experienced a change of heart?

Her own heart was knocking fast and furiously as she inched the car forward, all the while trying to curb the panic that was vibrating in her stomach. She could feel the buzz of it in her fingertips and along the inside of her arms.

The next few minutes were a blur as Blair went through the mechanics of parking the car and making her way up the walk.

When she came to a standstill in front of him, their eyes locked, the soft glow of the porch light giving them the power to pierce each other's souls.

But Blair could get no further than the bleak coldness of his eyes. In that instant she wanted to curl up and die, knowing that he couldn't possibly love her and look at her like that.

Finally Caleb spoke, his voice seeming to come from the depths of hell. "Blair, oh, Blair...I..." he croaked, taking a step forward.

Suddenly, Blair did see. She saw a lonely, self-sufficient man who'd never learned how to love and who was now terrified of giving himself, for fear of being hurt again, the sort of hurt from which he might never recover.

"Oh, Caleb," she whispered, "don't be afraid. I love you."

A sob tore from him as he met her halfway, crushing her in his arms, holding her so tight that the buttons on his shirt dug into her breasts.

"And I love you," he murmured fiercely. "More than life itself."

Blair raised her head, their mingled tears shining on her face. "And I you."

He kissed her deeply, his arms tightening still more, until she thought her ribs would crack. Then he was guiding her toward the door.

Once inside, everything else was forgotten. The passion that rose between them blotted out the weeks of pain, or perhaps it was all the more intense because of it.

Each caress, each movement, was both natural and new. Blair felt again that sense of completeness, of belonging, and knew that this man was the final step in that transformation. She had found her center. He had come home.

Blair lay beside him in the bed stroking his chest, awed by the simple fact of his reality.

"What are you thinking?" Caleb asked, smoothing out her hair, spreading it in patterns on the pillow.

"I'm bound to get pregnant," she said softly. "I haven't taken my pills for years. I'm surprised it hasn't already happened."

He raised her chin so she could see the smile breaking across his face.

"Good," he said happily. "Good!"

"You sure you wouldn't mind?" Blair asked. "I mean...it's so soon...."

"Wouldn't bother me," he said huskily. "I kinda like the thought of my baby growing inside you." He laid his hand across her stomach and began rubbing.

Blair went weak all over, giving in to the sensation his hands were creating.

"My love, my love," Caleb whispered into the silence.

"Mmm."

"About your...money." He stumbled over the words.

Blair soothed his brow. "What's mine is yours," she said huskily, "but if you want, we'll keep it in trust for our children. I don't care about money. I only care about you."

"I love you."

A hush fell over the room for a moment, then Blair spoke what was in her heart. "Your job... your being gone. I'm going to have to adjust to that all over again." She paused and then rushed on to say, "Not that I mind. It's just that..."

Caleb tweaked her nose, stopping her flow of words. "Glad you brought it up. I've been meaning to talk to you about that."

"Oh."

He grinned. "Worrell's stepping down and guess who's been recommended to take his place?"

Blair yelped, throwing herself back into his arms, their legs becoming tangled once again. "Oh, Caleb, that's wonderful. I'm so proud of you."

"At least now I'll be home and we won't starve," he teased. "But we won't be rich, either."

The smile faded from Blair's eyes and she pulled back. "You know that's never mattered to me," she said brokenly.

Caleb reached for her. "I know that," he said. "I was a damn fool for thinking otherwise."

Blair found his buttocks in the moonlight and cupped them in her hands. "No more than I," she whispered, kneading the firm skin.

He groaned, finding it difficult to speak. "Do you think your mother will ever accept me?"

"In time," Blair murmured, feeling his hardness press against her stomach. She clutched him between her thighs.

He groaned again, louder.

"It's because of her that I realized that I couldn't just let you walk out of my life."

His voice was thick and shaky. "Remind me to thank her... when I see her."

Blair's smile became a gasp as he thrust deep inside her.

"I love you," she responded, moving with him.

"For always."

"Is that a promise?"

"A promise of a lifetime," he whispered, filling her with his love.

And it was.

Silhouette Intimate Moments

COMING
NEXT MONTH

DOUBLE DEALINGS—Kathleen Creighton

Ex-spy Rose St. James was called out of retirement to
investigate Jade Castle, a man of wealth, power and danger.
He was lethal enough to cause Rose to fear for her life,
because he had already captured her heart.

MYSTIC—Lisa Jackson

What had begun on a hot summer night between Savannah
and Travis couldn't be denied. After nine years he wanted
her back, and despite her vows, she was falling in love with
him again.

KILLING MOON—Amanda Stevens

Could Maxwell Fiori be the double of Julie Ferris's late
husband? He was different, but he roused the fires of
passion in her all the same. During their escape through
the Colombian jungles, Julie began to believe she would
love again.

RISKY BUSINESS—Nora Roberts

All Liz Palmer wanted from Jonas Sharpe was to be left
alone. But if Liz was the link to his brother's murder, he
wanted revenge. In the process, he plunged them both into
the desperate world of drug smuggling and into the depths
of passion.

AVAILABLE NOW:

MAN FOR HIRE
Parris Afton Bonds

SWEET REASON
Sandy Steen

THE OLD FLAME
Alexandra Sellers

WHEN WE TOUCH
Mary Lynn Baxter

FOUR UNIQUE SERIES
FOR EVERY WOMAN YOU ARE . . .

Silhouette Romance

Heartwarming romances that will make you
laugh and cry as they bring you all the wonder
and magic of falling in love.

6 titles per month

Silhouette Special Edition

Expanded romances written with emotion and
heightened romantic tension to ensure
powerful stories. A rare blend of passion and
dramatic realism.

6 titles per month

Silhouette Desire

Believable, sensuous, compelling—and
above all, romantic—these stories deliver
the promise of love, the guarantee
of satisfaction.

6 titles per month

Silhouette Intimate Moments

Love stories that entice; longer, more
sensuous romances filled with adventure,
suspense, glamour and melodrama.

4 titles per month

Where passion and destiny meet...
there is love

Jesse's Lady

Veronica Sattler

Brianna Deveraux had a feisty spirit matched by that of only one man, Jesse Randall. In North Carolina, 1792, they dared to forge a love as vibrant and alive as life in their bold new land.